Adam looked across at Nicole and managed to catch her eye. She could not help but give him a lingering look, for she dearly wanted him by her side. Adam stood up sucking in his breath and thought. "Devil take it, the chit is flirting with me from across the room. Where did she learn to use her eyes like that?"

He strode over to her quickly and, ignoring the man who watched him from her side, took hold of her bare arm: "Come along, Nicole. I want a word with you!" It was a demand and he was in no mood for interference.

"Not now, my lord," she smiled saucily.

"Now, Nicole! You will soon learn that you cannot look across a room at a man as you just did, and not get exactly what you asked for."

Spring Gambit

Claudette Williams

FAWCETT CREST • NEW YORK

SPRING GAMBIT

Published by Fawcett Crest Books, a unit of CBS Publications,
the Consumer Publishing Division of CBS Inc.

ISBN 0-449-23891-2

Printed in the United States of America

10   9   8   7   6   5   4   3

dedicated to:

my husband, Gordon,
my parents, and
my brother Bobby

Chapter One

FEBRUARY, 1812

The Library In Sutland House was perhaps not its largest room, but it was most certainly decorated, as was the balance of the mansion, in the first style of elegance. One wall of this small but cozy room was lined with books, ranging from Shakespeare's complete works to the more recent novels and a collection of poems by Sir Walter Scott. The opposite wall boasted the family portraits. The third wall, which was made up almost entirely of windows, sported brown velvet draperies, tied back with gold ropings so that the extensive grounds of the Sutland estate glowed through, very much like a landscape picture.

There were two matched sofas that armed the huge fireplace (which occupied a good part of the fourth wall), now filled with crackling logs that gave forth an illuminating heat. The room had a much-used and comfortable feeling, as it was, indeed, the family gathering spot. Its only occupants at the moment, however, were two gentlemen sitting across from each other, an elegant writing desk standing firmly between them.

Lord Arthur Beaumont, eighth Earl of Sutland, leaned back heavily in his cushioned Chippendale chair, putting his hand to his chin. The habitual sweetness of his expression had vanished and he now wore a look of consternation. He had felt some mild surprise when just a few minutes before the butler had announced the Duke of Lyndham, for although they had for some months been working closely together in a branch of the foreign department, they had not as yet been on any social terms. This was due to the fact that Adam Roth, Duke of Lyndham, was a bachelor of eight and twenty years ... and until recently had been busy acquiring the reputation of being a fashionable rake.

A little more than a year ago the Duke's father had

7

died, leaving him the title and a considerable fortune. With his father's death, the Duke's libertine activities slowed down, and he turned his excessive energies toward politics, where he met the Earl of Sutland.

"Indeed, my boy, what you have just imparted to me must go no further! This is very distressing news and I do not at the moment perceive what is to be done," said the Earl.

The Duke pushed back his chair, stood up, and took a turn about the room. He gazed thoughtfully at the Earl, and then out the window. He had never been able to tolerate his own father, and many of the shocking excesses he had committed had proceeded from an overwhelming desire to shock the old gentleman whom he had been forced to call his sire. He had left Oxford earlier than his father had wished and plunged into a social whirl, where he found himself an intimate of the Prince Regent. In fact, he had been so much in the Carlton Set that he had gained the reputation of being able to drink Prinny himself "under the table," without becoming foxed. He had gambled at every Hell that St. James Street boasted for outrageous sums, seemingly unmindful of the outcome. His garments were cut to perfection and appeared to be molded to his form. His neckcloth was tied with an expertise that Beau Brummell himself often applauded. Yet . . . his shoulders and firm legs depicted the "Corinthian." He studied pugilism with the ex-champion Gentleman Jackson, was considered to be a nonpareil with a whip and four and a bruising rider to hounds. He had the felicity of being sought after by every matchmaking female in and out of the Beau Monde, and had thus far escaped them all.

His father deprecated these activities, shuddered at his son's dandyism of dress, and called down lectures upon his head for his predilection for sports. He would have forgiven him all these turns, however, if Roth had obeyed him by marrying and producing an heir. The late Duke had been a cruel, hard, and self-righteous man during his lifetime. When he discovered that he was dying, he became obsessed with the idea of having his son married off and begetting an heir. He had commanded his son to carry out his duty; a command that had been at first politely and then scornfully refused. It was inevitable that such a man would die refusing to be reconciled with his only son. It was also understandable that at eight and twenty Adam Roth had become withdrawn, cold, and cynical.

Gazing at the Earl now, he thought how very different this calm, sweet gentleman was in every way from the man he had called father. The Duke said quietly, his face grave, "Sir, I believe that there is a way to avoid a scandal being attached to the department, and of course to our names, but I fear that there is a great deal of risk involved."

"Well, Adam, let me hear your plan and between us we will try and minimize the risk," replied Beaumont sagely.

The Duke returned to the desk and pulled up the chair he had previously been occupying. "Yes, sir, but the thing is that in order to pull through this muddle, we will have to entail the risk of involving yet another person."

The Earl frowned and shook his head. "It's a tricky business, Adam, for as of now we have no idea who is entangled in this ugly mess and I do not countenance the idea of approaching anyone we are not sure of."

"No, sir, I agree, but I have reason to believe that young John Wellesly can be trusted and I should like to take him into our confidence ... indeed, I feel that we must."

The Earl sighed. "Yes, as far as trusting Wellesly, I am inclined to agree with you. However, Adam, I should first like to hear what you have in mind."

Lady Beaumont was at that moment looking out onto the drive for sign of her two wayward offspring. Her Ladyship was an enchanting beauty in her late forties. She wore her dusky curls cropped short in the prevailing mode. She had been considered a Diamond of the First Water in her day, and now, twenty-two years later, she was still a lively beauty, as well as one of the leaders of fashion amongst the Beau Monde.

The last week in February had brought freezing cold and rain, until this afternoon, when Harry had spotted the

9

sun. He had come rushing in calling for his sister Nicole, and their mother watched, amused, as they rushed out again, informing her gaily that they were going riding. Then the Duke had arrived, and now much to her Ladyship's exasperation, her children were overdue. She nervously wrung her hands and found herself ardently wishing Nicole would get back quickly and change her clothes, for although she had no wish for the Duke to cast his dangerous glance upon her precious daughter, neither did she wish for so important a man to form an ill opinion of her darling. Lady Beaumont was well aware that the Duke was a confirmed bachelor and that his flirts were generally ladies of unsavory reputation . . . one in particular being "that widow!" She was also aware that the Duke usually flirted with women close to his own age, making a wide circle round the "fledglings." Nevertheless, she was a little concerned that Nicole might find the handsome Duke—with his fashion and easy address—too attractive.

Lady Beaumont chided herself. After all, the Duke was staying only one night with them. She rang the bell for Grudsly, informed him when he appeared that the gentlemen should be called into the salon for tea, and went herself before them.

This spacious room was situated at the front of the house and had a panoramic view of the long wide drive that led to their front doors. She glanced up and smiled as her husband, followed by the Duke, entered the room and took seats beside her. Her Ladyship was in the process of pouring the tea when she quite visibly blanched. She stopped, holding the teapot in midair, and thought, *Dear God!*

She watched—indeed, they all watched—for there in full view were her children. Nicole, with her black tresses uncovered and falling in a disorderly fashion to her waist, was dressed in a short brown riding jacket that was more serviceable than stylish, but what forced her mother's mouth agape (along with that of their guest) was the fact that Nicole was dressed in her brother's breeches, perched upon the saddle with her legs tucked beneath her, and was riding at a reckless pace. Her Ladyship glanced at the Duke and observed with disquiet that his eyes were

10

riveted to this diverting spectacle, and she heartily regretted the installation of this new window, which was now affording them such an iniquitous vision. A fair-haired young man dressed somewhat more fashionably than the lady was seen to be attempting much of the same gymnastics without too much success.

The eighth Earl of Sutland slapped his knee and whooped with laughter, for he adored his children and looked fondly upon their antics. His lady prayed they would go straight to their rooms and change before entering the salon and shocking their noble guest further.

The Duke reclined in his chair, a hint of laughter lurking in his clear gray eyes. The front doors closed with a merry bang, and they heard a vexed male voice exclaim, "Devil take you, Nick, for you are small enough to maneuver that last with ease and it was most unhandsome of you to play such a dastardly trick!"

A musical giggle followed this reproach and two smiling faces peeped in at the salon threshold. The Duke felt a gasp form in his throat and quickly suppressed it, for he had been surprised to discover that what he had thought was a hoyden of a schoolgirl was in fact one of the loveliest creatures he had ever seen. Her green eyes twinkled gleefully, and even in her brother's breeches, her figure was alluring and lovely.

Perceiving that tea was being served, Nicole exclaimed, "Ah, Mama, tea!" She then turned an admonishing finger at her brother. "You see, Harry, if I had let you drag me to the west field, we would have been very late and probably missed our tea, which I am much in need of, depend on—"

Lady Nicole Beaumont cut herself short, suddenly aware of a new and most interesting presence. She eyed the Duke with undisguised zest, and although the thought came to her that he was extremely handsome, she would have then dismissed him from any further consideration (as he was clearly more than five and twenty) had she not met his smiling eyes. He stood up and she found herself being presented to the Duke of Lyndham.

Lady Beaumont heard her husband make the introductions and found her voice saying firmly, "Nicole, you will

11

go upstairs immediately and change into a dress." Then, shaking her head woefully, she continued, "Why, darling, you are to be presented to the *Ton* in less than three weeks, and here you stand . . . in breeches, smelling of the stables."

Nicole was clearly unabashed by her mother's rebuke and smiled impishly. "Oh pooh, Mama, I have three entire weeks of freedom left to me and the tea will very likely get cold. I am persuaded his Grace would not wish us to drink cold tea."

The Duke's lips twitched appreciatively and his eyes definitely held a chuckle. Lady Beaumont made as if to object when Lord Beaumont laughed and motioned for his wife to allow their spirited children to remain.

For the last few minutes Harry had been standing spellbound and in silence, gazing raptly at the Duke's neckcloth. He finally cleared his throat and ventured, "I say, Your Grace, that is a splendid cravat! I don't believe it's one of Brummell's . . . is it your own style, Duke?"

A slightly bored look crept back into the Duke's countenance and his answer was mechanical. "Yes, Viscount Beaumont . . . in fact, I call it the Lyndham fall."

"By Jove, Duke, if you are staying the night, I would feel privileged if you would allow me to watch you at it!" said Harry animatedly.

"Harry!" ejaculated his mother, shocked.

The Duke of Lyndham, amused at the lad's ingenuous request, smiled indulgently. "No . . . No . . . Lady Beaumont, I do not mind. Yes, Viscount, you may come up later, when I dress for dinner, and watch if you like."

Nicole smiled engagingly at the Duke. "Was that your gray that we saw in the stables, your Grace? He is one of the finest animals I have ever come across."

"Stap me if he isn't!" remarked Harry enthusiastically. "Tell you what, Nick, Ginger has met her match at last!"

Nicole turned a surprised countenance to her brother. "Why, Harry, how could you say so . . . when you know Ginger has never been beaten."

" 'Tis true, Nick ole girl, she ain't been beaten yet, but she has never run anything as fine as that gray!"

Nicole was now glaring at her brother. "Well, you cannot say that the gray will beat my Ginger, for you have never seen him race."

"Don't set your bristles up, Nick. I didn't say the gray will beat her—although I'm inclined to think he can—I said she'd met her match!" responded her recalcitrant brother.

Lady Beaumont, horrified at this interchange and what it was obviously leading up to, attempted to put a stop to the conversation by offering biscuits. Harry readily accepted the offer and leaned back in his chair, content to munch. His sister, however, declined the treat, turned to the Duke, her piquant face flushed with anger. "Well, your Grace, my Ginger against your gray?"

"No!" interjected her Ladyship violently.

Roth had been listening to the interplay between brother and sister with interest, and was now surprised to find himself feeling a disproportionate degree of disappointment as he responded in the only way propriety would allow. "I am afraid I must decline, for I could not lend myself to anything that would find disfavor in your mother's eyes."

Nicole rounded on her mother, exclaiming desperately, "Mama, you would not say no . . . you could not do anything so . . . so shabby. Did you not hear Harry? My Ginger must be defended. You could not wish me always to wonder whether she would have indeed been beaten? You could not wish me always to have to hear Harry say that she could have been? Ginger is a champion. It is not just for such an accusation to go forth undefended. Oh, Mama, do not say no. Surely there can be no impropriety in a race . . . here on Sutland grounds," she pleaded.

Lord Beaumont had been listening and watching his daughter quietly, and responded now before his lady had the chance to utter the strenuous refusal that was forming on her lips. "Well, my dear, I think after all Nicole does have a point there. There is not the least imprudence connected with a little race on our grounds and under our supervision."

Lady Beaumont looked from father to daughter and sighed, reluctantly giving way, and was immediately enveloped in her daughter's embrace. Nicole then bent

13

across to her father, planted a kiss, and turned sparkling green eyes upon the Duke. "Well, your Grace?"

"How can I now refuse?" Adam Roth laughed, genuinely amused.

"You cannot!" she answered happily and then sighed. "I suppose it will have to wait till morning though, for my Ginger has been about all day. Is that convenient, your Grace?"

His Grace, much diverted, nodded his consent, while Nicole found herself being firmly ushered out of the room by her harassed mama. Her Ladyship gave Nicole the order to bathe and wear her prettiest gown before descending at dinnertime, and then turned down the hall for her own chamber. There was no doubt in her mind that her children were by far the loveliest creatures imaginable. Harry, her eldest, was now twenty-one, endowed with blond locks that waved softly about his forehead and ears in a style that he called "windswept." His eyes were clear blue, and sincere. His nose was straight and aristocratic. He was blessed with the same sweetness of disposition that characterized his father. His mother sighed and reflected that he was all a mother could wish for. And there was Nicole, her baby, now eighteen ... Nicole, whose striking beauty was enhanced by the gift of charm. But Nicky's lively spirit filled her gentle mother with misgivings. Lady Beaumont felt certain of her daughter's success amongst the *Ton* in this, her first London Season ... and while she had no wish for the Duke to become overly interested in Nicole, she did not want him to leave with any erroneous impressions, for a few ill-chosen words said to the wrong party could damage her daughter's reputation and ruin her expectations. "Oh dear!" said Lady Beaumont out loud to her room, and then thought with a flutter of her hand, *But he did seem ... entertained ... so perhaps I am refining too much upon this awful race.*

Lord Beaumont's eyebrow went up as his gaze rested upon his son, for Harry had watched his mother and sister's departure, leaned forward, helped himself to another biscuit, and proceeded to munch, seemingly quite comfortable and disposed to remain in this relaxed setting. However, his father wished to continue the subject that had brought the Duke "posthaste" to Sutland, and directed a meaningful glance at his son. Harry gazed back at his father wonderingly, suddenly caught the gist of the "look," and stood up hastily. "I . . . I daresay I . . . er, should go up and wash now! Well, yes, then . . . I suppose I will. I look forward to seeing you later, your Grace." He bowed his head slightly and then turned back to his father—"Papa"—and proceeded to make good his escape.

As his son left the room without closing the door, the Earl rose, shut the door quietly, and then turned back to his guest, his expression once again grim.

The War with France was now in its tenth year, and while it had put little drain on the manhood of the country, it had been playing havoc with England's economy. The indigent felt the greatest of its tortures, and everywhere there was discontent. In contrast with the hapless impoverished country folk were the aristocracy. For during the Napoleonic struggle the nobility, encouraged by their Prince of Wales (now Regent), had set up hunting boxes, attended *roût* parties and assemblies, patronized cockfights and boxing matches. Sporting coaches could be seen everywhere on new and improved roads. Poets and novelists sprouted up, thriving on the paying aristocracy. To any observer, it would be a difficult task indeed to detect anything but mild concern on the faces of the *Ton* dancing at Almack's . . . or listening to the latest and favorite opera singers at Vauxhall Gardens. The War continued in the Peninsula . . . while the gaiety in London sparkled. However, there were those who worked to bring relief to the indigent, and a quick end to the War. The Duke of Lyndham and the Earl of Sutland belonged to those select few.

The Earl sat beside the Duke, silently waiting for his young guest to begin.

"In the meantime, my Lord, just before I left London this morning, I made arrangements for some discreet inquiries to be pursued. Our man is going to be in day after tomorrow, and I will be riding to the Coast to meet with him."

15

"As far as I can tell, you have done everything necessary . . . but still, there is no safety for us and we must beware. The sooner we can ascertain who the devil is behind this . . . this act of treason, the sooner we can enact your plan. The troublesome part is that without knowing whom we are dealing with, there is no way to keep any more billets from falling into his hands. Unless I issue an order that no further dispatches may be read by anyone other than ourselves."

"If you were to do such a thing, it would warn the scoundrel that we are aware of his activities. It is imperative that he feel free and unencumbered with suspicions."

"True, true . . . but, Adam, we must work out a method to keep the more urgent dispatches between ourselves." The Earl glanced across at Roth and noted the weariness about his eyes and exclaimed with self-reproach, "My dear boy, you are looking fagged to death. Please excuse me for not realizing earlier. I will show you to your room and send my valet to you at once."

"Thank you, sir, I can manage, if you will but point out the way," remarked the Duke gratefully, for he was indeed beginning to feel the strain of a long day.

The Earl showed him up the wide staircase, down the hall of the second floor, and into one of the larger guest rooms. Here the Duke found warm water awaiting him and thankfully washed, after pulling off his jacket and hessians, and then lay down upon the large oak-framed bed. The Duke had not slept well the night before, and the two-hour ride to Sutland had tired him more than he thought, so it was not long before he dozed off.

He had been dozing for no more than an hour when a knock sounded upon his door and he stirred.

"Hmmmm . . . yes," said he sleepily.

The door opened and Harry walked in, blinding him with a smile, and the Duke blinked.

"OH!" said Harry, surprised. "Did I wake you, your Grace? I am sorry . . . but you did say I should come and watch, and as I thought you'd be dressing by now—for it is quite late, you know—well . . . I came!" explained Harry.

The Duke, still not fully awake, perceived that the lad was apparently waiting for him to do something, and he blinked again.

"You came to . . . er, watch me?" he asked warily.

"Why yes, your Grace. You could not have forgotten?"

"No, no, of course not! You may certainly watch me, but is there something in particular that I should do?"

"Your cravat, Duke. I am most anxious to learn the trick of it," said Harry, mildly surprised at his Grace's lack of understanding.

Enlightenment dawned upon the Duke, and finding a considerable amount of relief in discovering what it was that this youth, smiling so blandly at him, required, he felt disposed to try and teach the boy the knack of tying a Lyndham fall.

The neckcloth that Roth pulled out of his portmanteau was nearly a foot in width, stiff with starch and gleamingly white, and produced an awed exclamation from Harry. This exclamation was followed by a series of *ahs, oohs,* and *by Joves* as the Duke manipulated the neckcloth by bringing his chin, which had been facing the ceiling, slowly down upon the crisp material, causing a very definite and perfect fold to form. He uttered no sound during this delicate operation, and when it had been completed, he viewed his creation in the mirror, giving it one final pinch, and then turned to face Harry, who was lost in silent admiration of so great a feat.

"It is merely a matter of infinite care and patience, and a clean and properly starched neckcloth," said Roth gravely, his eyes alight.

"Stap me, if that isn't the finest piece of work I have ever seen!" said Harry, beside himself. "Blister it, just look at this mess about my neck. Should like to retire to my room and have a go at it right now, but m'mother ordered me to bring you down to dinner by six, and it's close onto the hour now!"

The Beaumonts usually kept country hours while they were in residence at Sutland, adhering to the more fashionable dining hours only while in London.

Nicole found herself, after dressing with more care than

17

usual, feeling restless at being cooped up in her room. She went down to the library and sat thoughtfully by the fire. The Duke of Lyndham was certainly different from all the other young men she knew . . . and she was not quite certain what to make of him. Nicole was used to her brother's friends, and they treated her like "one of the boys," although recently they seemed to be acting silly, rushing to help her dismount, flushing and paying her odd compliments. They were . . . just boys. But the Duke, with his smiling eyes and his mocking tone, was indeed someone to be wary of; in fact, she was not sure she liked him very much. She stood up and walked to the window, gazing at the wide stretch of lawns, yellowed now from a long winter. One finger played with the cuff of her white lace, as Harry rambled into the room, leisurely followed by the Duke.

Adam Roth's eyebrows went up as his gaze rested on Nicole. She was wearing an emerald green velvet dress, high-waisted and falling in a straight line to her dainty ankles. It was trimmed with a wide white lace collar. The sleeves were long and narrow, cuffed in the same white lace. The dress fitted her trim figure to perfection, showing the alluring lines of her blooming womanhood. Her luxurious black hair had been brushed into a semblance of silk billowing down upon her shoulders and gliding down her back. Her black lashes curled around eyes that matched the color of her dress. She made a stunning picture, and the Duke's expression held undisguised admiration.

"Ah, can this be Lady Nicole? Allow me to say that while I found you adorable in your breeches, I find you enchanting in your gown." His mocking tone seemed to belie the words, and Nicole's eyes sparkled coldly at him.

"Yes, I imagine you would put such importance on clothes. I, your Grace, do *not*. One is what one is . . . regardless of one's raiments," she said haughtily.

Roth was surprised by this setdown. "Do you not think that one's character can be depicted by the clothes one chooses, when one is able to choose them?"

Nicole bit her lip and blushed. "Not when what you

wear is decided by a society you did not have the making of."

The corners of the Duke's lips quivered. "Er . . . I see your point, Lady Nicole, and still do not concede. For you will admit that while society does dictate . . . the fashions, shall we say . . . an individual does, in fact, display his personality in the manner he adopts by dressing within or without those confines."

Nicole answered this logic by putting up her chin and saying lightly, with the intent of dismissing what was fast becoming a disagreeable discussion, "I see your point, Duke . . . but I hold to mine!"

Lord and Lady Beaumont entered the room at that moment and the conversation took on a robust and congenial atmosphere with much raillery displayed between all three gentlemen. Lady Beaumont glanced fondly at her children, and feeling a twinge of parental pride, turned her eyes to those of her husband. Appraising him now, she could not refrain from thinking him perfect in every way. His Lordship, now forty-nine, was as handsome a man as he had been a boy. His curly black tresses were tinged with silver, adding luster rather than age. His eyes, which were black and penetrating, held depths of wisdom . . . quiet and loving. Impulsively, she touched his hand.

The Duke had been observing them with mixed emotions. He had found himself at first incredulous at stumbling upon what was evidently and obviously a love match, and one that had survived time and the depredations of a ruinous society. Adam Roth felt somehow warm . . . and yet empty all at once.

Dinner was announced and he turned to Nicole, offering his arm. She curtsied prettily and smiled saucily up at him. "Do not look so glum, Duke. Perhaps I won't beat you in the morning."

"As a gentleman, I should answer that sally by stating that I wish you may. As an honest man, I must tell you that I will make it extremely difficult for you to do so."

Nicole clapped her hands merrily before placing one upon his bent arm. "Wonderful, Duke. I am so excited that I doubt very much my ability to sleep tonight."

Chapter Two

The following morning was cold, but clear. A slight winter wind stroked the leafless trees, while the sun glistened through the bare branches, through the window of Roth's room, and came to rest upon his face. He awoke, applauded himself for having thought to draw his drapes, for the clock on his fireplace mantel was about to strike eight o'clock, and as his date with Lady Nicole had been fixed at eight-thirty, he scrambled out of his bed. He was feeling strangely exhilarated at the thought of the morning's prospect. He dressed without the assistance of a valet and managed in spite of this deficiency and the early hour to look the epitome of fashion. His superbly cut riding jacket made of blue superfine fit his body closely. His breeches, though buckskin, could have come only from the finest tailor in London, and his black hessians, which had been polished with a mixture of blacking and champagne, caught the glow of the sun's rays. He gave his tie one final pinch and walked slowly out of the house and toward the stables.

He reached his destination and gave the stable lads the order to have his horse readied, and then proceeded to take a short walk round the park grounds. Roth tilted his curly-brimmed top hat, giving him a raffish look, and gazed about him, aware of an absurd and titillating feeling of anticipation.

Nicole had, just as she had suspected, a very hard time at falling asleep, with the net consequence of having finally and exhaustedly dozed off in the early hours of the morning. This, of course, caused her to oversleep, and it was with some speed and little care that she brushed her hair and threw on her clothes, hesitating less than a second before donning her breeches, for she quickly surmised that this was no time to be riding sidesaddle! Nicole had raced most of Harry's friends, and had beaten them all, but she had never before raced such a horse . . . or such a man! Running out of the house, she caught sight of the Duke and waved her hand in greeting.

"Good morning, your Grace!" she exclaimed breathlessly. "My goodness ... I hope you have not been waiting long, for I must confess that I overslept." Then (not waiting for an answer) she hugged herself gaily. "Lud, but it is cold! A brisk ride is just what we need to warm us."

The Duke pulled a face. "I could think of several other methods that would do a considerably superior job at warming us, Lady Nicole," he responded teasingly.

"Oh no, Duke, I am persuaded you could not be so poor-spirited!" she countered.

He laughed. "No, I am sure you could not."

Nicole rubbed her gloved hands together and looked about her. "Now where is Harry?" Then she sighed as she observed her brother hurrying toward them, waving.

"Hullo! Dashed well too cold this morning. I think we'd better get on with it, for I'm devilishly hungry, didn't have my chocolate this morning, you know." He stopped short, eyeing his sister ruefully. "Damme, Nick, let's do the thing before m'mother wakes up and sees you in my breeches again!"

"Well!" exclaimed his indignant sister. "You arrive late and then dare to hurry us ... why, that is beyond everything, Harold!"

"Now, now, ole girl, no need to get fusty, you know." He turned to Roth and said with a boyish smile, "All set, your Grace? I see your mounts are waiting and I can tell you, Duke, I am most anxious to view this race."

"Just a moment," interjected Roth quietly, as he turned toward Nicole, who was standing at his elbow. "You have promised me a rare treat, but there is something lacking, you know."

Nicole's dark brows drew together, forming a puzzled frown, but Harry, more knowledgeable in these matters, grinned. "By Jove, of course, Nick. The wager! Not sporting without a wager, my girl."

Nicole's frown vanished. "Of course, your Grace. However, must we bet with money? For that would not be interesting to me at all."

"No, it need not be money. In fact, I have something else in mind." His eyes flirted with her, but she noted it not and looked shyly up at him, aware only that they were gray. *Mocking and gray*, she thought, but said, "Good! For if you do not object, I should like to have a snip of your steed's mane for a keepsake if I win." She said this wistfully, and the Duke noted the childlike innocence in her face and voice. He repressed the urge to flick her nose and looked back at her inquiringly. "A snip of my horse's mane? So be it!"

She responded by clapping her hands. "Thank you, your Grace, for I can think of no better keepsake!"

This time, he could not refrain from putting a finger to her nose and lightly twicking it, "You have not won it yet, imp!"

Nicole smiled up at him, seemingly pleased with this new form of address. "And what will you have, Duke . . . if I should lose?"

He smiled mysteriously. "Oh, I will name it when the race is won!"

She put up her chin and glared at him, for she had no liking for his self-assurance. "Done!"

They mounted their horses and Harry stepped to one side. He enthusiastically gave them the sign to start by bringing his uplifted arm down quite emphatically to his side.

Ginger was familiar with the park and eager for the run. Nicole glanced to the side and observed that the gray had bounded forward and was gaining easily. She leaned forward, cooing to Ginger softly, checking her speed ever so slightly, allowing the gray to come up abreast. Nicole could not contain her exhilaration and threw back her head with a laugh, letting the mare have her head. They bounded forward, again in the lead.

Having seen Lady Nicole's riding skill on the previous day, Roth had expected a good race, but he also expected to win. He now felt that some effort was needed to bring about this result. He had been holding his gray in check, but now gave the horse his rein and the stallion leaped to the challenge admirably. He had a strain of Arab in him

22

and was full of fire as he lunged forward, bringing his master abreast with Nicole.

Harry had run toward the center of the field to watch the performance and marveled at the grace and ease of the gray's long strides. Ginger was straining at the bit, for the gray had gained quickly and was now more than a head in the lead. The mare, a born leader and bred to win, was unused to following, and in a final desperate burst of energy brought herself forward . . . causing the distance between them to be less than half a head by the time they had reached the finish point.

Nicole drew up beside the Duke, smiling breathlessly. "Confound you, Duke! But he is a fine piece of flesh and blood!" She appraised the gray admiringly and continued in terms that would have appalled her mother, had she been privileged to hear her. "You are, in fact, a bruising rider, your Grace. Stap up to the mark, for there are not many that can ride the best out of their cattle! I own myself beaten by a notable whip."

"Well, that is what I told you, Nick," put in her brother unwisely. "But you wouldn't listen to me . . . however, it was worth it to see you beaten, for a finer race I have never seen!"

Nicole's understandable wrath was unleashed, and Roth had a moment to watch them as she attacked and Harry defended. The Duke had found that he had enjoyed the race immensely, much more than the outcome (which he had taken as a matter of course). He gazed at Lady Nicole animatedly disagreeing with her brother, and was surprised at the intense attraction he felt toward her. *Why good God, she is just a hoyden of a girl, a chit, not yet out;* he told himself chaffingly. He had never felt the slightest attraction for any of the debutantes who had been flung his way over the years. He found they giggled over naught and incessantly, he found their conversations stilted and uninteresting . . . and found, too, that most of them seemed passionless, and passion was one of his prerequisites when selecting a woman. He had turned to women who were both experienced and older . . . without any thought of marriage. However, here, too, he found he soon wearied of their company. Even his present flame, beautiful Lucy Beldon, was beginning to bore him. Six months ago he had pursued the lady relentlessly and had derived no little satisfaction when he had made her his ... stealing her, as it were, from under the noses of his friends. Lately, though, he had been feeling a strange desire to quit her company soon after he left her bed. She had become too predictable, and their relationship too routine.

He smiled to himself as he gazed at Nicole, now furiously berating her brother for disloyalty. At least the chit did not bore him ... yet. Harry had become quite incensed at his sister's rather thorough abuse of his person and had forgotten to assist her to dismount, which gave the Duke the opportunity to avail himself of this most agreeable task. Adam Roth's hands gripped Nicole's small waist and held her a moment before placing her feet firmly on the earth. In doing so, his eyes managed to engage her own.

"I believe my prize is now due, Lady Nicole," said he mockingly.

She blushed and lowered her lashes. She sensed the Duke was teasing her, treating her as though she were a child, and this both rankled and caused her to be shy.

"Why, of course, your Grace," she responded, her voice tight. "What will you have?"

He took a lock of her gleaming hair between his fingers, tilted his head, trying to engage her eyes. "I should like to ask for a lock of your hair ... but I fear your mama would be shocked, and I therefore will have to settle for less."

He succeeded in causing Nicole's gaze to leave his boots and fly to his face and was surprised to find her eyes flashing militantly at him. He had hurt her pride with his flippancy, and Nicole, inexperienced in the art of dalliance, was furious to find that he now appeared to be trifling with her. *So,* she thought. *He wants a lock of my hair, does he!* Her anger had left her bereft of speech, and for a moment she could only stand there and glare. Then suddenly she turned her back to him, and said pettishly, "Since you cannot ask for ... the lock of hair you men-

24

tioned, what will you have in its place? For I find that I am growing chilled waiting out here in the open."

His Grace regarded her between amusement and exasperation. For the second time in two days he had attempted a mild flirtation and had received a strange rebuff. He was piqued and his interest was fairly tickled. He thrust a bit of his best at her, his voice softening to the occasion, "Although such a contest as we have run today needs no memento to be remembered, I would like a keepsake ... your glove would do nicely, as it will serve as a splendid token of the finest race I have ever had with a woman."

Roth said this in a tone meant to bring the color to her lovely cheeks, and therefore was astonished to find that the lady, so far from blushing, laughed and quite merrily flung off a glove, throwing it lightly into his hands. She had taken him at his word, and believed that she had been mistaken when she thought he was poking fun at her. She noted neither the caress of his tone, nor the subtleness of his manner.

"Well earned, Duke, for you must know that Ginger, my poor beauty, has never before been beaten. Oh, I say, I am feeling ravenous," she said gaily.

Roth looked at her through his clear gray eyes and suddenly laughed heartily, shaking his head. The chit was a mystery.

Harry, however, agreed, readily remembering his unabated hunger. "By Jove, yes, cook has made something famous in honor of your visit, your Grace." Nicole then recalled her justifiable grievance against her brother and spun round, leveling an indignant look of reproach at him. "I am a good deal put out with you, Harry, for I must tell you that I do not think it very loyal of you to have taken so much delight in the fact that I have lost to his Grace."

"No need to take a pet, m'dear, not at all pleased with your losing. Simply happy his Grace didn't lose," replied her brother glibly.

"Oh ... oh ... you odious boy! It is one and the same thing! Do not speak to me, Harry, for if you do—and I tell you to your head—I shall cut you, cut you dead."

Harry regarded his sister from astonished and sulky

25

eyes, but was fortunately spared the necessity of a rejoinder, for when they entered the main hallway, their attention was caught by the sight of a somewhat stout young gentleman of average height and careless dress, pacing to and fro in a great deal of agitation. Sir Arnold Merdon, the only son of Lord Beaumont's elder sister Augusta, was a frequent visitor at Sutland, as his own estate was but seven miles to the south.

He had been holding his hat and gloves in his left hand, while he pulled fervently at them with his other. However, upon catching sight of his cousin Harry, he dropped them onto the center table, allowing Grudsly, who (poor soul) had been all the while trying to relieve Sir Arnold of these articles, the opportunity to put them away.

Sir Arnold came forward, catching hold of both of Harry's arms. "Harry, I have been driven to distraction waiting for you to come in. Where have you been? Isn't it just like you to be off somewhere when I need you most."

Harry eyed his cousin with feeling, removed the tight grasp from his coat sleeves, and replied caustically, "Been watching a race, and anyone can see that I *am* here now, so you needn't be in such a pucker."

Sir Arnold ran his hand through his fair hair. His chubby countenance wore a harassed expression. "Harry, I must speak with you . . . alone." His eyes moved significantly toward the library.

Harry gazed at his cousin suspiciously, "Quite, quite, ole boy, and so you shall, but first let us go in and breakfast. Devilishly hungry, you know."

"No! I will *never* eat again," Sir Arnold stated heroically.

"Don't think that would be too wise. I tell you what, Arnie ole boy, if you did it for a few weeks, might be a good thing, lose a little weight and buy that waistcoat you fancied," Harry replied practically.

Nicole, seeing that the situation needed a guiding hand, went over to her cousin, and taking him firmly by the arm, led him toward the breakfast parlor, saying soothingly, "Now, Arnie, if you are in another scrape, Harry and I will see you through . . . so, let us eat and be comfortable, for I promise you, I do not like to think on an empty stomach and we both know that Harry *will not!*"

As Harry quite vigorously approved of this speech, and Sir Arnold could see no way of putting it off, the party then went in for the morning meal. Just before sitting down, Arnie noticed the Duke and coughed meaningfully at Harry, who quickly made the introductions.

"Why . . . not the nonpareil!" said Arnie, overcome with awe. "The nonpareil . . . Harry, here!"

Harry nodded, looking somewhat superior, and lowered his voice, but not quite low enough to escape the Duke's hearing. "Taught me his Lyndham fall last night, you know."

This left his cousin speechless and it was several more minutes before anyone spoke, as cook had indeed prepared a feast. There was sirloin, and ham sliced paper thin. There were eggs, toast, buns, and an assortment of cakes. As they could not speak of Arnie's problems in front of the servants, they plunged in and enjoyed a hearty meal (Sir Arnold included).

It was sometime later, their youthful appetites assuaged, that they retired to the library. Harry, having taken additional fortification in the form of a sweetcake, sat down by the fire, stretching his lean body leisurely before him and enjoying his cake. His sister, having seated herself across from her brother and the Duke, requested Arnie to sit down and tell them what had happened to overset him.

Sir Arnold looked at the Duke and bit his lip, for he was clearly embarrassed at having to relate his problem in front of such a notable figure. Nicole observed his discomfiture and impatiently advised him not to be such a "nodcock," as the Duke was now a dear friend and could be depended upon to help.

It was at this moment that the Duke felt a strong inclination to take his leave of them, but alas, curiosity got the better of his good judgment and he allowed this remark to pass unchallenged.

Sir Arnold glanced once more at the Duke and was greeted with an encouraging smile, and so decided that such an experienced man as his Grace could indeed be of some service. He heaved a great sigh and then a groan

27

before he began his tale. "It's Mama!" he finally blurted out, and regarded the three pairs of eyes that looked back with interest. His face contorted into one of severe consternation and he paced about the room.

"Well, I assumed it had something to do with Aunt Augusta, but Arnie, what is it this time?" queried Nicole patiently.

"Wants me to offer for the Seldon chit and I don't want to."

"Did you advise her of your feelings on the matter?" said Nicole.

"Yes, I've told her all week, but she says I must. Says old Seldon is waiting for me to come over this morning to offer for her. Said I won't do it ... said I can't do it! Mama insisted I must, started blubbering at me, so I left the house and came here ... but Harry was out!" he said, looking accusingly at Harry.

Disregarding the latter remark of his cousin's, Harry replied impatiently, "Well, devil take it, Arnie, I can't see what all the bother is about. You are almost of age and you can't be made to marry anyone you don't fancy."

Arnie paced back toward them, throwing his hands in the air. "Cut me off ... said she will!" came his disjointed reply.

"Blister it!" interpolated Harry. "Can't cut you off, nodcock. You've already inherited. Talk sense, man!"

"But Harry, you don't understand. Said she will cut off my allowance, and she can, I tell you. She can!"

"Don't be a dolt, even Aunt Augusta can't stop your allowance. It's in the hands of the trustees and she wouldn't attempt to interfere simply because you won't marry to oblige her. Why, Arnie, she would look the fool," said Nicole reasonably.

"Yes, yes, Nick, I know all that, but there is more, I tell you! Oh, lord!" said Sir Arnold, and overcome with emotion, he took a quick turn about the room, whereby he noticed a nearby chair, decided he could no longer stand up, and flung himself quite vehemently downward. However, in so doing, he did not notice the small footstool directly in his path, tripped over this, causing both the chair and himself to fall backward violently.

28

There was some confusion while Harry came to the aid of his flustered cousin. "No, really, Arnie, must ask you not to overturn the furniture. M'mother wouldn't like it, you know," he protested as he helped his cousin into the uprighted chair.

Nicole, having satisfied herself that Arnie had sustained no serious injury (discounting the one to his pride), sank back onto the sofa and met the Duke's amused countenance. Recalling the matter at hand, she said soothingly, "Arnie, do calm down and tell us what more there is, for we can't possibly help you if we don't know what you are talking about."

"It's Mary!" replied Arnie in the way of an explanation.

"Mary? Didn't know Seldon had two girls ... only know of that one with the spots ... Sybil," put in Harry, surprised.

Arnie eyed his cousin scornfully. "*Not* a Seldon!"

"Mary Who?" asked Nicole in a more patient tone than she was feeling.

"Mary Melville ... sweetest ... loveliest, finest ... purest ..."

"Yes, yes, Arnie, devil a bit!" cut in Harry hurriedly. "I am sure she is a wonder ... but what has happened to the chit?"

"Nothing has happened to her ... yet," answered Arnie gloomily, then brightening: "Want to ... want to marry her ... *now!*"

Nicole put her hand to her eyes, shielding them, and shook her head. "Dear God ... oh, Arnie! Now listen to me and listen carefully. The Melvilles have five daughters and the dowry—if there is one—cannot be large. My aunt will never consent to it. Why, Sybil Seldon is an heiress, and a brilliant social connection ... and while you are not in any straits that you must needs marry an heiress, do not imagine that Aunt would allow such an alliance."

"I don't need to hang out for a rich wife," said Arnie unhappily. "I just want my Mary."

"I understand, Arnie, truly I do, but it's more than just the money. Arnie, are you aware that Melville is a ... a ..."

"Libertine," put in Roth softly.

"Yes ... thank you, your Grace. Arnie, Melville is loose with his money. Indeed, he is in debt and I have often heard Mama say something about his ... his ... amatory affairs. Oh, Arnie, Aunt will never consent!"

Arnie's face took on an expression of utter despair and they all remained in silence for a moment before Nicole spoke again. "Arnie, now listen, dear, in less than nine months' time you will be twenty-one, and by then Aunt will have forgotten her disappointment over the Seldon scheme, and if she hasn't"—she snapped her fingers—"the estate will come into your name and your hands, and then there will be no gainsaying whom you should marry."

Arnie groaned. "No, Nicky, don't get my inheritance till I am five and twenty. Mary don't want to wait till I am five and twenty, says she will be too old ... and I don't want to marry her when she is too old!"

The Duke had been reclining upon the sofa and watching the proceedings with a detached interest. The corners of his mouth had begun to twitch appreciatively, and he was obliged to turn his face away.

Harry was moved to expostulate, "No, really! What a tiresome entailment. How came that about, Arnie? I mean, really ... to be tied to your mama and a lot of damned trustees till you're twenty-five is the outside of enough, and what I call a dastardly trick."

Nicole was eyeing her cousin thoughtfully, "I have been thinking, Arnie, and while I believe I may have a plan, I do not want to voice it just yet. I must sit and work out the details. Please be calm in the knowledge that we shall see you through this as we have always seen you out of your scrapes. Go home now and tell your mama that you will never offer for the Seldon chit. Say you cannot like her ... and then just wait. We will all be in London tomorrow. Trust us—Harry and I will arrange something." This was said with more conviction than she felt. However, it did much to restore the color to Arnie's round cheeks, and with his spirits regained, he took his leave of them.

Nicole listened for the front doors to close, turned and

found the Duke's gray eyes twinkling. They both could no longer contain themselves and burst out laughing.

Harry regarded them with astonishment, and said reproachfully, "No, really! I don't see anything to laugh at. Devil of a will to live with. Imagine being tied to Aunt Augusta until one is twenty-five . . . and you, Nick, telling him we'd fix everything right and tight! What a coil. And the thing is . . . high sticklers these trustees . . . no saying what they might do. Don't see how we are to come about . . . and you sit there laughing." Instead of having recalled them to a sense of what was right, Harry was irked to find that his speech merely set them off into another round of mirth. Affronted, he got up and left them, shaking his head and feeling quite put out with their obvious lack of understanding and sensibility.

Lord and Lady Beaumont had slept late and breakfasted in the privacy of their boudoir. They had just descended the stairway together to find Harry donning his greatcoat, as he was preparing to join his friends at a nearby inn, where a cockfight was being held.

Lord Beaumont questioned his son idly with regards to his intended excursion, and received a jerk of the head and a sign with his hand, which clearly indicated that the answer was not for his mother's ears, as Lady Beaumont did not approve of either the "rabble" that attended such routs, or the cruelty of watching two animals peck each other to death. Lord Beaumont, understanding at once, smiled, and much to Harry's relief, declined from questioning him any further. Harry made good his exit.

Lady Beaumont looked at her lord as they heard laughter from the library, and remarked softly, "They seem to enjoy each other's company, Arthur. I noticed it at dinner last night. However, I am not sure I like it, although I must admit if he shows such a partiality toward her when we are in London, it will most certainly insure her Season."

"Nonsense! Nicky needs no one to insure her Season for her. Why, she will be the toast of St. James's inside a week's time!" He looked tenderly at his wife, taking her chin in his large hand. "Just as her mother was."

Lady Beaumont smiled with pleasure, but still asserted that the Duke's interest would most certainly be a boon to her daughter's first Season amongst the *Ton* ... if only his attentions did not go to her head.

"That is what most concerns me, Serena, my love, for it won't do for our Nicky to form any feeling for Roth. Fine boy, but she is not quite in his style and he seems to be set on remaining a bachelor. Nicky is a steady girl, and if she gives her heart, it won't mend easily. Perhaps you should drop a word of warning in her ear ... before she builds him into something he is not. For all her wit, she is still a green girl, and that lad has had his pick!"

"Oh, Arthur, I believe you are right, but you know what Nicole is. If I say he is unobtainable, it will only make him all the more desirable, for she dearly loves a challenge. I think we had better wait and see what occurs in London," sighed Lady Beaumont and left her husband, for they were leaving the next morning for town and there were many last-minute details she had to see to.

Nicole smiled at the Duke as she got up from the sofa. "I shall leave you to your own devices now, Duke, for I must run up and change into a dress before Mama comes down," she said saucily, her eyes dancing delightfully.

"That, I believe, would be advisable, imp," he replied with mock gravity. "However, I must bade you farewell now, for I fear I will not be here when you again return."

"Oh, are you leaving us so soon?" she said lightly, hiding the disappointment she felt.

"I regret that I must, as I have engagements in town that must be kept, but I understand from your father that you will be in London yourself tomorrow and I look forward to paying you a call when you are settled." His tone had become formal, for he was not sure he wanted this ... friendship to progress any further. She was sensitive to the change of his attitude and politely responded in kind, leaving him to his reflections and going to her room for her own.

Chapter Three

Upon arriving at his town house in Brook Street, some two and a half hours later, the Duke was met by his man of business, and became engrossed with that worthy gentleman for several hours, as there were many matters with regards to his estates in Hampshire that needed strong decisions. It was therefore not until some time later that Roth had the opportunity to thumb through his mail. When he was somewhat carelessly attending to this, he came across a scented pink note, and with a lift to his dark brow, opened it. He read the missive (which brought a slight curl to his lip, and the cynical look to his eyes).

Dearest Roth:

I have missed your company terribly. Please, darling, come to me at once, for your man tells me that he expects you back today, and I shall remain at home in the expectation of seeing you.

Your loving and impatient,
Lucy

At one time, some five or six months earlier, when he had been in strong pursuit of the lady, such an epistle would have sent him hot-foot to her door. Now, he felt the old boredom and restlessness descend upon him. He shrugged his broad shoulders and put the note aside. He had an engagement at White's that evening and would stop off to see Lucy on his way.

Roth entered the small hallway of Lady Beldon's lodgings and removed his greatcoat, handing it carelessly to the butler and advising him that he knew his way. He stood a moment at the entrance to Lucy's sitting room, which was done quite attractively in blue. This gave the widow the opportunity to gaze rapturously up at him, for he did indeed look his best. His black windswept locks framed his handsome face. His coat of dark blue super-fine, trimmed with sapphire buttons, showed his wide shoulders off to advantage. He wore a silk print waistcoat, and knee breeches of a fine pale blue knit. Lady Beldon had been waiting anxiously for his visit, as she was truly enamored of this tall handsome man. Looking at him now, she sucked in her breath and held out one elegant white hand. "Adam . . . love, do come to me! Oh, how I have missed you, darling," she said without getting up.

He thought her exquisitely lovely. Her pale blond hair was dressed Venetian style. She wore a blue negligee, which showed to perfection the loveliness of her pink and white skin. She was lounging on a blue satin settee near the fire, the folds of her negligee falling elegantly and carelessly to one side, revealing her shapely legs. She was a year older than the Duke and as practiced a flirt as he was himself! She made an enticing picture, lying there looking up at him provocatively. He went to her, thinking how desirable she would be, if only she weren't so pre-dictable! When he had first encountered the widow, he had had an overwhelming fancy to possess her. The first few months of their relationship had given him no little satisfaction and he had enjoyed their ardent lovemaking, but he had found that recently his need of her was no more . . . his desire for her had waned and his lovemaking had become mechanical. His desire to quit her had become heightened, for the widow was on the same social scale and had been hinting of making their relationship permanent. He had no intention of getting caught in such a trap.

She pulled at his hand. "Adam, kiss me, dearest."

He took her hand and held it to his lips while he sat down beside and facing her.

"You look charming as ever, Lucy," he said quietly.

She sensed something was wrong, and wishing the feeling away, she reached up for him, putting her arms around his neck and drawing him down to her. Their lips met and the desire within him was kindled as he felt her body move beneath him. His hand went to her exposed leg as he returned her kiss passionately. She threw back her head, lightly laughing, exhilarated by the fact that she had aroused him. "La, Adam ... for a moment there ... well, never mind, you are here and that is what I have been needing and wishing for, my darling. Shall we go upstairs now?" Her smile invited him, but the passion within him had died when he heard her laugh ... the moment was over. He looked up at the clock on the mantel. "I am afraid, Lucy, that I cannot remain long enough to ... go upstairs. I am engaged at White's tonight and cannot cry off."

She pouted at him. "No, Adam, I simply will not give you up again. La ... I do not see what there is at White's that needs you immediately. Can you not stay with me but thirty minutes more ... please, Adam, just a little while longer," she pleaded coaxingly.

He regarded her from thoughtful eyes. "Well, as I do expect to be gone again tomorrow evening, I suppose ... we must spend a little time together now." He put his hand about her waist and helped her to her feet. They were walking out of the room together when she spied a black jeweler's case lying elegantly on the stainwood table near the parlor door. "Oh, Adam, I have picked out my birthday present, if you please. I should so like you to have a look at it now."

"Why? Does it matter, Lucy?" he said drily.

"Adam, you are not put out?" she said, surprised. "For I saw the necklace and knew that it was just what you would have chosen for me yourself." She looked up innocently at him as she opened the case and handed it to him.

The Duke held the jewels in his hand and examined them indifferently. They were a simple but elegant arrangement of sapphires and diamonds, quite lovely and chosen in good taste.

"Do you approve, your Grace?" Lucy's smile embraced him.

"They are just what I would have chosen for you, Lucy—had I been allowed to do so!" he said drily. Then suddenly the Duke felt suffocated, and knew an urgency to escape. Things had become seedy and repulsive and he wanted fresh air! He turned to Lucy. "However, my dear, I see that it is much later than I had supposed and I must depart." He kissed her lightly on the cheek, called for his greatcoat, and left her standing in some bewilderment as he made his hasty departure.

As he walked the distance to White's he was not quite certain why he had been so peeved with her. For surely he had always allowed her to pick out such trifles and send him the bills. He had to admit that Lucy had not been greedy. She had an easy competence left to her by her late husband and did not depend on him for her living. She was a passionate woman and he had always enjoyed her lovemaking. He did not want to break with her and could not understand his speed in leaving her tonight. Roth was, in fact, bored . . . but there was something else that continually crept into his mind, nagging at him. Everywhere he went, his mind kept forming a picture of that damnable chit's face, alight with mischief. It brought a rueful smile to his lips. He shrugged his shoulders, reprimanding himself and thinking, *That's enough . . . you have spent an amusing time with a delightful and engaging family and you are allowing it to grow out of proportion.*

Roth entered White's somewhat more preoccupied than was his usual habit. He barely heard his friends regale him heartily until one gentleman in particular came laughingly toward him, slapping his arm good-naturedly. "Confound you, Roth, where have you been, for you were engaged to dine with me last night, you know, and never showed up!" The gentleman smiled reproachfully at the Duke.

"Why, James, I believe I sent you a note."

"Yes, but dash it, man, not good enough, running off at the last minute, and Brummell off God knows where. Left my party quite flat, let me tell you. Sending me a note saying you won't be back till the morrow explains very little . . . and it's an explanation I want!"

"Oh? I had rather thought my note did explain—but then, you were never very quick-witted, Jimmy my boy," rallied Roth, grinning.

"Why, if I thought I could I'd tip you a settler, you

rogue. Of all the unhandsome things to say," retorted Sir James Litchfield.

Sir James was an amiable young man of five and twenty. His brown locks were worn à la Brutus and framed a handsome if somewhat boyish countenance. He had been a constant and close friend of the Duke's for a little over three years. Jimmy, as his many friends called him, had been on the town since he had turned twenty-two. He aspired to the heights of dandyism, often donning a loud floral or striped waistcoat, heedless to the criticisms leveled at him by his cronies. His shirt points were always just a bit too high and his neckcloth was never exactly as it should be. Nevertheless, there was no hostess who did not put his name at the top of her list, no man who did not value his friendship. The patronesses of Almack's would never think to ask for his voucher. His happy disposition had won him many loyal friends. He now studied Roth musingly. "Eh, what's to do, man, you can't bamboozle me, Roth old fellow!"

"I'd like to wager you that I could if I wished. However, I have no wish to . . . er, bamboozle you, as you put it, Jimmy." Roth laughed.

"No, eh? Well, don't pitch your gammon at me, Roth, for I tell you to your head it won't fadge. There is something in the wind, so out with it, man."

The Duke had never been one to discuss his affairs. However, there was a deep friendship between the two men and he knew that Litchfield could be trusted and could in all probability be of some help. He lowered his voice, but smiled as if he were discussing nothing more important than the cut of his coat. "There's some bad dealings in the department over the tampering with one of our most important dispatches. In fact, we've got a traitorous spy amongst us and it's bound to cause trouble and scandal for the Regent."

Sir James gave a low whistle. "Felt something was afoot."

"That's another thing, James—how did you . . . *feel* there was something afoot?"

"To tell you the truth, Adam, I didn't hear a word, but all you fellows from the foreign department have been looking so damn serious and glum these last few days . . . well, bound to suspect something's wrong."

"Yes, yes, of course. Damned indiscreet bunch, aren't we?" Roth was clearly annoyed.

"No, but a fustier lot I have never seen. Not the way to go about a thing, if you ask me. Bound to make the fellow take a fright. Won't catch him if he lays low, Adam."

Roth put a hand to his chin, sighing. "Don't I know it, James. I have been trying to set things right these past few days and more. There is something you can do for me, my friend."

"Anything in my power, Adam."

"Jimmy, keep your ears open for me, and become my eyes. Men will say things to you which they would not say to me, and they might slip in front of you. They would not do so in front of me. I depend on you to be my ears and eyes through this mess."

Sir James grinned. "I wouldn't have to be if you weren't such a cold-hearted brute, Adam ole boy."

"How unkind of you, James, for I, on the other hand, have always thought myself a warm sort of fellow."

The two men's laughter was interrupted by a quizzing glass being leveled at them. They looked up to see Mr. George (Beau) Brummell. The quizzing glass fell and one fine eyebrow went up, a look of mock disappointment shown on the Beau's countenance.

"No, really, James, if you are to be a part of our set tonight for dinner, do go home and change that *thing* you are wearing and replace it with a waistcoat."

Roth laughed, Litchfield looked down at the offending garment and was come over with a feeling of dismay, for when he had bought it, he thought the stripes a bit too wide; and when he had put it on tonight for the first time, he felt sure they were too wide; now that Brummell himself had passed judgment, there was nothing for it, it must be cast with so many others into the cupboard until such time that Society's tastes should improve. He was now lost in the depths of indecision, for he was not sure whether he should return to his lodgings and change, which would surely make him late for dinner, or remain in the questionable waistcoat.

38

Brummell turned to Roth. "Ah, Adam, what a refreshing sight. Come, let us leave, for Alvanley dines with the Regent tonight, and so will not be with us."

"Oh, but I thought Prinny was in hot pursuit of Lady Hertford, and would not dine with any of us, for he declared to me that he was caught up in the throes of ardent love for her Ladyship and would not give up until he had won."

The Beau's lip curled. "Well, you have been out of town a day or so, haven't you, Adam?"

Roth threw back his head with a gusty laugh. "No, George . . . take care what you say." He chuckled again and linked an arm with "the Arbiter of Fashion," and as they turned to go, Roth turned his head, grinning at Litchfield. "Come on then, Jimmy, you can throw it away in the morning, for I am certain we can manage to keep our eyes averted tonight."

"No, this is too bad. I am persuaded you are both of you jealous, but if you feel so strongly, I'd just as lief go home and change to my—"

He was interrupted by a deep, anguished sigh from Brummell. "No, James, for you would then make us late for dinner. You may stay, dear boy . . . if you do not sit in front of me."

This brought Sir James back to his previous grievance. "Speaking of dinner, mine was ruined last night, for with Adam gone and your man saying you were already engaged, I was left with Derby. Damned flat for the two of us, I can tell you. Where were you, Beau?"

"I dined with a gentleman, whose name I shall not mention, a . . . Mr. R. I believe he wishes me to notice him, hence the dinner. But to give him his due, he begged me to make up the party myself, and I asked Alvanley, Mills, Pierrepoint, Mildmay, and a few others, and I assure you that the affair turned out quite unique. There was every delicacy in or out of Season. But, my dear fellows, conceive my astonishment when Mr. R. had the nerve to sit down and dine with us!"

The small group that had gathered round to hear this little story broke up laughing and the three men left the club in good spirits.

Chapter Four

With the departure of the Duke, the household at Sutland threw itself into preparations for the family's own leave-taking, which would be on the following morning. Nicole had been wandering about the park after she changed into a pretty muslin dress, one that she had wished the Duke could have seen her in. She felt strangely listless. She nodded to Grudsly as she entered the hall and he smiled at her with all the liberty allowed a retainer who had seen her grow to maidenhood.

"If you don't mind my saying so, Lady Nicole, it's mighty poor-spirited you are for a girl leaving for London in the morn."

Nicole put up her chin defensively. "I am never poor-spirited, Grudsly, not even when I am." She smiled at him and went into the library to find her mother, who was deep in invitations for her daughter's presentation ball. She sat down quietly beside her and said softly, "Mama?"

Lady Beaumont looked up at her daughter with a smile. "Hallo, darling. My goodness, if all these people accept our invitations—and they probably will—we will have over three hundred guests. It shall be the greatest squeeze of the Season."

"Yes, I am sure, but, Mama . . . I . . ."

Lady Beaumont was quick to catch the note of need in her daughter's voice, put down her pen, and looked up inquiringly. "Yes, love?"

"There is something of a very delicate nature that I wish to discuss with you, ma'am."

Lady Beaumont looked at her daughter intently. "Of course, love, what is it?"

"I have been thinking ever so much about my London Season and I have come to a very profound conclusion." She saw her mother looking at her somewhat surprised and hurried on. "I do not wish to be an ordinary miss. I know you and Papa say that I am pretty, but it is not enough, for I am persuaded that many pretty girls are presented. I simply do not want to be one of many. I want to remain myself, which means I do not want to wear clothing that is missish. I should like to dress in the height of fashion." She saw her mother draw back. "No, no, Mama, I would not wear anything you did not approve of or do anything that is not . . . not proper, but I do not want to look like a simple miss, for you know, Mama, I am not. The other thing which I want is to drive my own phaeton in London!" Seeing her mother's frown, she continued pleadingly. "Dear Mama, please do not say no, for Harry says that there is no impropriety in my driving a phaeton in the park, and it is so important for I am certain that while there is no impropriety in my doing so, not many girls my age have the skill and so it would make me somewhat special, don't you think?"

Lady Beaumont looked at her daughter's face and reached out for her, giving her a slight hug about the shoulders. "Well, dear, I cannot like it, and I must say that I don't think you need drive a phaeton in Hyde Park in order to be special." She clucked her tongue and frowned. "Nicole dearest, I should not like to have your name bandied about, as I fear it might be if you were to do such a thing."

"No one would dare, Mama, for Harry says that what might not be approved of in a . . . a nobody would probably set a fashion if done by a Beaumont."

"I am sure it is not proper for you to say so, although there is some truth in what you say. However, I should like to think about this."

"But, Mama, you do not understand the whole. You see, I am forever in the company of Harry and his friends, and while I adore being with them and find it excessively amusing, I always feel that they are such boys. I feel so much older, which is odd, for I am their junior. When I am in town, I do not want to be counted amongst the misses, for I do not feel missish. I want to wear clothes of my own style and drive about in a fashionable phaeton and—"

"And attract men such as the Duke of Lyndham?" finished her mother solemnly. "Dearest, the Duke is quite used to sophisticated women of his own age and has never succumbed to any of the young ladies presented to him. Not even Annerly's daughter, who was an exquisite blond much in his style and considered quite a beauty, got more than a waltz or two from him. That is not to say that I do not think you the lovelier of the two, for I do, and even if I were not your mama I should say that you have more countenance and more charm than the Annerly chit. However, darling, he is not the marrying kind."

"Mama, you mistake, I do not want to entrap the Duke. I merely want to be myself on the town and perhaps meet someone who is not a mere boy. Oh, Mama, please, for Papa will not object to your allowing me a little rein in London."

Her mother smiled ruefully for she could not refuse her daughter what in her heart she felt to be right. She sighed deeply, for she did not want Nicole hurt, yet there seemed to be nothing she could do and if a phaeton would give her a little confidence in town, then a phaeton she would have. "All right, love. You are a naughty puss, but I know you will behave just as you ought."

Lady Beaumont's elegantly styled coiffure was subjected to some harsh treatment as her daughter threw her arms about her mother, kissing her forehead excitedly, before running out of the room to find her father and inform him of his next expenditure.

The following morning Lord Beaumont left his family early, charging Harry with the office of escorting the ladies to their London town house. The Earl arrived before luncheon and stopped at Mount Street, where the Beaumonts' town house was situated. He assured himself that all had been prepared as his lady would wish, and then went on to Brooke's to meet with his colleagues. The Earl had been sitting with a few of these worthies when the Duke of Lyndham entered. Excusing himself, the Earl of Sutland went directly to him, as the Duke had called him silently with his eyes. "Adam," he said jovially, "how pleased I am to see you. Here, come let us sit down and have a chat." They chose a corner table that was quite secluded.

The two men seated themselves and the Earl lowered his voice, while his dark brows met over the bridge of his nose. "How is this, my boy? I thought you would be on your way to the Coast this morning."

"Received some disturbing news earlier this morning. Our man won't be at the Coast until later in the week."

"But why—what's amiss, Adam?" Lord Beaumont asked grimly.

The Duke let go a weary sigh, for he had been closeted at the Horse Guards all morning wrestling with this problem. "It's worse than we had anticipated, sir. As you know, Napoleon has discovered that we have agents installed in General Marmont's regiment. However, he has no way—yet—of knowing how many men we have entrenched, how close they are, and who they are. I received a billet this morning that General Marmont got our man—Major Goodwin, poor devil! He was at the line . . . had just gotten the information General Hill needed for the next maneuver, when Marmont's men (more fools they) shot Goodwin. It seems Goodwin's man had been standing some distance away with the horses and managed to get a message back. Marmont is no fool, though. He realizes that while his men made a serious blunder by shooting Goodwin, he put an end to some of our communication for a while. In the meantime, things are too tight for our men behind French lines. They daren't move . . . and we need to know what Marmont is about!"

"Damn these Frogs!" cursed the Earl angrily. "I am surprised that they didn't try to capture Major Goodwin alive!"

"It seems . . . that the Major gave them no choice!" the Duke said gruffly, aware that the Major had sacrificed his life.

The Earl frowned and pulled at his lip thoughtfully while the Duke reflected on the loss of his friend.

The War now being fought in the Peninsula had turned in favor of the British. Napoleon had the Tsar of Russia to contend with on one hand, and had begun to recall his troops from Spain in October of 1811. It was now the end of February of 1812 and more than thirty-thousand Frenchmen had been withdrawn from Spain. The Emperor underrated Wellington and the Tsar both! A mistake that was to prove fatal. Wellington seized his chance and replied by a swift concentration and pounced on Ciudad Rodrigo, carrying the fortress by a stupendous assault before Marmont could move! The English agents installed at Marmont's feet had done their work well ... and then once again, in January, Wellington struck at Badajoz. However, Napoleon had his spies as well—right in London, in fact—and he had discovered that there was a leak behind his lines. He had to repair that leak. Unfortunately, his men had killed Goodwin before they had time to ... question him, and he was dependent on the information he could get from his agents working in London.

The Duke gritted his teeth. "We've got Badajoz ... and there is no question that Wellington must take Salamanca now—for without Salamanca, he won't be able to capture Madrid. We need time. If Marmont should discover who is betraying his maneuvers, it will be the end of those poor devils ... and God knows we need them now!"

The Earl shook his head. "Does General Hill expect to send us another courier by the end of the week? It is extremely dangerous. We know that someone tampered with our last memorandum. Thank God, the document was of no significance, but if they are searching out the names of our agents ... well then, is this not a bad time to be drawing up their papers?"

"Yes, sir, it is! However, according to instructions, we must have their papers drawn up and signed by the Regent and given to our courier on his next trip ... for by the end of April, if our agents are able to get a hold of Marmont's campaign, then Hill will strike at Salamanca, and our men will have to slip back to us. They want no repeat of what happened to poor Whithrop."

Lord Whithrop had been labeled a traitor by his family as he had openly gone over to the French side. He had been, in fact, a British agent. He had been returning to General Hill when a regiment had stopped him and he had been recognized as "the English traitor." They did not believe his story ... and he had no documents to assist him. He had been given to the Portuguese, who had tortured and then killed him.

"You will have to be careful, sir," continued the Duke. "For the present, only you and I will know that you are working on such papers."

The Earl was looking past him and smiling, for suddenly there was an old friend approaching and he thought it wise to drop the subject immediately. "Well, Adam, you must call on my Lady tomorrow morning!" he said loudly.

The Duke took the cue immediately and stood up, promising that he would most certainly do so. He left the table, and finding that a group of his friends hailed him, went to join them.

The next morning brought forth three refreshed Beaumonts, none the worse for their rumbling journey. Lady Beaumont and both her offspring were gathered in the sitting room, which was decorated, as was much of the house, in the Adam style and neoclassical in its lines. It was hued in delicate shades of soft green, and well lighted by numerous candelabra and the large Regency bow window overlooking the streets. Deep green velvet hangings were drawn back so that the sun filtered in. The room was nobly furnished with two upholstered Regency sofas facing each other, a stainwood tea table centered between them. A large carpet of Spanish brown "oil floor cloth" covered much of the dark oak floor, and in a far corner reposed an elegant Thomas Hope work table and matching chair.

Harry yawned and stretched out one slim leg, placing it (with little heed) on the tea table. "Lord, Nicky, sit still, girl, it's not restful watching you pace about the room in that fashion," he complained.

"But, Harry, it is our first morning in London and here we are ... indoors! Why, just yesterday you were complaining that you wanted to be out riding ... and yet, here we sit doing nothing! Why ... it's really too bad! Mama, do let us go out."

Lady Beaumont was sitting on the sofa facing her fair son and working her needlepoint. "Now, what's all this fuss about, Nicole? You have been to London so very many times before." She clicked her tongue. "In fact, we have brought you every year since you were just a tot."

"Oh yes, but it is different this year, for I am out of the schoolroom and now a great lady!" she said dramatically, prancing about the room, mimicking her notion of a great lady's walk, causing both her mother and brother to laugh appreciatively.

"You are a zany, darling, but I must tell you that we are expecting some visitors this morning and I am persuaded that one at least will be of special interest to you both," said Lady Beaumont sagely, her dark eyes twinkling.

This brought Nicole's antics to a halt and she looked at her mother speculatively. Lady Beaumont looked back at her, meeting her eyes with amusement. "I am certain, in fact, that you and Harry would like to be here when *he* arrives."

Grudsly entered the room at that moment and announced the Duke of Lyndham waiting to pay a morning call. Lady Beaumont was taken aback, but quickly responded that his Grace should be shown in immediately.

Nicole whispered under her breath, "Surely, mama, you did not mean Roth?"

Her mother just had time to shake her head and turn a welcoming smile upon his Grace as he entered, looking extremely handsome in a dark brown cutaway coat, pale puff-colored breeches, and a waistcoat of cream silk. His neckcloth was tied with neat precision (which made Harry blink enviously) and his wondrous hessians glistened, while the gold tassels hanging from them captured the eye and held it. The Duke went directly to Lady Beaumont, bent over her hand perfunctorily, but gave her a warm smile. "I am delighted to see you so quickly established in London, Lady Beaumont." He turned to Nicole, who had been standing by the bay window, watching him with a strange agitation of nerves. She wondered that all her restlessness to be off had suddenly disappeared, for she was now perfectly happy to remain indoors.

The Duke again felt something stir within him as he regarded Nicole. She had chosen a morning dress of white muslin, trimmed at the high neck with a red band. The

46

hem and the cuffs of her tight-fitting sleeves carried the same red banding. The dress fitted her youthful well-shaped figure alluringly. Her luxurious black locks had been gathered at the top of her lovely head with a wide red ribbon, and then fell about her shoulders becomingly. Small wisps curled at her forehead. Her eyes looked up at him from under thick black lashes and he thought her the most enchanting creature he had ever seen. The Duke strode leisurely to her, picked up her hand, lightly brushing it with a kiss. "You look exceedingly lovely, Lady Nicole. Are we never to see you in breeches again, though?" he teased.

"I don't think London is ready for that quite yet . . . do you, your Grace?"

He laughed. "Definitely not, although it is something that London is most certainly missing!"

She looked saucily up at him but was unable to reply for the Duke was forced to turn to Harry who had been repeatedly calling his name and tugging at his arm.

"I say, Duke, devilish fine coat . . . cut by Weston? he asked engagingly.

"No, Harry, Davidson. Would you like his direction?"

"By Jove, I would that! Finest piece of work I ever clapped eyes on!" responded Harry, overjoyed.

This fruitful discourse was interrupted when the door was flung open with a flourish and a lady of middle age with a great deal of style and elegance entered, exclaiming, "Serena darling, it's been an age, you are a naughty girl! Staying out of London for so long. La, but I have missed your company." The fair-haired lady embraced Lady Beaumont and threw her kisses to Nicole and Harry, but when she caught sight of Roth, she looked somewhat astonished. "Why, Roth, how do you do? I wasn't aware that you were acquainted with the Beaumonts," exclaimed Lady Litchfield.

But once again there was a slight interruption as her son, Sir James, gaily entered the room.

Nicole screeched with delight and ran abandonedly to him, taking his hands into her own and saying gleefully, "Jimmy, how wonderful! Where have you been? You have not been to Sutland these many months and more!"

Sir James kissed both her hands and stood back, retaining his hold and gazing at her with frank admiration. "I'll tell you what, Nick, here I was thinking I was having the time of my life on the town . . . and instead, I have been miserable! Dash it, girl, you've grown into a woman and I haven't been around to see it happen!"

Harry stood up and gave Sir James a resounding slap on the back. "Jimmy, this is beyond everything great! We will have a capital time on the town together. Finished with Oxford, you know!"

Sir James smiled at Harry and responded in kind, but his eyes went back to Nicole's shining countenance. However, in so doing he caught sight of the Duke standing behind her, just to one side, pensively watching the scene being enacted before him.

"Roth, you devil! Well, isn't that just like you to steal a march on us with Lady Nicole!"

"I dislike correcting you, James. However, I feel I must, as in this case it is evident that it is *you* who have stolen a march on me!"

"What a fine morning this is turning out to be, Nicky," interpolated Harry amicably. "And *you* wanted to go out!"

"I was not aware that you were such close friends with Lady Nicole, James," continued Roth quietly.

"Lord, yes. Why, we used to romp quite a lot together at Sutland, for you must know m'mother and Lady Beaumont go back to their school days. Quite old friends . . . though we haven't seen much of each other this past year!" He returned his attention to Nicole, who had been standing beside him, watching him contentedly. "Shame, too, for I have quite missed your growing up, Nicole. You have left your rumble-tumble ways behind and turned into an enchantress." He smiled warmly at her and drew her to the sofa, situating himself beside her.

She smiled impishly up at Sir James, thoroughly delighted with this new form of gallantry. He had been a favorite with her for many years and she was genuinely pleased to have his company and his compliments.

"Why, Jimmy, I was not aware that my *ways,* as you were so uncivil to say, were rumble-tumble!"

Sir James leaned over the hand he was still clasping and looked into her eyes, for he was now seeing the woman. The child he had so often teased and laughed at had vanished. Jimmy's heart was by nature warm and affectionate. He had felt the pangs of love many times before. He now felt those pangs shoot prickly darts and was quite ready to bestow his frivolous heart upon the vision burning before his eyes. His mother glanced in their direction, and a look of satisfaction came over her face. Here was a match she was quite ready to promote. Nicole came from one of the Beau Monde's finest and oldest families. She was the daughter of her dearest friend, an heiress in her own right, and a beauty to boot! Lady Litchfield sighed. She was extremely pleased to note her son's capitulation.

Harry had for the past few minutes been altering his opinion and thinking the day was turning out not to be all he had thought. He had tried several times to gain Jimmy's attention and was about to give it up when the Duke suddenly came to his aid.

"James—if you are able to turn your concentration away from Lady Nicole a moment—you may find that Harry has been attempting a word with you," said Roth with a quiet air of authority.

Having successfully diverted his friend, he turned to Nicole. "I am afraid that I must depart now, but I would like to take you driving in my phaeton. May I call on you soon?"

Nicole flushed happily and replied in her candid way, "Oh, yes, I should like that, for Harry tells me your matched bays are famous, and I should like to see you tool them in London."

He laughed. "So it is my bays that have won your acquiscence! But I do not mind, for it is I that shall have the pleasure of your company."

Nicole laughingly gave him her hand, which he lingered over just a moment before turning to his hostess and taking his leave.

Jimmy, having made arrangements for that night's entertainment with Harry, was once again allowed to turn

49

his attentions to Nicole and the morning passed very creditably.

The next few days were spent shopping. The evenings were spent quietly at the Beaumonts' residence, with only their oldest and dearest friends for company. Each morning Nicole waited in the expectation of seeing the Duke drive up with his bays to take her for a drive as he had promised, and while her mornings were filled with visitors, she felt a restless anticipation within herself. It was on the third day of the Duke's defection that she found herself waiting outside a milliner's shop on Bond Street, for her mother had been undecided about a fetching bonnet that she felt to be somewhat too dear and was taking a bit too long to make up her mind. Nicole had become impatient and gone outside for a breath of fresh air. It was at that moment that the Duke of Lyndham, tooling his bays in the London traffic, caught sight of a neat figure in a smart blue redingote. There was something in the way she walked, more of a bounce, and the way she held her head that made him turn down Bond. He was rewarded by the sight of a pair of green eyes twinkling up at him and he quickly reined in his horses.

"My dear Duke of Lyndham, those are indeed a magnificent pair and they certainly are everything Harry said they were. Why, they handled that corner with a precision I have rarely seen. It is to be seen that that particular legend is indeed true."

Roth tipped his hat to her and smiled. "Lady Nicole, I thought it was you. How delightful to see you. Please allow me to take you up in my phaeton for a drive in Hyde Park."

All at once he saw the twinkle vanish, the green eyes grew distant and cool. "I am sorry, Duke, but I cannot. I am waiting for Mama."

"Then we will send your carriage home and I shall take you both for an airing."

"No, thank you, Duke, for Mama has other—"

She was interrupted by her Ladyship, who having decided in favor of the bonnet, came walking out of the shop quite pleased with her purchase. "Oh, hello, your Grace, how nice to see you."

Roth smiled his greeting and continued his entreaties. "Lady Beaumont, I have been urging your daughter to take a turn with me in the park. Please help me to persuade her," he said coaxingly.

Lady Beaumont did not catch the look her daughter shot at her and thought that this would be just the thing Nicole needed to curb her restlessness. "I think that would be delightful, Nicole, for I am sure you are heartily sick of shopping."

Nicole felt that to persist in her refusal would be too obvious and so allowed Roth to help her up into the phaeton. He watched her wave to her mother, thinking, *Whatever is the matter with the chit, for there was no mistaking her aloofness. Why, devil take it, she is reproving me for not having called on her these past few days.* He hesitated and then said in his quiet manner, "I have just returned to London this morning, but I imagine your father must have mentioned that I was away on some business."

Her expression immediately brightened and she sat back, ready to enjoy the ride. "No, no, he did not mention it. Lud, but you handle your steeds far better than anyone I know."

"You overwhelm me, imp." He smiled at her and began sighting some points of interest.

Nicole had not been in town more than a day when she had heard about the Duke's amorous adventures and had become determined not to allow herself to be one of his many flirts. Her guard was up, and while she allowed herself to enjoy his company, she remained somewhat detached and formal. Roth had been called a "deep 'un" by many a man, and so he was quick to note her change in attitude.

He sighed and looked at her, his eyes dancing, his countenance grave. "Ah, what have I done, Lady Nicole, to have turned those warm green eyes so cold against me."

"Why, your Grace, you have done nothing. How could you when you have not been here?" she replied blandly.

The Duke decided that something was needed to bring this cold mood to an end and put the reins into her hands.

She gasped. "You would trust me with your bays?"

"I would," he replied steadily.

The remainder of the drive was accomplished with Nicole in high fettle, bathing the Duke in her sparkling high spirits. It was seen that they both indulged in spurts of uncontrolled mirth. They drove back to Mount Street, each quite happy with the other, and his Grace promised faithfully to call on her soon. He had not meant to flirt with her seriously; however, when he lifted her down from his phaeton, he could not keep his eyes away from her own. Nicole quickly averted her gaze and accepted his promise to call on her as she hurriedly excused herself and ran up the steps to her door.

Roth reflected on the little Beaumont as he drove his bays homeward. If he had been but a few years younger, his heart most certainly would have been captured. But he was not a boy, he was eight and twenty, and he had no intentions of giving up his freedom. Nevertheless, he enjoyed the little Beaumont's company and saw no reason why he should refrain from this particular pleasure. He therefore did indeed call on Mount Street the following day, only to find that Lady Nicole had already gone out. He left his card. In fact, he was not to meet her again until two weeks later at her presentation ball.

The Duke usually avoided all such affairs. However, he rationalized that this was no ordinary affair. This was being given by the Earl of Sutland, a friend and colleague. Yes, the Duke prepared for the ball with a ridiculous feeling of anticipation, for it had been some time since he had seen Lady Nicole and he was cognizant of the fact that he had missed the chit. He arrived at the ball quite early and took up a strategic position at the foot of the grand staircase. Here he was joined by Sir James Litchfield, who, it seems, had also been looking forward to this evening. They stood talking pleasantly, awaiting Nicole's entrance.

This was done with an air and grace that held her audience captive. She stood for a moment under the staircase chandelier, the lights catching and reflecting the shimmering beauty of her glossy hair and the sparkle of her green eyes. She held them spellbound, for she was a ravishing sight.

The wide carpeted staircase curved toward the east part of the house, which held the enormous ballroom, whose doors were now flung open to receive her. The ballroom was lit with tapiers of every size, on nearly every wall. The floor was made of a glossy pink-veined marble. One wall, completely of mirrors, made the room seem twice its size. There was a huge fire crackling wildly from the marble-framed fireplace, which seemed to fill the far wall. The Windsor chairs had been pushed back into corners and against walls to make room for the dancers. There was a five-piece band playing in one corner of the room, but the people nearest the entrance had eyes only for the new debutante. Mamas encouraged their sons to go and stand near the doorway and engage her attention when she descended, for Nicole Beaumont was not only from one of the oldest houses of England . . . but she was also an heiress!

Nicole's hair was dressed in Grecian curls from which protruded little white silk roses. Her dress, which was cut lower than her mama had wished, was of white gauze, over a white satin underskirt, high-waisted and embroidered all over with branches of green leaves made up of small green emeralds that matched the color of her eyes. Around her neck she wore a choke necklace of emeralds and pearls. There were matching earrings hanging from her small white ears. She was an instantaneous hit and was to become the joy and despair of every eligible London buck unfortunate enough to meet her.

Roth leaned back against the wall, watching her dance with a few of these overanxious young fellows, and then quietly and unobtrusively made his way toward her. Without a word he took her hand and led her onto the floor just as a waltz was struck up. He looked sadly down into her radiant face. "I predict that they will be toasting your name in St. James's by the morrow, imp!"

"Lud, but you say it as if I have lost something, your Grace." She eyed him beneath a puzzled frown.

"No, imp, I do not think you could ever lose that which makes you what you are."

The waltz drew to an end, bringing Sir James Litchfield up to them and he exclaimed with an indignant smile, "Now, Roth, take yourself off! For what do you mean stealing a dance from me, for that last—and devil take you for your unaccountable luck at getting a waltz—was promised to me!"

They all laughed, and after a few minutes' conversation, Roth did take his leave. Nicole felt a disappointment as she saw him make his way toward the door, but it was understandable that this disappointment was alleviated throughout the night by her new and many admirers. One in particular, Count Louis D'Agout, a son of a French *émigré*, was constantly by her side, with Sir James ranged on the other. The Count maneuvered her into a corner of the room that had momentarily become unoccupied and found an empty settee. He was smiling tenderly at her, his shining black silky hair falling (with a practiced carelessness) about his handsome florid face. He was suave, seductive, and expert at the art of dalliance. He whispered to Nicole caressingly, "My little dove ... to think that I was almost unable to attend tonight. Ah, but you are too lovely, you steal my heart. *Non,* you have captured my soul. *Mon Dieu,* I want only to gaze into your eyes, my little dove!"

The smooth-spoken Count was used to having his ardent blandishments received with deep sighs ... or returned with no little passion. Lady Nicole Beaumont *giggled*! For this tickled her sense of the absurd. "Silly man, how dull to be obliged to sit and look into my eyes all night, for what must I be doing ... but sitting and staring back."

"Aah, but you wound me, my dove," he cried, "for that is precisely what I most ardently wish. If I could but capture your gaze and keep it upon me, I would be the happiest man in the world," he countered, not to be abashed.

It was then that Sir James Litchfield discovered where the Count had hidden his Nicky and came upon them, his usual good humor somewhat impaired.

"So! There you are, Count," he said dramatically. "Here, Nicky, do not listen to the fellow's gibberish!"

"Hallo, Jimmy, I am so glad you have come, for the Count here has been turning my head and I am persuaded you, sir, would not do so!" she said, smiling playfully at him.

"Here now, Nicky, as for turning your head, I surely would not do so, but I own, I would have to tell you the truth ... and that is that you are the most enchanting creature in all of England!" said Sir James, not to be outdone by his rival. This idle banter continued for some time until Nicole's attention was caught by the announcement of Lord Byron. The young poet had become an overnight success with the publication of *Childe Harold*. He was *the* rage with the Beau Monde. Nicole had read and liked *Childe Harold* and was curious about the poet. He had been described to her in many ways, but none of these descriptions had prepared her for the beautiful, disdainful man she saw before her. She was at first surprised by the unconventionality of his dress ... but her eyes went at once to his auburn locks, curled so amazingly around his beautiful face that Nicole suspicioned he set them with curlers. She watched Lady Caroline Lamb float toward him and saw by the expression on her face her obvious adoration of the poet.

Nicole turned to Jimmy, who shook his head ruefully. The London women adored Byron ... the men wondered about him.

"I had not realized Mama had sent him an invitation." Then, frowning: "Jimmy, I do not understand why Caro throws herself at Byron that way ... when her husband is so very nice. Why, how can he bear it, to see her so open about her love for another man?"

Jimmy grunted. "You know nothing about the Lamb family, my dear. They are bred for such situations."

Lady Caroline Lamb, or the Fairy Queen, as London had dubbed her, had married William Lamb ... and all had declared it was a love match! Certainly the child bride had adored her tall, dark, handsome husband. But it was not long before she had taken a lover. It was not to be surprised at, for she was the niece of the Duchess of shire, who had kept a *ménage à trois* with her husband and her best friend. Lady Caro's mother had for the last decade lived with a man far younger than herself, and her mother-in-law believed in the principle that once a woman had given her lord a legitimate heir, she was free to bestow her favors elsewhere. Therefore William Lamb appeared not in the least interested in his wife's rather open affair with Byron.

"Making a fool of herself with that libertine!" remarked Sir James caustically.

Caro, who was not many years older than Nicole, glided up to them, holding tightly to Lord Byron's arm.

"Dearest Nicole, allow me to introduce Lord Byron to you," she said, smiling mischievously.

Nicole nodded politely, and Caro laughed rather loudly, and gutterly. "Do you see, my Lord, my friend Nicky does not swoon at your feet ... like all the rest. Her Calvinistic heart does not approve of you!"

Lord Byron smiled sadly. "Then I shall have to do something to correct your opinion of me, Lady Nicole, for how can I allow one so charming and beautiful to have a disgust of me."

"No ... please, my Lord Byron, Caro jests. I have no dislike of you. Why, how could I when we have never met before? Indeed, your poetry recommends you!" replied Nicole, blushing and glaring angrily at Caro, who simply laughed at her discomfiture.

A waltz had been struck up and Lady Caroline Lamb took Sir James by the arm. "You will dance with me, James!" said she, glancing naughtily at Byron, who frowned slightly before turning his penetrating gaze full upon Nicole's piquant face. He smiled ... again sadly. "Please excuse me, Lady Nicole, for not leading you out, as one of the advantages of being lame, is *not* having to dance."

Nicky felt the bravado behind this remark and a sudden twinge of compassion shot through her. She answered him saucily, the sternness of her words not tallying with the merriment in her voice, "Why how very unflattering of you, my Lord. Don't you wish to dance with me?"

He smiled appreciatively at her. "Why, how so, lovely

lady? I find it far more gratifying to stand here beside you in sweet conversation than to try to catch your eye and hear your voice through the machinations of the dance steps."

She laughed. "Yes, that's true of the country dances . . . but what of the waltz?"

"Ah—now you have aroused a feeling of regret for my inability. Yes, most certainly I shall and do miss the chance of holding you in my arms, fair beauty! Do you think perhaps we could walk out on the terrace so that you may console me?"

She liked his soft voice and his manner and responded cheerily, "But Lord Byron, it is March and quite cold . . . we should freeze!"

"Never! Not with your sweet soul to warm us," replied Byron, ever gallant.

Sir James had led Lady Caroline Lamb back to them and had come upon Lord Byron's elbow in time to hear his last remark. He glared at the poet, who smirked back, but as Caro was quick to reclaim his Lordship, Sir James was again at ease.

"Come on, Nick, here's a country dance!" said he, offering his arm.

"Oh no, Jimmy, I am quite sure we shouldn't . . . for this is my third dance with you!" said Nicky.

"Lord, Nick, are you counting? For I promise you I am *not!*"

"No, you probably are not, but I am sure the dowagers are!" replied Nicole, laughing.

"Oh gadzooks, child, let them!" scoffed Sir James. "After all what can they say . . . it is only a country dance."

As this seemed to wave aside her objections, Sir James led his Nicky off for their country dance. The remainder of the evening was as exciting as Nicole could have hoped, and it was easily seen that she was in high spirits.

Her parents, watching her, sighed and locked hands. Their party, and their daughter, were a complete success. They looked at each other, for this was the end of an era and the beginning of another . . . and as much strength would be needed for the new as had been for the old!

Chapter Five

Sir James Litchfield, looking smart (if somewhat tired) in his natty coat of olive green superfine and yellow pantaloons, walked into the study to find the Duke of Lyndham engrossed with his morning mail. Roth heard the door open and looked up from the pile of papers on his desk and blinked at the vision approaching him. A slow grin covered his handsome face and he rose with an outstretched hand.

"James . . . how, er, bright you look." He released his friend's hand and said with a twinkle, "I did not expect to find you up and around so very early this morning."

"Good morning, Adam. And no, I wouldn't be here if it weren't so important that I speak with you, I can tell you that, for I was one of the last to leave Nick . . . Lady Nicole Beaumont's ball last night."

"Yes, I somehow thought you would be, for she was looking exceedingly pretty last night, wasn't she?" he said gravely, his eyes full with amusement.

Sir James expostulated heatedly, "Exceedingly pretty?! Is that all you can say? You? Why they call you a judge of beauty is beyond me if that is all you can say of Nick! Why, she is ravishing, she is . . . is the incomparable . . . enchanting . . ."

Roth's deep laughter interrupted him. "Yes, yes, Jimmy, do stop. There is no need to extoll on Lady Nicole's beauty to me, for I most humbly beg pardon. 'Exceedingly pretty' was not the term to use at all!"

This piece of happy agreement should have mollified Sir James; however, seemingly it did not, for he stood back and eyed his friend warily. "Eh? What's that you say, Roth? You agree, do you? Well, I'll tell you plainly, Adam, she is not for you! Why, Lady Nicole is a . . . a child, an innocent. Not in your style." He completed this reprimand by grunting gruffly and sitting down.

Roth laughed again, giving his friend a pat on his shoulder, and leaned back against the desk, putting one leg over the side and swinging it unconsciously. "There is no pleasing you this morning, James! But come now, tell me what has brought you here, when clearly you should have been sleeping off the ills of a long evening."

Sir James released a heavy sigh and eyed his friend seriously. "Observed something last night. Didn't like it and I thought you should know without any delay. It was a few minutes after you left. I was looking for Nick—I mean Lady Nicole. Dash it, Adam, it's hard to refer to someone you've known all your life by her proper term of address, but now that she's out, I suppose I shall have to. Ah well, as I was saying, I was looking for her, for I noticed that fellow (daresay you've seen him) Count D'Agout paying too much court to her. He managed somehow to whisk her off somewhere. Well, I happened to go into the library ... and I tell you, Adam, I have never been so surprised, for what do you think I found?"

Roth stiffened, not aware why he was feeling this seering pain shoot through him. He eyed his friend gravely. "Ah, James, never say that our little Lady Nicole was locked in seclusion with the evil Count?"

Sir James rose angrily, his face flushed. "Devil take you, Adam! Certainly not! How could you suggest such a thing? Dash it, man, do you think that even if such a thing were true, I would come here first thing in the morning to gossip about it!"

"No, certainly not at this hour!" replied the Duke gravely.

"My lord, if you are going to continue along in this vein, I will bid you good day!" replied Sir James grandly.

Roth controlled his laughter and said with as much solemnity as he could muster, "Dear James, as I cannot conceive of anything that would bring you here this morning at this time and in such a mood, I do most humbly beg that you will enlighten me. So please, my friend, sit down again and pray forgive me for my stupidity this morning."

Sir James grumbled but sat down, a smile slowly dawning, for he was of a sweet nature and was beginning to be aware of his ill-humor and was already sorry for it. "Well, Adam, I walked into the library and had a queer start, for there he was, Sir Charles Barnaby you know, Lord Boothe's cousin, or whatever he is—standing over the Earl's desk!"

"There is nothing queer in that, Jim, for Barnaby is in the department with us and it is only natural that the Earl would invite him to the ball, although I must admit that a bigger fool I have yet to meet and I have always felt ashamed that he should be connected to our department. By the by, you've got it wrong. He's not a cousin of Boothe's, he's the cousin of Boothe's wife. Have an idea that Lady Boothe nagged her husband to appoint him, for he would never have done so on his own."

Sir James stood up and waved this information aside excitedly. "To be sure, Adam, but all that does not signify. It was what he was doing in the library that I found to be unusual . . . to say the least, for I found him leaning over the Earl's desk, thumbing through the drawer. When I asked him what the devil he was about, he claimed that he had dropped his snuff box in the drawer, and demme if he didn't come up with it in his hand. Too smoky by half, Adam. Didn't like the look and feel of the thing . . . thought you should know."

Roth's black brows met, his square jaw was set in a hard line, his gray eyes inscrutable. He got up, pushing his chair back, and took a turn about the room while Sir James watched him expectantly.

"You say he was in one of the Earl's drawers . . . which drawer, James?"

Litchfield pursed his lips. "Let me think now." He stood up and walked across the room, one finger to his forehead and positioned himself. Then, taking his finger from his head, he pointed it to the south wall. "That's it, it was the right-hand drawer—top one, a rather deep one, I think."

"Hmmmm" was all the response this bit of information elicited.

"Hmmmm, what?"

"I was just thinking. I have had my eye on Barnaby, and yet, I still find it hard to think of him having the cunning or the nerve for the manner of game this is. Deuce take it, James, what can he have been searching for?"

"I'll tell you what, Adam. Fellow is a loose screw. Have known it these past two years and more. Why, Alvanley was just telling me that Barnaby lost a cool thousand to him at Hazard two months ago, and demme, the fellow hasn't come up with the blunt yet. No honor!"

Roth clasped his hands behind his back and stood gazing at Sir James without really seeing him. He said quietly, more to himself than to his friend, "The thing is, what made him look in the desk . . . and what made him think anything was hidden at the Earl's home?"

Sir James made a sound close to a snort. "You said yourself the man's a fool. Who's to know what's in the mind of a fool?"

"But James, don't you see? He must be desperate. I had not thought of that. Something, or someone, must be pressing him badly, for him to take such a step, and you can be sure Barnaby is answerable to someone."

"Oh no, not Boothe. Surely, Adam, that is impossible."

"No, no, of course not Boothe. Lord Boothe is in no way connected with this mess, discounting the fact that he appointed Barnaby to his position, which is probably the only obtuse thing he has ever done."

Roth shrugged his shoulders, straightened himself, and turned an intent gaze on Sir James as if seeing him for the first time. "This is a damnable business, James, for you must know that the Regent appointed Lord Boothe, and should a scandal arise out of this mess, it will do him great harm. I know you will excuse me, for I must at once repair to Mount Street and speak with the Earl."

That same morning found the servants in Mount Street quite busy, some delivering notes of adulation, posies, and morning callers anxious to further their acquaintance with the Rich New Beauty, while others picked up after the remains of a successful but disorderly ball. Toward the latter part of the morning, Harry, understandably, became quite indignant, exclaiming at his sister, "Dash it, Nick, tell those fellows to go about their business. Why so many of them must come and go all morning is beyond me. It is most unnerving!"

"But, Harry, they are going about their business. They are courting me," came the happy reply.

This response only added to her brother's disgust and he proceeded to leave the house in search of better entertainment.

The Earl had come downstairs to find his household in a state of confused bustle and quickly retired to the library. His Lady reclined in her bed, fully aware that her party had been a splendid triumph, sure to be envied by all the hostesses of the Beau Monde. She had no fault to find with the busy aftermath of the previous evening. She had the gratification of knowing that their ball had been a social triumph. What more could she want at this moment? She sighed happily and lay back upon her pillows.

Harry, escaping down the front steps in some haste, nearly collided with Nicole's next visitor. The young Viscount found himself looking down into a pair of lovely brown eyes. He felt a sudden need to take in more air, and stood frozen in his tracks.

"Why, Harry, how are you? I declare it's been an age since we've met. How good it is to see you."

Harry regarded Arabella Wellesly from eyes that had grown warm with tenderness, and a distant yearning. When he had first set eyes on her, it had been two Christmases ago, for she had come home with Nicky for the holiday. He had instantaneously been cast into transports of admiration, declaring to himself, and then to her, his undying affection and devotion. She had been seventeen and flattered by his attention. She was brought out shortly thereafter, as she was more than a year older than Nicole. He had continued to court her whenever he was able to get away from Oxford, but then came John Wellesly, and from the moment Bella had met him, she had eyes and heart for no one else. Harry, quick to comprehend, quietly withdrew. He fretted for a time in his gentle way, but then he thought he had forgotten her . . . until today.

He tipped his hat and smiled broadly at her. "Happy, Bella? But here, no need to ask . . . you are looking radiant. Marriage agrees with you, child."

"Oh yes, Harry. I . . . we are ecstatically happy. But la, how I have missed you and dear Nicole."

He felt something inside of him twist and a pain that he thought had died shot through him. He had to get away. "Here now, Bella, get yourself in the house or you will be catching a chill, and then John will in all probability call me out." He stepped down and then turned round again. "Bella?"

"Yes, Harry?"

"It's grand seeing you again."

"Thank you, Harry."

He turned and walked down the rest of the steps to his waiting curricle, and she did not see him put his hand over his eyes momentarily, or the look of painful resignation as he drove away.

Lady Wellesly was announced and ran in to embrace her friend, who had jumped up at the sound of her name.

"Bella . . . Bella, how glad I am to see you. Why weren't you at my ball, for I was a devastating success."

"Oh, Nick, your tongue is as always so naughty. I wish I had been there, but dearest John was out of town and he would not allow me to drive here from Wellesly Court after dark."

The two girls were deep in conversation, their heads bent toward each other and their hands clasped, when the Duke of Lyndham was shown in. Nicky's eyes danced, for she had just been describing him to Bella and was quite happy to see that he lived up to the very thorough description she had given.

Upon being presented to Lady Wellesly, Roth bowed with a genuine smile. "This is indeed a pleasure, Lady Wellesly, for John and I have been very close these past few months and I have been looking forward to meeting the lovely wife he raves about."

Bella laughed. "I have heard of you often, your Grace, for you, too, seem to be continually on my husband's lips. He never ceases to sing your praises and the fine work you are doing in the foreign department."

"I can see that the praises he bestows upon you, at least, are not imagination," he replied lightly.

She laughed, allowing him to turn toward Nicole, who was frowning slightly. "No, no, I agree with Lord Wellesly, for I must say that of all the London beaus and bucks I have met thus far, you, your Grace, are the most sensible."

Roth raised his eyebrows. "What is this, imp? Do not tell me that all our pretty bucks have missed their mark?" he said, his tone that of mock dismay.

"Well, what am I to think when I must endure being told that their only desire is to sit and gaze into my eyes all night. Why, that is nothing but a round tale, Duke."

"And what did you reply upon hearing this, er . . . *round tale*?" grinned the Duke amused.

"Why, but that it seemed a singularly boring occupation," she said mischievously.

The Duke whooped with laughter and took Lady Nicole's hand, putting it briefly to his lips, quite forgetting their company and looking deep into her eyes. " 'She is a phantom of Delight,' " he said quietly.

" 'When first she gleamed upon my sight,' " supplied Nicole saucily. "Wordsworth . . . and so prettily said, Duke. You know, though, I like his poetry far less than Byron's."

"Where is your father, imp?" he said with severity, his eyes twinkling.

"Oh, and I thought you came to pay me court! Ah well . . . so you do not join the lists." She smiled adorably up at him. "In the library, and looking sulky as a bear."

He bowed his way out and no sooner did the door close behind him than Arabella grinned knowingly at her friend. "Uh-huh!"

"Uh-huh what?" demanded Nicole, glaring.

"Oh nothing, Nicole . . . just uh-huh! But never mind, I have some news of my own I want to share with you, so do not look as though you would eat me."

"Well . . . all right," Nicole relented, "but then, do not gaze at me in that odious knowing manner! Now tell me . . . what news?"

Lady Arabella Wellesly imparted the happy news that she was now with child, and the two girls spent the morning discussing the blissfulness of this state of affairs. Lady Wellesly left sometime after luncheon, taking with her a solemn promise that Nicky would visit her at Wellesly

Court in the near future, and they parted on the happiest of terms.

Roth had been shown into the library, situated at the rear of the house on the first floor, to find the Earl frowning over some correspondence he was holding.

"I regret having to disturb you, sir, but it is extremely urgent that I do," said the Duke gravely.

The Earl eyed Roth and motioned for him to sit down. "What's to do, Adam?"

The Duke plunged right in. "It seems . . . Sir Charles Barnaby found his way to this room last night and James—Sir James Litchfield—came here in search of your daughter and found him instead, evidently rifling through your desk drawer. He advised Litchfield that he was looking for his snuff box, which he claims fell into the drawer—which he also claims was ajar. There can be only two possibilities, sir: either he was telling the truth, which I doubt, or he was searching for something he believed to be housed in your desk drawer. If that is so, how did he get such an idea? I had no notion that you were bringing any documents with you to Mount Street."

The Earl's frown deepened, he leaned heavily back in his chair, one hand playing idly with a quill. "I can see that you are angry with me, Adam, but what I did was necessary. I had to know for certain whether Barnaby was our man . . . so I let him think that the list of names that Napoleon wants *does* exist, and that I had it here in Mount Street. I have had my suspicions about Barnaby, as you have had, and when the chance came up yesterday afternoon, I snatched it up. No lists of any kind exist . . . but he is not aware of that. I let him know that we had discovered someone had broken into the files, and that I could no longer take chances. I actually told him, quite indiscreetly, that I was obliged to draw up some papers for our agents behind French lines, and that I was taking the list home with me to this library to work on. I watched him enter the library last night and knew he was our man." The Earl stopped and looked at the angry young man now facing him. The Duke pushed back his chair roughly and got up, striding angrily toward the window and giving the Earl his back, saying low, over his shoulder, "And you did not deem fit to trust me?"

"Trust? My dear lad, this is not a matter of trust. If it came to that, Adam, I would trust you with my life. I have told you there was no time. I came across Barnaby just as I was leaving the Horse Guards . . . and knew suddenly what I had to do. I took up the chance . . . watched him last night, and sent a note round to your lodging this morning asking you to stop by here and discuss the matter with me. Evidently you left your place before you received my note."

The Duke said nothing, for he was still angry. He shrugged his shoulders and turned to face the Earl.

"Sit down, Adam. We should not be bickering about trust and other outlandish notions you have taken into your head. What next is to be done?"

Roth did sit down. "To be sure, sir, our agents need time in which to work freely . . . and find out Marmont's next maneuver. Napoleon wants a list of our agents. Why not arrange to let him have one?"

Nicole entered Lady Jersey's drawing room that evening to find the Duke of Lyndham already present and evidently waiting for her, as he came immediately to her side and engaged her attention with an amusing anecdote. This, of course, caused several dowagers to raise their eyebrows, and one in particular to utter venomously, "Pretty enough, but not quite enough reserve for my liking."

Unfortunately she had made this remark to the sweet-natured Lady Sefton, who was also a friend of long standing to the Beaumonts. Renowned for her gentle loyalties, Lady Sefton smiled a frosty smile and addressed the dowager sweetly. "No, but then you have never had superior taste . . . have you?" She then stood up and went in search of more congenial company.

Roth continued to amuse Nicole, both of them blissfully unaware of the attack and rebuff committed on her behalf. Nicole's eyes swept the room and twinkled delightfully when she noticed her Aunt Augusta sitting on the sidelines, dressed in regal purple and casting languishing glances at the Seldon heiress.

Sir Arnold Merdon, happily unconscious that his mama was casting him looks of reproach, weaved his way toward Harry with every intention of avoiding both his mother and Sybil Seldon. The situation seemed so ridiculous that Nicole giggled lightly, and barely refrained from going off into a peal of uncontrollable laughter when her eyes met those of Roth's. He, too, had been privileged to witness the thwarted lady's melancholy. Nicole twinkled naughtily up at him. "No, really, Duke, one should indeed feel sorry for my poor Aunt Augusta, for you must know that Sybil Seldon is to inherit some eighty-thousand pounds, and while Arnold has an easy competence, one cannot compare it with a fortune."

"No, one cannot," he said drily, "However, I must say, imp, that I cannot envision your aunt being reconciled to Arnie's alliance with Mary Melville. In fact, after seeing your aunt I am certain that she would—if she had to choose—prefer a rich cit to a penniless lady of quality."

"It is a terrible reflection to find one's relatives have so little sensibility, but it is not anything I can deny. However—" She stopped suddenly, her face lighting up, as a thought struck her. "Duke, I think I have an answer. Yes, oh yes, of course. Now do listen carefully, Duke," she cried excitedly.

A warm sensation shot through him, for in her excitement, she had placed her hand upon his.

"I am all ears, imp. Do proceed," he said, smiling.

"All right—now, imagine that Aunt thought that Arnie was stealing away to meet some lovely girl . . . who lives in the wrong part of London . . . a . . . a tradesman's daughter, a *poor* tradesman's daughter, and this girl was . . . a terrible person, in fact, an adventuress. If we could bring Aunt to believe that Arnie was so befuddled that he was on the verge of eloping to Gretna Green, would she not be grateful to anyone who rescued him from such a scrape?" She yanked the hand she was holding, motioning him to silence, for she meant to answer her own question. "Well, of course she would. We will make it appear that Arnie is on the verge of creating a *mésalliance,* and then we will present Mary to him for the first time." She frowned, apparently going over this in her mind. "Mary will have to become a particular friend of mine. Well, obviously, Arnie will recognize the finer points of Miss Melville, realize that he has been only infatuated with the other girl, and Aunt, having to choose, will not choose a penniless cit, I warrant you," she finished triumphantly.

Roth laughed. "Very resourceful, my dear, but there is one flaw."

"No! Oh, what is it?"

"Will not your adventuress have to be real? Your aunt will not believe a story told from Arnie's lips ... and it would not do for you to be the bearer of such tidings. Therefore, Arnie will actually have to be seen abroad with this creature of your imagination."

Nicole frowned, putting a pensive finger to her lips, but not to be dashed so quickly, she brightened almost at once. "But, Duke, you will have to get us an adventuress who will play the part, for I am sure you must know many of them, and we will tell Arnie to take her about with him and let himself be charmed publicly."

"What an estimation of my character! Are you suggesting that I am on easy terms with ladies of ill repute?" he said severely, the severity belied by the amusement in his eyes.

Nicole blushed. "As you have been on the town for so long, I assumed that you were acquainted with at least one bit of muslin. So please do not be so disobliging," she replied, looking up at him through lowered lashes, her voice soft and small.

"Well, as a matter of fact, I do know a 'bit of muslin,' although it is most improper for you to know about it and to use that term. However, the ones I know are not available for such ... schemes. I daresay, I can endeavor to locate a female who will accept to play the part, but will not Arnie object?"

"From what I hear, it is very fashionable for a man to go about town with his bit—I mean lady—under his protection, so I do not see why he would object."

"Well, imp, just to further your education, a gentleman

does not go about town with a . . . lady of that sort when he is on the verge of matrimony," he informed her.

"What is that to anything, when no one knows that Arnie is promised to Mary? Besides I don't see why that should shock the Beau Monde, for what about Devonshire and his *maison à trois*, and beautiful Lady Devonshire never minding a bit."

"Nicole! Where the devil do you hear such things? That is not the type of gossip you picked up in your mama's drawing room," he exclaimed, amused and just a little surprised, for girls were protected from such knowledge until they were wed.

"Oh well, your Grace, I have been treated as a boy for so long by Harry's friends that I am forever hearing all manner of things—at least I used to. It was not until I'd been on the town that I started to really understand all the little things that are dropped about so easily. However, that is getting away from the issue. The fact is that Arnie must be seen in the park, in the Bond Street shops, with the lady in question, and he will not object, for it is all a hoax, and if Mary should object—for when I think about it, she may—I shall just have to bring her round, won't I?"

Roth smiled at her self-assurance and would have continued his attempts to dissuade her but their attention was brought round by the announcement of Mr. George Brummell's arrival. Beau Brummell's reign over Regency London was at its height and he remained supreme arbiter of fashion. His name amongst the *Haut Ton* brought to mind a young man of considerable luster and wit. In fact, Byron had written, "I would rather be Brummell than Napoleon," at a time when Napoleon had conquered most of Europe. Nicole had never had the privilege of observing the Dandy before, and was astonished to find he was totally different from anything she had expected. She knew him to be a leader of fashion, the "Supreme Dandy," and so had conjured up a person decked out in bright colors, jewels, fobs, and outrageous styles. She found, instead, an exceptional and unobtrusive man of about five and thirty, wearing a dark blue cutaway long-tailed coat that fit him unusually well, over a white silk

69

waistcoat, black dress knee breeches, and a cravat that was as neat as it was unusual in its crispness and intricate folds.

He scanned the room, his eyes finding Roth, his quizzing glass finding Nicole. He dropped it languidly and walked toward them in a leisurely manner.

Having reached them, he smiled at Roth and requested his friend to introduce him. The Beau bowed over Nicole's hand and said in a tone that belied the words, "I have come tonight with the express purpose of making your acquaintance, for I have been informed that you are a work of art, and now I most heartily concur with my colleagues. I certainly regret the circumstances that prevented me from attending your ball, Lady Nicole, and hope that my sincere apologies will find acceptance with you."

Nicole was so much astonished by his overwhelming address that she quite forgot to blush, and in fact appraised him in her frank, open manner. "This is, indeed, a pleasure, Mr. Brummell, for I am glad that you have come here tonight, for you must know that I have heard you were a dandy . . . and I have been thinking all manner of falsehoods. But I can see that you are no such thing. Why the term 'dandy' should never be used in conjunction with your name, for I find your taste in dress to be exceptional, sir."

Her voice was sincere, and her smile genuine. His inscrutable gaze lingered on her. *So the chit has style as well as beauty. No wonder Roth has taken up with her,* he thought.

Roth grinned. "He is called a dandy because he thinks of little else but the cut of his coat, Nick—but granted, that coat is superb."

"No, no, your Grace, do but look at him. I think he has fooled you all. For what purpose, I know not, but I will not ever think of Mr. Brummell as a dandy."

The Beau turned to Roth, putting one elegant hand to his heart. "Oh, my dear Roth, I regret that I must have my horses put to immediately, for if I remain in Lady Nicole's company any longer, I will fall in love!"

Nicole, somewhat taken aback, looked across at him, surprised.

Roth grinned. "You must know, Lady Nicole, that Mr. Brummell here has never been susceptible to the passions of love, for passion would most definitely crease his coat!"

"You are jesting. I cannot believe that not one of England's lovely maids—and many must have cast out their lures—has managed to stir your heart," she said saucily.

"Once I was in love—but what could I do, my dear, but cut the connection? I discovered that my lady actually ate cabbage," replied Brummell with his whimsical smile.

Roth choked on his wine and Nicole shook her head in disbelief.

Sir James Litchfield joined them with a smile and a reminder to Nick that she had promised the country dance to him. It was during this dance that Nicole observed with a sigh of regret the departure of the Duke of Lyndham, accompanied by the Beau.

Chapter Six

Grudsly opened the door to find two young gentlemen eyeing each other with polite hostility.

"Hallo, Grudsly my friend. Where is Lady Nicole?" asked Sir James Litchfield with a broad grin.

Grudsly had known Sir James since the lad had sported nankins, and there was ever a warm spot for the young man. However, he was a high stickler for convention and would not allow such liberties in the presense of a total stranger, so he replied in frigid tones, "Lady Nicole is in the morning room, Sir James, and if you will but wait for one moment, I will announce you . . . and . . ." He turned his stolid expression toward the gentleman at Sir James' elbow.

"Count D'Agout," responded the Count hastily.

"Very good, Count. If you will both wait in the—"

"Oh, to the devil with that, Grudsly. I've no need to be on such formal terms, and if the Count here insists on coming in, well, I might as well take him along with me."

Sir James turned to the Count and said ruefully, "Well, come on then." Whereby he pushed past the butler, who sighed, resigned to this most irregular behavior.

It was thus that Nicole received and enjoyed the company of her two callers, each trying to outdo the other, and staying rather longer than was seemly. Lady Beaumont interrupted them with a smile and an accomplished dismissal.

However, Sir James was determined not to leave without the Count, and turned to his rival, offering him a ride, which was politely declined. Loath to withdraw from the room without the Frenchman, Sir James stood his ground, eyeing his rival pointedly until D'Agout felt it incumbent upon him to follow slowly in his wake, allowing the lackey to bring his coat and hat to Grudsly, who, in turn, helped both gentlemen into their coats. Having thus satisfied himself that D'Agout was leaving the premises, Sir James called for his curricle, donned his hat, and made his departure. The Count smiled to himself, turned slowly from the open door, and saying over his shoulder to the shocked butler that there was something he had forgotten, reentered the morning room.

Lady Beaumont looked surprised and eyed him with a look of disapproval. "Yes, Count, is there something wrong?"

"Please forgive me, Lady Beaumont, but I was unable to make known to you my wish to take your daughter for an airing in the park. I came in my phaeton solely for that purpose, but had I voiced such an intention with ... that puppy here, he would have most certainly demanded that Lady Nicole accompany him, and I would not have put Lady Nicole to the task of choosing, for fear that she would not choose me."

His frank appeal to her made her Ladyship smile. It sent her excitable daughter into a peal of laughter. "Nicole!" admonished Lady Beaumont. "Really!"

"I know, but Mama, the Count is absolutely right. Jimmy would have been so angry. I would dearly love to ride in your phaeton, Count D'Agout. May I, Mama?"

Lady Beaumont did not like the Count. He was certainly to be seen at everyone's house, and she could not think of anything really objectionable about him, and yet ... But to refuse him after Nicole had expressed a wish to ride out would not only appear rude, but most certainly, and more importantly, it would set up her daughter's bristles. She had no wish to encourage the Count's attention or her daughter's interest in him. Were she to refuse a simple ride for no apparent reason, Nicky would most certainly label it "ill treatment" and perhaps take a greater interest in the Count. She sighed. "Well then, hurry up, child ... go get your pelisse. And Count, please do not be too long."

He bowed to her. "As you wish, Lady Beaumont," he replied suavely.

Nicole raced up the stairs, laughingly shouting down to the Count that she would only be five minutes. True to her word, she reappeared within a short space of time, wearing a peacock blue pelisse, fashionably trimmed about the hood with white ermine.

The Count looked at her with gallant admiration. "Allow me to tell you, Lady Nicole, that your taste is as wonderful as your ravishing beauty."

Nicole was enjoying this new form of address, and although she had been the petted, spoiled baby of the family, she was unused to such lavish compliments. She thought the Count extremely charming. He smiled down into her upturned face as they left the house and she was conscious of a flutter in her breast.

They had reached Hyde Park, and the Count brought his horses to a slow walk, enabling him to cast his enraptured glances at Nicole. It was thus that Harry, who had been out for a ride with his cousin and the Duke of Lyndham, had a full view of his sister looking up in a somewhat hypnotized manner at D'Agout, who was speaking quiet words of adoration.

Harry cursed under his breath and called out to them to wait.

"Hallo, Nick." He merely nodded at the Count, whom he instinctively disliked. "Thought you'd like to know that Papa has chosen your phaeton this morning and they are bringing it round to the house for your inspection right now."

Nicole clapped her hands, her face alight with excitement. "Oh, Harry, really? Count D'Agout, do turn around this moment and take me home, for I am most anxious to see it. What does it look like? Did Papa find one with the upholstery I wanted?" She was animated and looked adorable in this display of innocent anticipation.

"You shall have to go home and see for yourself," replied her brother severely. He did not want her riding about with that Frenchie looking at her in that possessive way and whispering into her ear for all the town to observe.

She turned her brilliant eyes to the Duke. "Your Grace, did you see it?"

"Yes, imp. In fact, I helped your papa with its selection and am just returning from the carriage house. I am most anxious to hear your reaction, after you have seen the phaeton."

"Well then, Count, if you please, take me home at once."

"But, of course, Lady Nicole, anything your sweet heart desires."

He turned, nodding to the men. "Gentlemen." He then maneuvered his curricle in the direction of Mount Street.

Roth tilted his head and regarded Harry. "What is it, Harry? There is no harm in her driving in Hyde Park with the Count, you know."

"Don't like him, and I won't have him chasing after my sister. Surprised m'mother let them go out together alone. Why the man's a libertine and she's a green girl, in spite of all her knowing ways. Devil take him, where was his groom?"

"I imagine, he ... er, dismissed him for the express purpose of catching a few moments alone with Lady Nicole, but there's no impropriety in that, not at this hour and in the park. Don't put yourself out, Harry. She's not interested in the Count, merely amused."

"Well, I'd as lief she weren't amused. Mind now, not saying the fellow means any harm by her, but I am saying that if ever I saw a loose screw—say what you will, Duke, but she ain't your sister!"

"No, she isn't," came the quiet reply.

74

Sir Arnold Merdon coughed, hoping to make his presence known, and was rewarded with Harry's acknowledgment. "Arnie. Duke, I think I'll take my leave of you . . . should like to go home . . . but first there's someone I have to see." He left them in somewhat of a hurry and headed toward White's in search of his father. He drew a blank and then decided to take matters into his own hands and proceeded to Mount Street.

Finding her new phaeton to be everything she had hoped for, Nicole, thoroughly satisfied, retired to her bedroom with the intention of taking a short nap before luncheon.

Harry entered the house shortly thereafter, and upon being told that his sister was sleeping, strode up the stairs, two at a time, and barged into her room unceremoniously, exclaiming impatiently, "Nick, Nick, do wake up, for we have something to discuss, you and I!"

Nicole had only been dozing and the tone of his voice caused her to sit up alert. "Why, what has happened?"

"It's Arnie, he is driving himself and me abstracted."

"But why? What is the matter?"

"Well, I must say Nick, you go and tell poor ole Arn that you'll fix everything right and tight and then forget all about him!"

"I have not forgotten!" retorted Nicole, indignant. "I was about to tell you last night, but then Mr. Brummell appeared, and later when I looked for you, you and Arnie both had left the party, so there was no chance!"

"Yes, well, that is all very well, but Arnie is in the devil of a pucker, and says something must be done immediately because Mary has received an offer from Sir Thomas Sudley, and I tell you plainly, my girl, this is no time to be napping!"

"Dear God, Harry, no! Sudley is at least sixty. They cannot match poor little Mary with him. What an infamous thing to do!"

"That's what Arnie has been jabbering at me all morning. Seems Sudley has plenty of the ready and is prepared to make a handsome settlement for Mary."

"But . . . but Harry, would not Arnie's settlement be

75

just as good as Sudley's? I know Arnie is not as wealthy, but could he not match whatever Sudley is doing?"

"Don't be ridiculous, Nick, you know better. Sudley is settling all of Melville's debts, and even if Arnie *could* do it, he can't! Aunt Augusta is not going to put out any blunt for a girl she don't want."

Nicole jumped out of bed and clasped her hands together, her face lit with excitement. "Harry, Harry, listen, we have thought of a plan that will make Aunt Augusta want Arnie to marry his Mary." With which she proceeded to explain how the Duke was to find an adventuress for Sir Arnold to threaten to elope with, and how Mary would save him from such a fate.

Harry listened quietly, eyeing his sister with no little respect. "By Jove, Nick! Must admit, for a while there I dashed well thought you had landed us at *point non plus,* but must say . . . proud of you, girl. It's just the type of thing that would work with Aunt. But the devil's in it, you know, for what we are to do about Sudley is more than I can say."

"Yes, that was a piece of unexpected news, but after all, the Melvilles cannot force poor Mary to the altar. The thing is, Harry, she is such a meek child. That settles it! I must send a note round to her and arrange a meeting. You leave Mary to me and go off and tell Arnie what we have arranged."

Harry stood up and took a worried step toward his sister, for the entire purpose of his visit had not yet been accomplished. Aware of Nicole's quick temper, he was concerned lest she fly into a rage and do just the opposite of what he wanted. Thus he said gently, "By the by, Nick, I don't like that Frenchie fellow who's been making up to you. Tell you what it is, if he keeps whispering in your ear everywhere we go, I'll box his for him!" he ended emphatically, looking at his sister with a challenge in his usually placid countenance.

Nicole was extremely fond of her brother and this show of concern warmed her rather than angered her. "Why, Harry, there is no harm in him. Why don't you like him?" she asked, surprised.

"I just don't! Don't like his set either. Queer group.

Seem to go about with the raffish set of London. Saw him smoking a cloud at Cribb's Parlor the other day with Sir Charles Barnaby—and I don't like Barnaby. He looked at her intently as another thought struck him. "And don't let Barnaby whisper in your ear either, Nick!"

Nicole laughed and clapped her hands together. "Barnaby! Barnaby!" she exclaimed, disgusted but amused. "Why he is a coxcomb. I can't understand how he came to be in the same department with Papa and the Duke. Why, the man is a fool. Papa and the Duke barely tolerate him."

"Roth—nice chap, Roth. A Corinthian, you know, Nick. If you want your ear whispered in, let him do it. He's a right un!"

She pushed him out of her room, laughing, and turned a thoughtful finger to her lips. Clearly there was no time to be wasted. She went to her writing desk and quickly jotted down a few lines and called to her maid. "Marcy, take this note round to Mary Melville. See that she gets it and then come back here for me."

"Oh, Lady Nicole, it's trouble we're in for. You have that look in your eye."

"Don't be absurd, I am simply meeting an old friend in the park for a little chat. Now quickly, girl, it's late and there is no time to be wasted."

Marcy had grown up at Sutland and was just a few years older than Nicole. Although she was not in Nicky's confidence, she often became involved in her escapades. She shook her head now for this had all the signs of yet another scrape, and she had no wish for her mistress to be embroiled in any such larks now that she had been presented to the Polite World. She arrived at the Melville's, gave the note to the butler, and sniffed to that austere fellow that she had instructions to wait for a reply. A reply came in the presence of Mary Melville. Mary was a pretty little creature with light brown hair and large soft brown eyes. Her nature was both gentle and meek. She looked at Marcy now and spoke softly, "Tell your mistress that I will be in the park in less than half an hour. Will that be enough time for her to meet me?"

"Oh yes, miss, for she is home waiting for me to return and accompany her to the park."

"Good, I shall leave immediately. Thank you."

Marcy hurried home to find Lady Nicole waiting for her in the grand hallway. She had already donned her pelisse and held her reticule in her hand. "She will be there?"

"Yes, Lady Nicole."

"Now listen to me, Marcy. Her maid will be there and I do not want to be overheard when I am talking with Mary. Therefore you will lag back with her abigail and carry on a lively conversation so that you will not be nearby when Mary and I ... er, talk! Is that understood?"

Marcy was well aware that there was nothing for it but to consent to this, as Lady Nicole could be very stubborn, and listening to wise advice once her mind was set was something Marcy could not hope for. She sighed and nodded her head, venturing to say, "I don't know what ye be planning, Lady Nicole, but I'll tell ye to yer pretty head, I ain't going to let ye get into trouble."

"No and I shall not, but our poor Mary is in trouble, for they mean to marry her to a man past sixty, and I want to try and calm her down without anyone hearing what I am saying."

"Calm her, is it? Not that I hold marrying a little chit like that to an old rake—such as I fear this man must be, seeing as he wants a girl forty years his junior—but it's not calming her yer about, Lady Nicole."

"Marcy," came the desperate appeal and one that her kindly maid could not refuse.

They approached Mary and her abigail, who had been sitting on the park bench watching their approach. Nicole impulsively went to Mary, as she could see she was looking quite pale and withdrawn. Taking her hands, she drew her aside and led her down the path while their maids followed at a distance in the rear.

"Mary, it has been some time since we were in school together and you look as lovely as ever!" Nicole said warmly, hoping to cheer her. Mary smiled shyly but said nothing.

"Buck up, Mary," said Nicole boyishly, "for I am sure that when you hear what we are planning, you will believe that all will be set to rights and you and my cousin Arnold can tie the knot right and tight."

"Oh pray, Nicole, what and how can you contrive such a thing, for I am feeling quite sick with apprehension, for you must know that Papa is arranging a marriage between Sir Thomas Sudley and myself."

"Yes I do, but you will forestall your papa and tell him that you hold any thought of marriage with Sudley in such disgust that you could not enter into such a thing. Your papa will not force you into a repugnant marriage, after all!" Nicole having been the spoiled and petted baby of loving parents could not imagine that Mary's father cared very little for this, the least attractive of his five daughters. That he looked with relish upon Sudley's mercenary offer and thought very little of his daughter's feelings in the matter. No, Nicole could not imagine such a father. Mary, however, knew her father.

"Nicole, Nicole, I am afraid that our circumstances are such that Papa does not ... does not concern himself with my feelings. He needs the money, and that is ... just that."

"Upon my word, Mary, you cannot tell me that your father would ... would force you down the aisle!" said Nicole in shocked accents. Miss Melville, well acquainted with her papa, thought he would do just this, and so stated.

Nicole, much struck by this aspect, said nothing for a moment, then putting her hand on her friend's arm, said firmly, "Nevertheless, you will advise your father that you will not marry Sudley. He will not, I am persuaded, drag you down the aisle, for it would cause a scandal. Can you imagine his ... his dragging you while you cried and wailed in front of everyone. No! He would not do it, and you will tell him that is precisely what you should do!"

"I ... I have suggested to Papa that my feelings of revulsion may overcome me in church, and he has advised me that we will have a private ceremony."

Much daunted, Nicole exclaimed, "Oh really, Mary, your papa is extremely vexing. But we will not be undone.

You will advise your papa that you will scream *I don't* when you are supposed to say I do, and then the minister will not be able to marry you . . . not in good conscience."

"Oh . . . oh, Nicky, I dare not."

"Oh, you were ever such a meek child. You *must dare*. Think, Mary. You have said yourself that your papa is not thinking of you in this affair. He is thinking only of settling his debts. Therefore you must think of you. I tell you to your head the only way out of this is to stall your father. Make him see that you need time, lots of time to adjust yourself to the idea of marrying Sudley. Hint to him that while you absolutely refuse to marry the old fellow now, you might not be so averse to it at a later date when you have had time to get to know him. That will give us time to launch our plans and get them into full swing. When they work—and they will—Arnie will approach your father and offer the same settlement—if not a better one—and your papa will accept his offer. *Voilà*, it is wonderful, I think. Do you not?" exclaimed Nicole, much taken up with the picture this presented.

Mary regarded her rather doubtfully. "I . . . I am sorry, Nicole. Perhaps you think me rather slow-witted, but I do not see how you are to convince Lady Merdon to allow Arnold to offer for me."

"No, of course you don't, dear, so listen and try not to speak until I am finished, for I daresay you will not like the things I am planning, but believe me, it is the only way."

She then proceeded to explain that Arnie would be pretending to be infatuated with a beautiful lady of a doubtful reputation. As was to be expected, this did not find favor with Miss Melville. "I can not like this idea. In fact, I do not like to think of my Arnold driving about with some beautiful creature. What if she does ensnare his heart?" She clutched at Nicole, as this thought took fearful hold of her. "Oh, oh, Nicole, could you not find another way?"

"No, dear, I cannot," replied Nicole gently.

"But people will say he is in love with her, and I could not bear it."

"My sweet Mary, you were ever a simple child. We

want them to say he is in love with her. Most young men have bits of muslins. Oh, excuse me, dear, I know I shouldn't say that, but nonetheless it is true. There is nothing in that, you know. The only way it would disturb my aunt's peace of mind is if she were to hear that her son was smitten by his bit . . . his—oh, confound it, there is no better way to say it—his light-o'-love. She must be made to think that he is about to actually marry her. Then . . . you will be introduced to him. He will begin to see that he really loves you and tell his mother that if he cannot have his light-o'-love, he must have you. Aunt will choose you, dear!"

Mary appeared much struck with the romance this implied, but replied that she feared people would think her dear Arnold rather fickle.

"What does that signify? All young men are fickle. There is nothing in that, Mary. Young bucks are expected to make mistakes before they settle down," replied Nicole knowingly.

Mary put her gentle hand out and took hold of Nicole's, giving it a light squeeze. "Whether this works or fails, I want you to know, Nicole, that I shall forever be in your debt."

"Nonsense! It would not do for us to talk too long, though, as we have never been on close terms in the past. Let us wait for our maids and separate now. We will say that we have discussed mutual friends and found pleasure in our renewed acquaintanceship."

As Marcy and Mary's maid had come upon them, Nicole smiled and said more loudly, "Well, then, this has been pleasant. Will I see you at Lady Sefton's? Good! I shall look forward to it." Then turning to her maid, she said benignly, "Come along, Marcy."

Feeling quite accomplished, Nicole bounced happily back to Mount Street with a sighing, head-shaking Marcy beside her.

Chapter Seven

Having done justice to what cook prided himself was one of his most supurb menus, the Earl bade his family good evening and went happily off to his club for an evening of cards. He luckily took his leave in time to miss the bustle that began in his kitchens and that rushed, with growing boisterousness, to his wife's horrified reception. Evidently the cook, a man of delicate sensibilities, had taken a strong dislike to Harry's latest waif. The creature, a disreputable parrot that Harry had come across on one of his evening's adventures, seemed to return the cook's disdain. It then followed that each objected to being left in the other's company. However, Harry was anxious to keep the bird's presence in the household from his mother's ears and left the parrot below stairs.

Unfortunately the parrot had been educated by a rather rough individual, and cook's sensibilities were further affronted by the bird's lamentable stream of abuses. This was aggravated when the parrot repeatedly requested a biscuit and was ignored. The bird hurled its caustic dialogue at the cook, who, in turn, came face to face with the parrot and began a flow of guttural French curses. The bird, quick to take offense, returned curse for curse. It was inevitable that the wooden spoon cook had been swirling in the air would finally be flung at the bird's head. The squawks and noise that followed soon brought Lady Beaumont to the scene. It was some time before she was able to smooth the feathers of both participants in the dispute, and this only after she had banished the bird to the stables!

Lady Beaumont then hurried back to the parlor and flung a tirade of her sternest at her only son. This caused him to chuckle appreciatively and a lively conversation ensued. He was finally able to divert her by looking meaningfully at the clock and saying, "Lord, Mama, would you believe it is ten o'clock already!"

"What?" shrieked her Ladyship. "Hurry, children, we

must rush if we are to arrive at Almack's before the prescribed hour!"

Harry stood up and stretched, an act that caused his mama severe palpitations. She shrieked again, causing her son to jump some two feet in the air and gaze at her with astonishment.

"Harry, you horrid boy! Go at once and change into your dress breeches. You will never be allowed into Almack's in pantaloons! Do, in fact, put on your new black satins ... white stockings ... and don't be above one minute ... we are so dreadfully late!"

Harry made a hasty retreat while his sister looked on. Laughing, she turned to her mother. "Why, Mama, what is all the fuss? What if we are a little late!" exclaimed Nicole, surprised.

"My dearest child, Sarah Jersey is one of my closest and dearest friends, but if we were to arrive but one minute past the hour of eleven, we would not be allowed admittance. In fact, our own dear Wellington appeared one night at the door seven minutes after eleven. She sent word by an attendant, 'Give Lady Jersey's compliments to the Duke of Wellington and say that she is very glad that the first enforcement of the rule of exclusion is such that hereafter no one can complain of its application. He *cannot* be admitted.'"

"You don't say," exclaimed Nicole, much struck. "I believe Lady Jersey is the veriest tyrant that ever governed fashion's fools," she said after a moment. For she was always impatient with rules and regulations for which she could find no useful reason.

Harry hailed them and the three bustled out and into their waiting coach. Nicole leaned out of the window and called to the postilion, with a mischievous smile, "Spring 'em, Becky."

They arrived at Almack's very close to the dreaded hour and rushed in with as much decorum as possible. Lady Jersey glided over to greet them, extending her hand and sweeping them with her warmest smile.

"Ah, Sarah, what an evening we have had. Simply awful, and then this terrible son of mine must delay us further by forgetting to don breeches. What a fatiguing rush we have had to make."

"Yes, it is true. Mama has been telling us what a tyrant you are, Lady Jersey, with regards to the rules."

Lady Jersey tweaked Nicole's nose. "Naughty puss, how unkind of you to say so. Go along with Harry and enjoy yourselves. Serena, come sit with me, for I have the choicest piece of gossip to impart to you."

Nicole, satisfied that her mama would be happily occupied, did go off on her brother's arm, to be met by Sir James Litchfield. He led her to Lady Sefton, where they received the sanction to waltz. Nicole noticed the Duke of Lyndham deeply engrossed in conversation with a gentleman, and knew a little pique for he did not look her way. Mr. Dereck then claimed her hand for a country dance, and then the Count D'Agout for a waltz. All the while she was waiting for the Duke to approach her for a dance, but he stood ... not looking at her and in conversation with that awful man. She could have screamed with vexation. It was with understandable coolness that she met him for the fourth dance, happily a waltz.

"He is an old friend, just arrived in London, and I could not break away from him sooner, for it would have been most rude of me, don't you think?" he said.

Her gaze was intent on the buttons of his waistcoat. She was caught between relief at knowing that he was aware of her presence and chagrin at knowing that he was aware of her agitation. "How nice," was all she could find to say, and that in a voice barely audible.

He laughed, but pursued. "I had almost given up hope of your arriving here tonight. What kept you?"

She giggled, remembering the events of the evening. "Harry's odious parrot."

"What?" asked his Grace, eyebrows and interest raised.

"Harry had gone out to some ... terrible place the other night and came back with this parrot. I think they must have been foxed—which is unusual, as Harry doesn't really like to drink—but he must have been, for he came back with this bird. When he brought it to me, it ... it swore quite vigorously. I like animals very much. But I did not like this bird."

"Understandable," replied the Duke gravely.

"Yes. Well, after Harry saw that the bird was so unfriendly, he was not sure what to do with it, for if Mama heard the things it was saying . . . ! Well, you can imagine, he had to do something with it."

"Definitely," the Duke agreed solemnly, biting at his lower lip.

"So, we put it in the kitchen. It seems the bird got hungry and asked for food. Our cook is French and he did not like the bird and thought it beneath him to feed it. So he didn't. The bird became quite violent and swore at him. Our cook swore back . . . in French, you know. The two ended up having rather a row, which caused Mama to hear and she settled matters quite comfortably."

"Amazing, your mother. How did she manage to settle the matter," asked his Grace.

"She ordered the bird to be fed, which kept it quiet. Then she promised cook that the bird would be sent away and she sent it to the stables. Becky is in charge of it now."

"Who is Becky?"

"Our groom. He will know how to handle the parrot."

"Courageous fellow, your groom." With which he threw back his head and gave a shout of laughter. "I can just imagine your mama telling the bird to watch his manners." At which he went off into another peal of laughter.

He led Nicole back toward her brother, who had been recounting very much the same tale to his cronies, but they were intercepted by the Count. "Lady Nicole, allow me to escort you in the country dance now forming."

Roth's eyelids flickered, he bowed and released Nicole's arm. Only his intimates would have sensed his annoyance.

It was some time later that Harry, having escorted his mother and sister home, bade them good night. He went thoughtfully toward the library in hopes of finding his father home. He opened the library door and put in his head, saying with a heavy sigh, "Sir, if you are not too tired or busy, I should like a word with you."

Lord Beaumont raised an eyebrow, surprised. "Of course, son. Here, sit beside me." He pulled out a chair, motioning his son to it.

Harry sank into the chair and looked seriously across at his father. His father looked inquiringly back at him, waiting for his son to proceed.

"It's this, sir," said Harry, plunging. "Nick is a fine ole girl. Grand, really, but she is not up to snuff yet. Daresay you haven't noticed, but there is this French Count ... D'Agout. Follows her about everywhere, danced with her twice tonight. Nick doesn't seem to mind. Well, Papa, the thing is the fellow's a loose screw. Not the sort for Nicky. Thought you might like to drop a hint in Nicky's ear. I tried, but you know what she is. Laughed and said I was silly. If I told her again, it's likely she'd take a pet. Wouldn't from you, though."

The Earl studied his son with renewed interest. Here were depths hitherto unknown in his lively son. That his daughter and son were fond of each other, he had always been aware. That his son would appoint himself Nicky's chaperone was something new indeed.

"What makes you say Count D'Agout is a ... a loose screw, for as far as I know, he comes from a good family. French *émigrés,* but nevertheless good blood there. He has an easy competence, and travels in the best circles. On what basis can I raise an objection to his admiration of your sister, for at this point it has gone no further than that."

"Dash it, Papa, there's something havey-cavey about the fellow. You'll know how to say the thing to Nick, always do. You're a knowing one."

"It is extremely gratifying to have your confidence, Harry. However, although I have felt the same about the Count, there are no facts to support our suspicions, and you know as well as I do that if I forbid Nick without good cause, it will stir up the devil in her. I don't think she is interested in the Count, and I fully intend to watch them both."

Harry looked doubtful, clearly not satisfied. "Yes, sir, but ... he whispers in her ear! You can watch all you want, but you won't know what he is saying, and Nick is just a green girl! It could turn her head."

The Earl of Sutland roared with laughter. His son

looked affronted. "Harry, I daresay any number of young men are whispering in Nick's ear—your friend Sir James Litchfield being one of the leaders in this superior occupation."

"Jimmy? No, you don't say," remarked Harry, evidently much struck with this new piece of information. He shrugged his shoulders. "Well, as long as you know."

His father smiled. "Harry, why all this concern? Nicole is no fool!"

"Gad no! Not she! Nick's a right un, but thing is, sir, the only bucks she has ever known are my friends, and they never whispered in her ear. Bound to believe what she hears, for she's not used to anyone being sly with her. It's bound to turn her head, and I don't want to see her hurt."

"No, nor do I, son, and I don't think she will be. She's always had her head square on her shoulders."

The Earl smiled, stood up, and gazed fondly at his son. The candlelight flickered across Harry's fair curls and he looked sweetly boyish.

"Harry," called the Earl softly.

"Yes, sir?"

The Earl came quietly over and put an arm about him, while the other ruffled his hair, much in the way he had done when his son was but a child. "I love you, son."

Harry blushed happily and father and son said a fond good night before retiring.

Nicole met Harry on their way downstairs, but before entering the morning room, Nick put a restraining hand on her brother's arm. "Harry, I want to do some sightseeing this morning. Will you be so obliging as to take me to the Museum?" she said cajolingly.

Harry eyed her with no little horror and responded immediately. "No! What a thing to ask a fellow first thing in the morning. Besides, Nick, you won't like it. Really, fusty old place. Surprised at you, dear girl." He saw that she was about to fling a tirade of pleading at him and hastily added, "Tell you what, Nick. Take you to see that 'Push me-Pull me.' Daresay you'll like that much better. Should like to see it myself, you know."

She gave him an arched look that clearly indicated she did not agree, but as Harry could be stubborn on certain things, she conceded.

They left in the family curricle. However, they neglected to take along the guidebook and it was not long before they realized they were quite lost. Harry had been wielding his team down a narrow and heavily trafficked thoroughfare when they were hailed by familiar voices. Harry reined in and smilingly awaited their owners' approach. They greeted Harry and Nicole with much affection, as they had been acquainted from the cradle. Archie and Robert Wychburn exclaimed in one voice, "By Jupiter, the Beaumonts!"

As these two young men were identical twins, with carrot-colored hair and round faces covered with freckles, this ejaculation, said in unison, set the Beaumonts off into explosive laughter.

"What is so funny?" inquired Archie, much surprised.

"Oh, nothing . . . nothing! Never mind," replied Nicole between convulsive fits of laughter.

"I know . . . you two must be off to the fair, but you have turned down the wrong lane, Harry. You'll find much easier access down Whitmore Street, to your left. I say, it's first rate, you will like it excessively, for we did the whole thing yesterday in bang-up style," said Archie enthusiastically.

"Fair? What fair? Did you hear that, Nick? There is a fair!" exclaimed Harry joyously. "Where did you say, Arch?

As Archie was now engaged in an animated description of the hideous freaks who were on display at the fair (to which Nicole was pulling a strong face), it was Robby who answered him. The four youths conversed happily for a while.

"Didn't you know about the fair, Harry? But then, where were you off to?" asked Archie, surprised.

"To find that damnable thing the 'Push me-Pull me,' but devil take the thing, we've been going round in circles for some ten minutes now without a trace of it."

"Hmmm . . . well, shouldn't think you would like it half

as much as the fair. Do better to take Nicky there instead. Not the thing, but you're her brother so there can't be any harm in it," supplied Robby thoughtfully.

"Thank you, Robby, for telling us, I am sure we will like it, but if you have seen it already, what are you two doing down this way?" asked Harry curiously.

The honorable Robert Wychburn cocked an eyebrow and a warning glance at Harry, and whispered, "Visiting Archie's bit of muslin, ole boy. No need to mention it to Nicky."

As Nicole was ever on the alert when Harry's friends lowered their voices, she had not failed to hear this bit of news and looked up at Archie's freckled face. "Why, Archie, and you just out of Oxford."

Archie blushed to the roots of his red hair and scowled at his brother; he then turned a pleading look to Nicole. "Don't pay attention to anything Robby says, for all I have to do is to talk to a female and he will have it all over town that she is my latest flirt!"

"Then I shall take care not to talk to you, sir." Nicole laughed.

"Oh, you do not count!" replied Archie blithely, then realizing what he had said by the expression on Nicole's face, he hastily continued, "That is, Robby and I hold you as our closest and dearest friends and therefore I cannot be thought to be flirting with you."

"Well, I think you should know, Archie, that I have become all the crack and some of our dearest and oldest friends have been, as you put it, flirting with me," cried Nicole indignantly.

"No? You cannot mean it?" said Archie before thinking, and once again, observing the fire in Nicole's eyes, made an awkward attempt to retrieve himself. "I mean . . . that is . . . devilishly handsome girl, Nick, but you . . . you're our Nick after all. One does not think of his . . . his friend . . . but looking at you now, by Jove, you *are* looking beautiful."

This somewhat disjointed speech sent Nicole into another peal of laughter. They parted from their friends, arranging to meet on the morrow.

Having successfully found the fairgrounds, the Beaumonts spent the next two hours heartily enjoying themselves.

"I say, Nick, dashed good idea to come out with you this morning. This is beyond everything wonderful."

Nicole had not been attending, as her attention had been caught by something else. She put out her finger to his lips, and said in a whisper, "Ssh."

Harry glanced at her, much surprised, but listened quietly.

"Harry, I did . . . I did hear it. Did you?"

"Yes, m'girl. Come on, then, it's coming from over here."

Harry led her round a huge tent and stopped short as their eyes focused on a small boy of no more than eleven or twelve years, bleeding at the nose and covered all over with bruises.

Nicole gasped and immediately rushed over to the whimpering boy, kneeling beside him. The urchin cringed visibly, and she stifled another gasp and said soberly to Harry, "Oh, oh, Harry, the poor . . . poor boy!"

Harry's face was flushed with anger and he was scowling. "How have you come by those bruises, boy?" he demanded harshly.

This made the boy cringe further into the corner and whimper.

"You must not be afraid of us, child, for we mean to help you," instantly put in Nicole kindly. The sight of this battered child pulled at her tender heartstrings and the kindness shown in her eyes reassured him. The boy, who had not known a single day's kindness since the death of his parents, regarded her through a half-amazed and half-suspicious countenance. He coughed and said feebly, "He bashed me about again, ma'am, but 'tweren't nuthin' to what he does most times."

"What?" ejaculated Harry, incensed. "Who bashed you about?" Harry's mild temper had been replaced by a feeling of outraged fury, and this frightened the child further.

The boy whimpered, "Please, govn'r, don't make me tell ye, for he'll beat me again, he will."

"No one shall touch you, child. Tell us now, who beats you?" Nicole questioned gently.

"Ole Hookum, m'sister's husband. Hates me fierce, he does. Says I eats more than I'm worth. Says I be lazy. But I ain't. I work, I work hard. I run his dirty errands for 'em, I does, and I never blabs a word of what I hears. But he beats me. Says nuthin' pleasures him more."

Nicole seethed with indignation. "Well, he shall never do so again."

Harry's initial anger had abated and he looked thoughtfully at the miserable creature before him. He reached out for his sister and pulled her to him, saying low, "If this fellow Hookum is his lawful guardian, Nick, we won't be able to do much about it. As his guardian, he has the right to beat him, you know. Wait now, I'm not saying it's right. Of course not. It's wrong, but it's the law! Don't see what we can do about it."

Nicky stared at her brother, a martial gleam in her eyes. "Harry, I tell you now that this man, guardian or no, will never lay a hand on this boy again. Law or not, I will not allow it. Do you hear me?"

"Easy, girl. I don't intend to let him touch the poor tot again, either, but what can we do about it? There's just one thing! Buy the lad. Confound it, it goes against the grain, but there's nothing else we can do."

"Harry. I will not pay that . . . that brute a penny, and we will still save the child. When we finish with that man, it will be a long time before he raises his hand to anyone again, I assure you!"

Harry regarded his sister and saw that she was indeed determined, which brought no small amount of alarm into his heart. It was at this moment that a large burly man, smelling of gin and grease, approached them. The boy scrambled deeper into the corner and whined, "That be 'em now, please don't let em bash m' 'ead again."

Nicole turned and stood between the man and the boy. "Am I to understand that you are Mr. Hookum and that this boy is your ward?"

Hookum knew the quality when he saw them, and these two upstarts were unquestionably the quality. There was no telling what such as them would take into their heads, and so he eyed them warily and answered cautiously, "Ay, my name is Barney Hookum and that there's my boy—not that it be any of your business, one way t'other."

"And, sir, as his guardian—his protector, so to speak —you feel the right . . . the need to beat him to the point where he lies bleeding and swollen upon the ground?" she continued austerely, her eyes glinting.

Barney Hookum looked a little uneasy, he knew that by the English laws he had the right to beat the boy, but he also knew that the quality were a queer set, and there was no telling what they could do if they had a mind to.

"Well, answer me, sir!" demanded Nicole, enjoying his discomfiture.

"I have the right to beat him as I sees fit!" he answered defiantly.

"Then, that settles the matter. I am taking this boy with me, for he is clearly of no use to you, as I understand that he received his beatings for being lazy. A lazy child can do you no good, and since he eats more than he is worth, I really should ask you to pay me for taking him. However, I will relieve you of this burden, and *you* will *never* attempt to see him again."

Mr. Hookum put up his hands in protest. "Here now, you can't up and take him. If you want him, I'll sell him at a price. Mind you, he's my wife's brother, only brother, so he don't come cheap."

Nicole sneered for the first time in her life and dearly wanted to box his ears. "How happy I am to hear you say so. However, I will not pay you one groat for the boy. He is worth it, mind. However, you deserve it not. Now listen to me, Barney Hookum. If you in any way attempt to see the lad, or to try and retrieve him, I shall make it my business to discover what yours is, and if I cannot have you put away for brutality against a child—for my father is a member of Parliament and I am sure he would be able to discover a law, even an unpracticed law that would cover your crimes—however, if he cannot, I will most definitely discover what business you deal in—for something tells me that your *work* is not altogether legitimate—and then, sir, we will see how long we can put you

92

away for. I suggest that you count yourself lucky you now have one mouth less to feed."

Mr. Hookum moved nervously away from them and said in a whining tone, "This ain't the last of this thing. You'll be hearing from me."

"I think not! The boy means nothing to you. You will not risk what most definitely is planned for you, should you entertain the thought of disturbing any of us again. Good day, sir." Nicole turned to her brother.

Harry lifted the boy tenderly into his arms and turned to go, but before leaving, he looked at Hookum and said ominously, "Forget the child and this incident. It will go hard on you if you do not!"

He carried the boy, who seemed to be weightless, to their waiting curricle. Once safely away from the fairgrounds, Harry looked at his sister admiringly. "You were dashed wonderful, Nick. Proud of you. Why, you were a complete hand. I must remember everything you said, for it was grandly done, my girl. Grand! Should like to spout off a speech like that. Fine piece of work."

Nicole, quite pleased with herself and her brother's praise, nevertheless ignored his tribute and returned to the matter at hand. She looked kindly down at the bewildered child beside her. "What is your name, child?"

"Jed . . . I be Jed Scortch, m'lady, and I be ferever beholden to ye."

"Well, Jed, that was very prettily said, but you need not be 'beholden' to me or to my brother, for it is not necessary. Now I do not want you frightened, for we are taking you to our home, where you will be fed, bathed, and clothed, and then you will rest. In the morning you will tell us whether you prefer to go to Sutland, our country home, or remain with us in Mount Street."

"Please, m'lady, I want to stay with ye." His large eyes looked pleadingly up at her.

"Of course you shall." Then her face brightened with a sudden thought. "Tell me, Jed, do you like horses?"

" 'Orses . . . ay, I do love 'em dearly."

"That settles it. I shall have Becky train him, Harry, what a wonderful thing. Jed can be my tiger, for Becky cannot sit behind me when I take out the phaeton, he will be needed by Mama. Jed will learn from Beck and be my tiger, as soon as Becky says he has learned enough."

"By Jove, Nick, that is a capital idea." Then his brow darkened. "No, you can't trust this urchin with your blood cattle. Could ruin them."

"Well, I won't let him drive them till Beck says he is able. And I shall watch his progress and will not let him have charge until I am satisfied with his progress. Anyway, I don't have my 'blood cattle' yet. I do not want Papa to choose them, for I would end up with a pair of meek mares. When will you do the thing, Harry?"

"Oh no, not I!"

"Well, why not?"

"I'll not having you breathing down my neck that I've chosen you ones that're all show and no go. Papa will have to do it."

As another thought struck Nicole, she let the issue drop.

They reached the Beaumont residence in Mount Street and entered their home with all the excitement of children back from a marvelous adventure. Nicole handed Jed over to Marcy with instructions to bathe him, feed him, and put him to bed. Marcy took the dirty urchin by the hand and cooed softly to the lad. Jed showed some reluctance to go with her, but Harry put his firm foot forward and the boy grinned for the first time that day, promising to do anything his new master wanted of him. Brother and sister then went in search of their mother and excitedly made known to her the activities of the day.

Lady Beaumont rarely frowned, but her countenance came very close to this, and her eyes held concern. She said in her gravest tone, "Oh, my dear children, to be sure, you evidently had no choice in the matter, I suppose." Secretly she wondered how all other people seemed to avoid this type of scrape that her children were evidently drawn to like magnets. "I do hope that odious Mr. Hooky will not come here making a fuss over the boy."

Her son snorted, which showed that he thought this very unlikely.

Nicole stood up and approached her mother, laying a gentle hand on her shoulder. "Mama, rest assured that nothing more will come of this, other than one poor boy being spared the type of life he would have had to live under that brute's guardianship."

Lady Beaumont regarded her daughter from troubled eyes. She had often thought that her daughter's heart would lead into things much better avoided. To be sure, the state of things for orphans was not what it should be. Lady Beaumont had often winced when she saw the urchins of London's poorer quarters, dressed in rags, their eyes betraying fear and hunger. She sighed. No, Nicole would never look away from such a sight as she herself did. Nicole would plunge right in, demanding to know why such things existed. Why people could stuff themselves day and night with all manner of foods, and allow children to walk about in such a state.

"To be sure, my darlings, I have already stated that you have done the only thing you could. However, you must realize that it is not the proper thing for you, Nicole, to have attended such a fair in the first place, and I am much put out with you, Harold, for having taken her to such a dreadful place. It is not the thing, and if anyone of consequence has seen you there . . . why . . ."

Nicole's gay laughter rang out, interrupting her and stopping her brother from defending himself. "Oh, Mama, how very absurb! You say it is not at all the thing to be seen at the fair, so if anyone of consequence has seen me there, well then, it was not the thing for them to be there either and I am very sure they will have little to say."

Harry laughed, giving his mother an affectionate hug. "She has got you there, ma'am!"

Lady Beaumont smiled ruefully. "I do not know how it is that you manage to always turn things about, Nicole, for that is what you have done, and I must still insist that you do not attend such places in the future, for it is *not* the thing, for all you may say. Then, having gone to the fair, you should have avoided people like that . . . that odious Mr. Hooky, for from what you have told me, he was a . . . a vile creature!"

"Well, for one thing, his name is Mr. Hookum, and for another, we did not involve ourselves with him. We, in fact, told him to never come nigh us again," retorted Harry.

"Hooky, Hookum, I am sure it makes no great odds, Harold," replied Lady Beaumont haughtily.

"Lord, Mama, we've told you, we took care of the fellow right and tight, so don't be in such a pucker about the thing. Jed is ours and Hookum will never come near us after Nicky threatened him. Hookum is a scoundrel and up to no good. When Nick threw in the possibility that we would investigate his activities, the man took fright, so I tell you frankly he won't risk the chance of incurring our wrath, eh, Nick?" He finished by winking at his sister.

Lady Beaumont sighed, resigned, for there was little that she could do now. What had happened, had in fact happened. Her children kissed her consolingly before taking their leave of her. She knew their arguments to be logical, and yet there was this fear that gripped her heart when she thought of the evil Mr. Hookum.

Nicole rushed up to her room and took pen in hand to dash off a note, reading it, signing it, and hastily calling Marcy and asking her to deliver it to the recipient's house.

The Duke was again closeted with his agent and they were evidently disagreeing over some expense that Roth wanted to incur on behalf of his tenants when the butler entered the room and coughed.

"Excuse me, your Grace, but this note has just been delivered and there is a servant from Mount Street waiting for a reply."

His Grace took the note from the silver salver extended to him and walked away to a corner of the window, opening the note as he did so. His expression showed surprise, for it was on pink paper and therefore *not* from the Earl. He read it with a slight smile spreading over his countenance.

Dear Duke of Lyndham:

As you have been so kind and have helped my father choose a phaeton that is precisely the vehicle I wanted, for you must know it is just in my style and I am quite pleased with it, I thought perhaps you could assist me with this new problem I now have.

I have just found this poor boy and have decided to make him my tiger, so there is no time to waste with regards to obtaining the horses for my phaeton. Harry says that I may not go to Tattersall's myself, as it is not seemly for a female to do so, and as he is not willing to oblige me, and I would rather Papa did not choose my horses . . . I thought perhaps you would do so.

Allow me to tell you, your Grace, that I am paying you no little compliment in trusting you above all others to choose my pair of horseflesh and feel confident that you will be able to do so. However, if you cannot find the time, and if you feel that I am perhaps imposing upon you (and I am), I will perfectly understand and then I will ask Papa to choose them for me.

My servant will await your response, and again, if for any reason you cannot do this favor for me, I will really understand and will hardly be angry with you at all.

Nicole Beaumont

He read the note through and then read it once again, wondering, *What boy?* He sent an answer that advised Lady Nicole Beaumont of his sincere desire to do her bidding, and advising her also that he was deeply honored.

Chapter Eight

Nicole forgot about the excitement of the day when she sat that evening beside Sir James Litchfield in his box at the theatre. Her head darted this way and that as she watched the progression of the glittering fashionables. The stage was well lit by fixed strips of candles behind the proscenium arch, but the curtain was down, and all Nicole's attention was on the bejeweled women now filling the boxes. Here were the most beautifully dressed women she had ever seen.

Sir James watched her with amusement. "So, Nick, what do you think of the New Drury Lane?"

"Oh, Jimmy, it . . . it sparkles so. I have always imagined it would be like this. Do you know, I think that most of the people here come to see each other dressed up in all their finery rather than the play!" she exclaimed ingenuously. Lady Litchfield had leaned forward, anxious to hear how her son's relationship with her best friend's daughter was progressing, for she hoped soon that her James would be placing Nicole's name next to his in the *Gazette*. Here was a match that would bring him social prestige and add to his already sizable fortune. She laughed lightly and turned her attention back to Lady Beaumont, for the Earl was not with them that night.

Nicole pulled at Sir James' sleeve, an elegant light blue creation. "Jimmy, who is that strange man yelling at the top of his lungs, for I must tell you that he looks as if he is going to give that poor fellow a facer!"

Sir James chuckled. "Nick, do refrain from using boxing cant or your mama will scold me, and *he* is Hellgate, always goes about screaming and kicking up a fuss."

"Mama will not scold you, for it was Harry that taught me boxing cant and she doesn't scold him . . . fact is, will probably scold me and me alone, but why does he yell?"

"Lord, Nicky, no one knows! Look there . . . that's Roth waving to us. Confound him, he is coming over," he said, annoyed.

Roth entered their box smiling and made his bows to the ladies and then turned to Sir James with a grin.

"Hallo, James. Lady Nicole, I think my friend here has chosen just the play for you tonight. You will like it excessively, for it is a comedy. Just what I would have taken you to see."

"Well, you haven't, so take yourself off, Adam," Sir James retorted caustically.

"Now, James, that is most inhospitable of you." He looked at Nicole, whose eyes were dancing at this interchange.

"Lady Nicole, I would be honored if you would allow me to introduce you to my Aunt Elizabeth in the adjoining box. She has an overwhelming desire to make your acquaintance." His eyes held hers as she rose, exclaiming that she would be happy to meet his aunt.

Nicole entered the Duke's box, one hand resting on his arm, and made curtsy to the elderly woman sitting before her. She found a woman with steel gray hair piled high upon her head. A pair of bright gray eyes regarded her from a thin drawn face.

"Hmmm, so you're the beauty all of London is prattling about. Well, well, you are indeed, my child. I like your chin and your eyes." She patted the chair beside her, and Nicole sat down, while the older lady swished her satin skirt aside. Lady Elizabeth Dowling turned to Roth and motioned him to sit down as well.

"Well, child, they say my nevvy here has been seen in your company more than is his custom. Not in his style, you know. Favors another set altogether. There is nothing in it, so don't go getting your hopes up," she said roughly, cackling slightly.

Nicole was shocked, for the woman spoke as if Roth wasn't sitting there, and what she said angered her almost to the point of forgetting the older woman's age and the respect that was due her. In time, she remembered this and modified her temper, but nothing could keep her from putting her chin up and stiffening. "I find it strange that you should say that to me, Lady Elizabeth, for I have never held *hopes,* as you put it, or placed the least significance in his Grace's company . . . for his . . . er . . . company"—she mocked the word—"comes so easily that one is persuaded not to set any store by it. One knows that things that come too easily . . . leave just as easily, and therefore should not, shall we say, be cherished."

Lady Elizabeth Dowling threw back her bony neck and gave a cackle of laughter, odd in someone so frail. "Why, child, you have a tongue. Did you hear her, Adam? She don't care a fig for your attendance. Now tell me, girl, what do you think of your first London Season?"

Nicole sighed, Roth leaned forward, his languid expression belied only by the alertness in his eyes.

"Well, Lady Elizabeth, would you like to hear the truth or should I say simply what is expected of me?"

Her Ladyship once again gave that strange cackle of laughter. "The truth, child. It will be most refreshing to hear a bit for a change."

"Then I must own that I dislike it excessively. Oh, not coming to the play and going to parties. They are quite nice, although I imagine I would tire of it soon. It is just that I feel I am being auctioned off to the highest bidder—which, of course, I am not, as Mama and Papa would never contemplate marrying me to anyone I am not partial to, like ... well, like other girls I know. It is just that I must do this and not say that and not gallop through the park, and so many other dos and don'ts that seem quite ridiculous."

Lady Elizabeth smiled and patted her hand. "Yes, child, I felt very much the same during my first Season. Any female with a head on her shoulders must to some degree feel as you do, but however will you meet your ... your Prince Charming if you are buried in the country?"

Nicole smiled. "If there is a Prince Charming, why can he not fulfill the legend and ride up to find me?"

Lady Elizabeth chuckled. "Yes, dear, to be sure, that would be much more romantic, but our Prince Charmings are lured by the thrills of London, and so we poor females must present ourselves in order that they might discover us."

"Yes, but it does spoil the story, and is not what I had ... imagined."

She looked up to find Roth's lips quivering. He managed to control himself, but not before Nicole felt his mirth. She blushed hotly and looked away.

Roth stood up and offered his arm, advising his aunt that he had to return Lady Nicole to her party before the curtain went up.

Roth pressed Nicole's arm warmly as they left his box. "Thank you, imp."

"Whatever for?"

His expression was tender, his voice soft. "For being you!"

She blushed becomingly as he led her to her seat.

"I say, Adam, really, what the devil do you mean keeping Nicky in your box for so long?" demanded Sir James, much incensed.

"Yes, that was rather bad of me, but I cannot in truth say I am sorry, James."

As Sir James showed signs of retaliating further, Nicole hastily interrupted, "Jimmy, do sit down, the play is about to start." Roth bowed and went slowly back to take his seat beside his aunt.

She looked at him archly. "Well, Adam, if you don't marry that chit, you are a fool indeed, something I thought you would never be again. Why, she's the most refreshing child I have ever met ... very much like your own dear mama."

"She is a taking little thing, but I am not the marrying kind. It wouldn't do for me."

His aunt's eyes narrowed. "Humbug! Don't talk fustian to me, Adam. I saw the look in your eyes when they rested on her. It's more than half in love you are!"

He looked at his aunt and said slowly, "She is too young. I am ten years her senior. It will not do, my dearest Aunt. I must and will get over this."

"Ha! Say what you will, Adam, but I tell you to your fine handsome head, she's just the thing for you. If you let her be wasted on some young fool like James Litchfield ... well, it does not bear thinking of."

He patted her knee gently and sat back, but his eyes strayed to the box adjoining his own. Nicole on impulse turned her head in time to meet his gaze. Their eyes met and held and she felt a thrill rush through her. Heedless of the propriety and given to impulse, she waved to him, and he inclined his head, thinking ruefully, *The naughty puss, she would probably tumble me from one mess into another. No, I cannot marry her.* He turned away and sighed audibly, which made his aunt grunt with satisfaction.

Chapter Nine

Grudsly opened the door to find Sir James Litchfield looking gay and handsome in his greatcoat, which boasted no less than five capes. His hat tilted at a rakish angle gave him a boyish rather than libertine countenance. Grudsly smiled indulgently at him and bade "Master James" a good morning. By using Sir James' name in such a way, he had reduced him to the boy he was, thereby putting him in his proper place. This, however, in no way discomposed Sir James, as it suited him very well to be on easy terms. He removed his hat and coat and handed them, together with his gloves and cane, to Grudsly and announced that he would show himself in.

Nicole sat alone at the writing desk in the morning room. She was dressed in a yellow-dotted muslin gown. Her hair was tied at the top of her head, with the long, thick curls falling down to her neck and framing her pretty face. Sir James gazed at her rapturously. Nicky looked up to find him staring at her and stared right back with a smile. "Hallo, Jimmy. My, you are looking fine as fivepence this morning!"

He grinned back at her, coming further into the room. "I do, indeed, thank you, Nicky, but you should not use those terms, you know."

"Oh pooh! Should I say, instead, 'You are looking very smart this morning, Sir James?' If so, I do indeed beg your pardon." She sighed. "But you know, Jimmy, it is most tiresome being what one is not!"

"What you are, Nicky, is perfect and do not worry your head about my silly notions of what you should and shouldn't say. You say whatever you wish to say—however you wish to say it." He suddenly took her hand, giving it a slight squeeze. His face looked serious, his eyes were full with concern.

"Oh, I am quite sure you would not wish me to say everything that comes into my head, for it would most assuredly put you to the blush." She laughed up at him and changed the subject abruptly for he was looking strange and she sensed he had come with a special purpose, a purpose she would have him forget. "How did you come here, Jimmy?"

"I rode. Should I call for Ginger to be saddled? We could ride together in the park, for it is a clear day, Nick."

"That is just what I should like. It will take me but a few minutes to change into my riding habit, though it would take me less time to change into my breeches." She giggled at his expression and continued, "No, do not worry, Jimmy my friend, I will not don my brother's breeches. London's *Ton* will not allow me to gallop in Hyde Park, and so I need no breeches, do I?" She laughed gaily and ran out of the room and up the stairs to change.

His eyes followed her and once again he thought her the loveliest, most alive little creature he had ever seen. To be sure, there was just a bit too much levity about her. Nicole never seemed to be serious, but he felt there was no fault to find in this. He was sure that with time this would change. He knew that his mother wished for the match and he believed he ardently wanted to call Nicole his wife. The thought thrilled him. At times, he thought she was not at all averse to him. He wanted to coddle, fondle, and protect her. Yes, oh yes, he wanted to marry her with all his heart.

A few minutes later Nicole strengthened this resolve by appearing in a black velvet riding habit and a blouse of a white flimsy material held high at the neck by a thin black velvet band. Her hat was a black velvet chip hat, twilled with a long white scarf that fell down the back of her head. Her curls protruded from all sides and she was indeed an exquisite sight. She smiled merrily at Sir James and extended her hand, which he took reverently and kissed. *God, but I love her*, he thought.

They rode down a wide lane in the park at a slow pace. He looked round and noted that the park was thin of company. *Well,* he thought, *this* is the time. I'll do it now.

He said quietly with ever a slight nervous inflection, "Nicole, darling Nicole, I find that . . . that I . . ."

"Jimmy, wait just a moment, my friend, for there is Princess Esterhazy waving to us. Do let us ride to her carriage, for it would be most rude to ignore her as she is one of Mama's dearest friends."

Jimmy looked sullen, but there was no getting away from it, so he silently swore and rode beside Nicole to the waiting carriage.

Nicole greeted her mother's friend with an amiable smile and started to introduce Sir James Litchfield, but the Princess quickly interrupted. "Oh, there is no need to introduce Sir James, we are very well acquainted. Hallo, James, how are you?"

He responded that he, his mother, and all the family were very well. The Princess then turned back to Nicole and said with a sweet smile, "My sweet Nicole, you are looking charming in that habit. I do not believe you have yet met Mrs. Drummond Burrel." She turned to the woman sitting haughtily beside her and said softly, "This is our dear Lady Beaumont's daughter Nicole." They exchanged greetings and then the Princess continued, "Nicole, I am sure I have no need to warn you that you *will not* gallop in Hyde Park. I am sure your mama has already told you this, but you were ever a headstrong little girl and you did appear to be on the verge of such a disastrous thing."

"Oh no, Princess Esterhazy, I was thinking of it, but I would not do so."

"Good, my child. Be off now and enjoy yourselves."

She smiled her dismissal and the carriage moved on. Jimmy led the way back down toward the path that led deeper into the park.

"Oh dear," complained Nicole, "I shall have to arrange a little expedition to the country soon if I am going to have a good run on Ginger. Oh, Jimmy, a picnic would be just the thing. Don't you think we could arrange one?"

"No . . . I mean yes, of course, but forget that for a moment, Nick. There is something very particular I should like to ask you. Nick . . . Nicole, I am very much in love with you. I would be greatly honored if you—" He was once again interrupted by a small hand that clutched at his arm. "No, James, do *not,* I beg of you, for we would not suit!"

He looked at her quietly for a moment. "I . . . it was too soon. You were not prepared. I am exceedingly sorry, Nicole, I did not mean to rush you."

"Oh, Jimmy, Jimmy, do you not know me better than that? I have always known my own mind. I do not need time. I adore you, Jimmy. I have never felt closer to you than I do now . . . and *no,* I cannot say I regard you as a brother, for I *do not!* I regard you as a wonderful, wonderful friend. But I would not suit you as a wife, my dear. I am really a sad romp, and that would not do for you. I must always have my own way, and should plunge you into one wild scrape after another. I am forever getting embroiled in other people's affairs. Do not imagine me a small creature in need of your loving protection, for I am not, and that is precisely the type of female you do need. I will always long for my breeches . . . long to run madly across the park with the wind in my face . . . gallop at a reckless pace . . . say what I should not, for I am still the 'rumble-tumble' girl that I was, and you would soon tire of me."

"Never! I should never tire of you. I love you, Nicole. I worship you, and you are not a sad romp! Never describe yourself to me in those terms. I know better. You are sweet and your heart is too tender. You are young and you are of a happy disposition, which leads you into what you call scrapes. I call them adventures and I . . . I do not wish to prohibit or stifle these. I wish to join you in your adventures. You are everything I wish for . . . everything I have dreamed—"

He was again interrupted. "No, James, pray do not press me any further. Trust me, instead. I know myself, and what is more important, I know you. Please, my friend, let us stay *friends.*" She looked up pleadingly at him.

While he wanted most ardently to extoll her many virtues and continue along this line, he was wise enough to realize that she was not in the mood to listen to him yet. He stopped immediately and smiled at her tenderly, and gave her hand a pat. "Do not fret, Nick, for I shall not bother you any further now. I know I was too soon. Look there, is that not Harry riding toward us with Roth?"

She looked up quickly and felt relief when she saw her brother and Roth approach. Harry was beaming happily at Sir James. Roth was gazing at her intently.

Roth had seen his friend and Nicole engrossed with each other and had no doubt as to its meaning, for he was well aware of Litchfield's interest in Lady Nicole. He allowed Harry to draw Sir James ahead. The Duke slowed his gray to a walk beside Nicole. He smiled at her and received a smile back, but he was quick to note the agitation in her eyes.

Nicole was extremely fond of Sir James. She had for a long while been infatuated with him when she was a schoolgirl. She knew a need to stop him from regarding her as anything more than a friend. She wanted their easy friendship to continue, and now ... this was spoiling it. She felt an urge to burst into tears and Roth, quick to sense her mood, engaged her in idle conversation. As she barely responded to his remarks, he became rather direct and quizzed her with an upraised brow. "What's amiss? Did you not want our poor James to come up to scratch?"

She turned at that, her face flushed with anger. "What an odious thing to say! How could you, for I am sure I have never given Jimmy reason to think ... never! Why, he has always been such a dear friend ... I never thought ..." She turned away in some agitation as she felt a large tear forming.

He had wanted to draw her out, not make her cry, and this new turn startled him and yet softened him. He thought ruefully, *Her tender heart will probably be the ruin of me*, and, resigned, continued. "No, Nicole, do not distress yourself. James will come about. It is your beauty he is in love with, not your soul, and I do not think it will be a lasting thing!"

This is precisely what she thought herself. However, Roth's confirmation of this mode of thought did nothing to relieve her agitation. She turned on him somewhat angrily. "Oh, do you think so, indeed? You are not very flattering!"

106

"Why, Lady Nicole, how is this, you have just led me to believe that you do not wish him to be deeply in love with you," he mocked.

She looked murderously up at him. "I will not discuss the matter with you any longer, for I am certain it is most improper for me to do so, and you, Duke, do not seem to have any sensibility whatsoever!"

He laughed and would have leaned over to flick her dainty nose, had he the chance, but Nicole had lightly kicked her horse into a trot and caught up to her brother. "James, the Duke desires a word with you."

She waited for Sir James to fall back before once again turning toward her brother. "Harry, are you engaged with the Duke for the rest of the morning?"

"Lord, no. Good fellow, the Duke, met him by chance, but I'm not in his set, you know. Told you before, he's a Corinthian . . . the nonpareil!"

"Well, then, you will tell Jimmy that you are going to escort me home and then you will do so, for it is time that I returned home. Mama wants to take me shopping and I must leave for Mount Street now and do not wish to trouble Jimmy to take me home."

"Dash it, Nick, wasn't planning on returning to Mount Street just yet." He saw the obstinate set of her mouth and the pleading look in her eyes and capitulated with a heavy sigh. "All right, dear girl, don't take a pet. Don't know what's in your head this time, for I know Jimmy would be pleased to take you home. Dash it, Nick, he likes you. Don't know why, for he's sensible, Jimmy, but there it is. All right, all right, let's take our leave," he said, exasperated.

Too emotionally exhausted to take exception to her brother's stating that James was too sensible for her, she meekly waited for him to make their excuses.

Sir James wistfully watched them ride away, but was brought back to cold reality by a firm, strong voice. "It would not do for you, James." His companion smiled.

"Oh, go to the devil, Roth. How should you know what would and wouldn't do for me?"

"Stop and think, James. What is wonderfully attractive in a female you are pursuing would be most tiresome in one that is your wife. For now, you are not encumbered by her faults, and while you may not now realize it, Nicole is not the perfect little sweetheart you think her."

Sir James turned wrathfully upon his friend. "How dare you, Adam! Really, Roth, you go to far. Nicole is the sweetest, warmest, kindest, finest person alive. Why ... she is as honest as she is beautiful. Where are the faults you speak of?"

"Yes, James, I agree, Nicole is everything you have said, but you must admit that she is not, shall we say, a restful female. In fact, she is forever on the go. She will always find herself and her spouse involved in a lark of some sort. That, my dear friend, while it may do for some, would not do for *you!*"

"Ha! So that is it. You want her for yourself. Well, let me tell you, Adam, that I do not want a *restful female*. I want Nicole, and I never thought it of you to ... to try and convince me that sweet little angel is besotted with faults simply to clear the way for yourself. I tell you frankly, if you were not the better shot, I would have met you in the morning for this ... this treachery. So in the future, Adam, do not try me, for I am out of patience with you and being beaten to a pulp would be worth the facer I am itching to give you."

He was answered by a hearty laugh and a hand on his shoulder, which he angrily shrugged off. However, Sir James was of too mild a disposition to remain angry for long, and by the time they reached St. James Street, he had been talked out of the sullens and spent a very good sort of morning in his friend's company.

Lady Beaumont had been patiently awaiting her daughter in Mount Street, and no sooner did Nicole arrive, but she was whisked out again and taken to Madame Bertin's on Bond Street.

She tried on gown after gown, deciding on the pink silk, the flowered muslin, and the yellow chiffon. A decision had to be made, for Nicole wanted a peacock blue dress that was cut very daringly at the bodice, and Lady Beaumont thought it too womanly for her daughter. Nicole was at the moment trying to convince her mother that it was all the crack to be just a little daring when her attention was caught by voices in the adjoining room.

"Why, Lucy, do but look at this silver sarsnet. It is the very gown you need to compliment the jewels Roth has given you."

"Yes, it is quite stunning. I am sure Adam will like it excessively."

Nicky felt something in the pit of her stomach twist. Her face froze into immobility, her hand fluttered unconsciously to her eyes as if to ward off a flush hit. Lady Beaumont watched her daughter and her own heart felt the anguish that was tearing at Nicky's. She reached out and gave Nicky's hand a squeeze and said quietly, "Shall we leave the peacock blue, darling? We can always decide on it another time. I declare I am fatigued and should like to go home and rest."

"Oh, yes, please, Mama, for I cannot ... I would rather we leave now," came her voice softly, barely audible.

Lady Beaumont turned away and was obliged to open the door in order to advise Madame Bertin that they were leaving and to have the dresses they had selected sent round to Mount Street later, as they would not wait for them to be packed. Nicole then caught sight of Lady Lucy Beldon elegantly walking across to call Madame Bertin's attention. Nicky felt the room go suddenly suffocatingly hot and bit back a sob. Here was the loveliest, most sophisticated woman she had ever seen. She felt an overwhelming urge to run, run madly, when all at once she felt the arms of her mother steady her and lead her downstairs toward their waiting coach. Inside the carriage Nicole was silent. Her thoughts could be read in her eyes, and Lady Beaumont felt her heart wrung with what she read in her daughter's eyes.

So ... this was the Lucy Beldon she had heard of. That ravishing, beautiful woman whose name she had heard coupled with the Duke's on so many occasion. She had been a fool not to believe—for she hadn't, *not* in her heart of hearts. She had thought, oh maybe in the past, but not now, not since they had met. *God what a silly little chit you are,* Nicole Beaumont, she told herself, *how could you think he cared for you when he had her!* He had given her jewels ... jewels so lovely that Lady Beldon was buying a dress to complement them. *Oh God, you little fool, Nick,* she thought, *how could you think he would be interested in a girl who wore breeches ... how could you think he had a special look in his eyes for you? How did you see what never existed and be blind to what does exist? But he did look at me so ... so ... oh, stupid girl, he was being kind to a friend's daughter. Nothing more. He has always treated you as a child, nothing more. Why should he not be involved with that woman. He is free!* A sob stuck in her throat as these thoughts whirled round her head.

Lady Beaumont reached out and patted her hand, saying softly, "Look, Nicole, Harry is just arriving home. Perhaps you would like to go out riding with him."

"Oh no, Mama. I am very tired. I just want to go to my room and lie down."

Nicole walked to her room like one caught in a trance. She eyed her bed for a moment and then threw herself downward, sobbing into her pillow.

Her mother stopped by her door a short while afterward and sighed. "My poor darling. You have had your first illusion shattered. Would that I could spare you," she said softly.

This state of affairs was not allowed to continue, for Harry arrived, full of news, as he had just attended what he called a splendid cockfight and wanted to describe all the marvelous details to his sister, who had never had a liking for such things but had nevertheless always lent an ear to his adventures. She opened the door for him and he was much shocked to find her red-eyed and looking listless.

"Lord, Nick, whatever is the matter? You look terrible."

"Oh, I was just tired from shopping," she replied quietly, not looking at him. She had never kept secrets from Harry, but she could not bring herself to tell him what had brought her to the real world.

"Really? Never knew you to ever get so tired from shopping. Well, never mind. Guess what has happened? I daresay you may, for you have seen Archie's red cock before. Thing is I've won a bundle on him. The gray was a famous little fellow, lots of pluck, but the poor bird didn't stand a chance against Archie's red. Never have thought much about gray cocks. Here, Nick, are you listening? What's to do, girl?" he asked solicitously, for he was not use to seeing her look so despondent.

"Oh, nothing. Harry, do you think Roth is . . . is very much in love with Lady Beldon?"

Harry looked much struck. "Dash it, girl, how should I know?" He looked at her searchingly and then added thoughtfully, "I'll tell you what, though. Heard that Roth hasn't been near the Beldon widow in weeks. They are laying odds that Dameral will be her next victim."

Nicole pounced on this bit of news eagerly. "Oh, Harry! But Harry, does a man give a woman jewels if he doesn't love her?"

"Lord, Nick, thought you had more sense than that. A man of Roth's stamp could give jewels to a lady just for being a beauty. There's nothing in that. Mind now, not saying he don't care for the Beldon woman, but haven't heard any news of wedding bells, and she's free enough. Should like to see you make a love match, Nick, so you won't have to worry about things like that. I can't see you looking the other way. God, you'd kick up the devil of a fuss if you ever caught your hubby sending jewels off to some pretty lady. Feel sorry for the poor devil."

"Harry, do you mean husbands send jewels to other women?" she asked, shocked.

"Most of them do. Oh, not Papa, but theirs is an unusual setup. Married for love, you know. Papa told me once that the moment he saw Mama, he walked right up to her and said, 'Very soon I will ask you to marry me,' and she said, 'Then very soon I will accept.' "

Nicole sighed. "Oh yes, I know. Mama has often told me of their romance. It was beautiful. I should . . . like to marry someone I love and who loves me."

"Good, now that we have settled that up right and tight, I wish you would attend to me, girl, for I have quite a story to tell you about today's cocking."

Nicole gave a gurgle of laughter and was subjected for the next twenty minutes to his tale of triumph.

Roth, quite oblivious to the events that had taken place at Madame Bertin's, visited Tattersall's, a visit that was not successful as he did not approve of the livestock they had ready for his inspection. He left strict instructions on the type of horses he wanted, which they promised to try and furnish. He then continued along his merry way for a round at Gentleman Jackson's boxing saloon and was hailed by Lord Alvanley.

"Heard there's some nasty trouble in your department, Roth ole boy!" he said, his voice low, his head inclined toward Roth.

The Duke of Lyndham cursed under his breath. "Was that a question or a statement?" came the dry response.

"Eh? Oh yes, quite. No need to pucker up, Roth. Not being curious, you know. Have something to tell you. Think you should know."

"Well, then, what is it, man?"

"It's the Regent. He put that fellow Boothe in your department this year, you know. A favor to Lady Hertford, related in some way or other. Well, damn indiscreet Boothe has been, blabs to his wife. Has a cousin of hers working for him—you know, Sir Charles Barnaby."

"Yes, I know all that, Alvanley," put in Roth testily.

"You do? Yes, of course you do. Well, the thing is Barnaby had a bad run of luck and the devil was in it, owed money everywhere! Owed me quite a bundle. He's a loose screw, for he owed it to me for months. Promised to pay, but he had run through his fortune—mortgaged his estates. How the devil was he to pay? Shouldn't play if you can't pay, but there he was. Bad sort of fellow."

"Yes, yes, but what has that to say to anything?"

"He came in to see me the other day, Roth. Laid the blunt on the table. Paid me that debt, and from what I can make out, has paid off quite a lot of debts. Where'd he get the money? That's what I should like to know!"

Roth's lips curled and he hissed, "The bloodsucking traitor."

112

"Have a care, Roth. Prinny's attached to this thing. We don't want him launched into any scandal just now."

"God, man, do you think I'm daft? Don't worry yourself over this matter, let it rest with me. I'll handle the situation now that he's been so unwise as to show himself on two occasions."

"Two occasions? What else?"

"Never mind that. I need some additional help from you, Alvanley."

"Anything in my power, Roth."

Roth grinned. "Can you put me in the way of a pretty adventuress?"

"Upon my word!" exclaimed his startled friend.

Chapter Ten

Nicole stood chatting with Mr. Dereck as if she had no other care in the world when, in fact, she had been stunned that very afternoon to find that she had to admit to herself that she was in love. In love with a man who in all probability loved another woman, and thought of her as a child. Her eyes darted to the ballroom door every now and then, when at last she was rewarded with the sight of a pair of gray twinkling eyes. She turned abruptly away and started behaving coquettishly with the startled young Dereck (who had been trying to get her to behave this way all night and was at a loss to understand how he had managed the feat).

The new arrival made his unhurried way to Lady Nicole's side and she found that she could not ignore the cherished face that grinned so merrily at her. Roth had taken up a position of advantage directly facing her and had extended his hand in a friendly gesture. "Come, Lady Nicole, I should like a word with you," for he had not had the chance the previous evening to question her about the mysterious "boy." Nor had he had the chance when he had met her that morning.

"No, really, Duke!" objected Mr. Dereck, affronted.

The Duke raised an imperious eyebrow, and poor

113

young Dereck blushed miserably and refrained from saying anything further. Nicole took pity upon him, put up her chin at the Duke, and requested him to fetch her a glass of lemonade. Young Dereck saw his chance to outshine his noble rival, and responded that he would fetch her the drink and ran off hurriedly.

His Grace took Lady Nicole's arm, gently leading her to a quieter room, just off to the side of the ballroom. "Come, then, we have much to discuss and I would like to do so now, while we can."

"What do you mean? Why did you not tell me what you had in mind this morning when we met in the park?" She looked up at him somewhat puzzled, thinking that the morning seemed years away.

"I seem to remember a very rude young hoyden advising me that I had no sensibility, and then riding off leaving me to cope with my poor friend Sir James, while she went off to adventure with her brother!"

She giggled. "Oh yes, that was very rude of me, but you know you had none whatsoever."

"I had enough to calm poor James after you broke his young heart."

"No . . . oh please, do not say so, for I could not break his heart. He has not really lost it to me. You know he is merely infatuated with me because I have become all the rage."

He cocked an amused eyebrow at her. "Shall I agree with you again and risk the chance of being told that I have no sensibility, for when I told you the very same thing this morning, that is precisely what happened."

She laughed. "No, I shall not be so unjust twice in one day. Pray, Duke, what did you wish to speak to me about?"

"It is about your horses. In fact, how you can have forgotten is quite beyond me." He grinned at her.

Her eyes sparkled at him. "Oh, Adam, Adam, have you managed to find a pair of blood cattle for me already? Why that is beyond everything great! I was sure it would be no easy task."

"No, I have not found them yet, but consider it done,

imp, for it must always be an object with me to make you happy." He said this looking tenderly at her.

She blushed. "It is not your job to make me happy—and in all other matters I believe you could *not*, for you divide your favors and I do not accept part of anything, it is all or nothing for me, Duke. But I do, indeed, thank you and I am sure that my father will thank you, for I am persuaded no other man could choose the horses for my phaeton to my satisfaction."

His Grace regarded her thoughtfully. No fool, she! So she had heard about Lucy. He decided it best to ignore her remark as there was no delicate way of imparting the information that he was no longer interested in the beautiful widow without declaring himself, and he had no intention of giving over to what he hoped was a passing passion. They had found an empty sofa and sat down together. He was facing her, his clear gray eyes had become soft and warm. "Say my name again, for I have never heard it sound so charming."

"No! I will not, for it was a slip and I am sure it was most improper for me to do so," she said gravely.

"How you can ask me to choose your horses one minute and then the next say it is improper to use my given name is a wonder."

"Yes, I see what you mean, but the thing is that while Harry is a bruising rider and ... well, he would not be able to choose just the type of horses I want. Besides, he said he couldn't be bothered with the job, and Papa would do the thing and I would end up with a pair suitable for a lady. My father was quite pleased to hear that you were setting about the task for me, so you needn't worry on that score."

"And you do not in fact wish a pair of horses suitable for a lady?"

"Oh no, Duke, I want a matched pair just like your bays, if you please." It was so enchantingly said, all air of reserve dropped, that he was hard put to refrain from catching her up in his arms then and there. He said instead, "Now, Lady Nicole, you will oblige my curiosity and tell me all about this ... er, boy, you said you found."

"Oh, Jed. Yes, to be sure. The worst thing of all, and which distresses me greatly, is to think that all over London things of that nature are occurring. Papa says that although some reforms have been introduced, none have really gone over because of this awful war with Boney. Parliament appears to be ignoring a situation that cannot be allowed to continue and I wish . . . I wish I could do something more."

Roth was slightly taken aback. "To be sure, my dear, but what things are happening all over London . . . and what boy?"

"Did I not tell you just now? His name is Jed—poor beaten, underfed Jed Scortch." She saw the astonished expression on his face and continued hastily, "I see that I had better start at the beginning."

"It would help." He laughed.

"It is not at all funny, Duke, so do be quiet and listen," she said sternly.

"I do most humbly beg pardon," he said gravely.

She then related the activities of the previous day, which had caused her to acquire one tiger.

In the meantime, Mr. Dereck had returned with the lemonade. He looked about him for a moment and then found that the only graceful way of disposing of it would be to drink it himself, which he retired to an empty corner to do.

Harry caught sight of his sister with Roth on the sofa, yanked Arnie by the sleeve, and bore down upon them. As they approached the couple on the sofa, Harry overheard a part of the story she was recounting to the Duke and exclaimed gaily, "Is Nick telling you about our Jed? Oh, but that was a fine piece of work. Nick spouted off a rare speech to that brute. Daresay I shall forget it before ever I get the chance to use it."

"What speech is that?" asked his Grace, looking inquiringly at Nicole.

As she had omitted that part of the tale purposely, she now flushed and glared at her brother, who went happily on to tell with animated pride almost word for word the barbed speech Nicole had rendered to Mr. Hookum.

Roth looked at Nicole tenderly. "So, my dear, are you a defender of the people?"

"Well, it does seem that while this awful War is being fought, the poor are the only ones to suffer and their children suffer the most."

The Duke regarded her affectionately. He took her chin in his hand. "Your heart is as lovely as your face."

Arnold, finding that *his* problem was being ignored, put in a hasty reminder that something had to be done.

"Yes, well, that is precisely what I have been saying," replied Nicole, surprised.

"No, no, Nick, I mean ... well, something must be done about the children, but right now something must be done about *my Mary*."

"Oh, did not Harry tell you? I have settled everything with Mary, and all we need now is for Roth to find an adventuress."

All eyes turned to the Duke, who looked back at them with raised brows and a roguish smile.

"I have found you an adventuress, Sir Arnold. However, I will not discuss it with you now. You will present yourself at my home in the morning—make it ten o'clock—and I will give you all the information you need. In fact, you may start seeing your little woman tomorrow afternoon if you like."

Nicole had been staring at him, both happy that an adventuress had been found and strangely upset that the Duke had indeed known a woman willing to carry out this part of the deed. "You ... you found her quickly, Duke. Was she a ... a friend of yours?"

He flicked her nose with one finger, laughing. "*No*. In fact, I have never seen her before. She was made known to me by Lord Alvanley."

"Oh, that is wonderful. I mean it is wonderful that you have been able to find a lady to play the part so quickly."

Harry caught sight of some friends and went in their direction, with Arnold following in his wake.

Nicole glanced about her and said softly, "I think, Duke, that we had better return to the ballroom, for I am sure I have been here with you far too long."

"No? Have we? Time passes so incredibly fast when I am in your company, my lovely imp!"

She tilted her head at him. "Why, Duke, do I detect yet another compliment? Upon my word, I am stunned—so many and all in one night!" she said saucily.

The Duke's eyebrows rose. "But my dear Lady Nicole, have I not always paid you desirable compliments?"

"No, Duke, you have not!"

"Then I must remind you it is only because you once advised me that you thought the praises uttered by London's young bucks to be quite ridiculous, boring, and silly," he said glibly.

"Ah, but Duke, you are not a young buck," she said mischievously.

His face fell ludicrously and for the first time in many years he felt nonplused. No other woman had ever told him he was too old. He wanted to wring her neck and advise her that he was but eight and twenty, when she clapped her hands and steadied his world by saying gaily, "Oh, Duke, I meant only that you are a . . . a man of the world, not a mere boy, and I should never, I am persuaded, find *your* compliments silly, boring, or ridiculous."

"Well, then, I shall no longer be backward, for I see I must live up to my reputation or you will be sadly disappointed in me."

A sigh escaped her, for these last words of his reminded her of all his flirtations . . . and of Lady Lucy Beldon. But when she looked into his eyes, she could not believe that they lied to her, that they did not caress her. She banished these thoughts almost with a shake.

He had seen the consternation on her face. "What is it, imp? What has brought that look to your eyes?" His voice was gentle.

She was about to give him a noncommittal answer when they were interrupted by a lovely voice. "Ah, Adam dearest, there you are, for I have been wanting a word with you." Lucy Beldon looked provocatively at Roth, completely ignoring Nicole.

"Yes, Lucy, of course, in a moment," replied Roth impatiently.

Nicole's eyes flashed, while her body stiffened. "Pray, Duke, do not keep my Lady waiting, for I believe this dance is promised and I have already sat here too long." She stood up and left the room, her head held high and a firm control over her legs, which were itching to run. She turned into the ballroom and was met by Mr. Dereck. Jealous and upset, Nicole readily accepted his invitation to be led into the waltz.

"Damnation, Lucy, was that piece of work contrived, for I do not thank you for it!" Roth said acidly.

"I have come to see you, Adam, as you have not come to see me for several weeks, and, oh dearest, I have missed you. Tell me all is well, my darling, please."

He looked at her, she was a lovely woman, but he found his eyes straying past her to a dark-haired child waltzing about the ballroom.

"I am afraid, Lucy, there is no way to end a relationship kindly when one of the two people is still involved, but I find I must tell you that for many reasons we cannot continue to see one another as we have in the past." His expression was grave, for he liked Lucy and had no wish to hurt her.

"Ah. So the chit has won your heart, has she? Well, if I am not mistaken, Adam, she will lead you a pretty dance."

"She already has, my dear." He smiled ruefully at her as he led her onto the floor for their last waltz.

Nicole could not help turning her head to catch sight of the Duke twirling about the floor with Lady Beldon in his arms. She felt a fury she had never known before and it showed on her flushed countenance and in her eyes. He caught sight of her and thought she looked magnificent when she was angry. His lips twitched appreciatively, for he was rather enjoying her jealousy. This attitude of his did nothing to mollify Nicole's agitation, and when she left the floor on Mr. Dereck's arm, she looked quite flushed.

Count D'Agout had entered the ballroom in time to see Nicole leaving the floor and rushed up to intercept her.

"Lady Nicole, you are looking adorable tonight, but I

119

fear that it is too warm for you here. May I escort you for a short walk about the house?"

"Oh, Louis, please do take me away, for I should like to leave this stuffy room." She turned to Mr. Dereck. "Thank you, sir, for the lovely waltz, and pray do excuse us."

Mr. Dereck bowed, and as he was evidently defeated, he turned on his heel and left them.

The Count smiled. "Impudent puppy!"

"Oh come, Louis, do let us leave, but where we can go I do not know!"

"Have you seen Mrs. Ombersly's garden room? I promise you it is a treat worth the viewing."

"Yes, that would be nice." She took his arm and was pleased to find that the Duke's eyes followed them as they left the room.

It was a great hobby of their hostess, Mrs. Ombersly, to collect exotic plants from all over the world and to fill her garden room with them. This room, which consisted almost entirely of windows, was built on the south side of the building and received the sun all day. The overpowering scent of orchids now filled it.

Nicole sank onto a garden bench and the Count sat beside her. When he had first seen Nicole, he had speculated that it would be diverting to flirt with such an unusual beauty. When he learned that she was an heiress, he thought it would also be profitable. It was not long after that he decided he would have her for himself, for he was more than just a little attracted to her piquant face and alluring figure. He wanted to possess her . . . desired her more than he had ever desired any woman. He was quite used to getting the woman he cast his eyes toward.

The Count murmured her name, his eyes roved over her body. "My dearest angel, my beautiful little darling. I have been in love with you since the first moment of our meeting. What am I saying? I have loved you even before we met, for you were always in my dreams. You drive me mad with desire for you. I want to make you mine. Do not, I beg of you, hold me at bay. Nicole my pet, I can wait no longer." He put both arms about her, drawing her closer to him. His voice had become husky with passion.

Nicole had never had a man hold her in this manner, she had never had an experienced man make love to her. Jealousy of Lady Beldon still raged within her. She felt stimulated by the Count and his words aroused her. For a moment, she allowed herself to be drawn to him. She looked up at his handsome face and all at once knew she had to get away.

"No, Louis, do not say such things to me and let me go."

The Count laughed low in his throat. He was carried away with his own fire and held her pinned against him, while his lips sought hers hungrily. She pulled away slightly and had to stifle a scream. "Louis, please let me go." She hit at his chest ineffectually, and began to feel terrified. "Louis, I beg of you, let me go at once!" She was almost sobbing now, and then all at once she was free. She stood up, standing riveted before two angry men.

Roth stood very still, his two fists clenched at his side, his gray eyes like two steel darts, his square jaw set in a hard line. His voice came, low and deadly quiet. "I believe the lady requested you to remove your hold on her!"

Flushed with humiliation and anger, the Count glared back at him and expostulated, "This is none of your affair, Roth."

Then a little foot stamped loudly at them both. "Stop it, both of you. Louis, you may leave this room at once, before your angry voice brings down the house around us."

He turned toward her and bowed. "Your servant, Lady Nicole." And then he stalked out of the room. Nicole turned her indignant fury on the Duke. She was blushing hotly. The fact that her anger toward Roth was both unjust and unreasonable made her all the more enraged.

"How dare you? How could you?" she gasped. Her face had gone white suddenly and her eyes were sparkling pools of green ice.

Roth regarded her through narrowed eyes. He had suddenly discovered that he was a jealous man. The sight of the Count's arms around Nicole was fresh in his mind and

121

caused his anger to mount and match her own. His eyes glinted at her.

"How dare I?" he exclaimed incredulously. "You allow yourself to be put in a situation you could not control, and when I come and find that you are indeed in need of assistance, you fling your anger at me! No doubt I was mistaken and have interrupted a much sought after *tête-à-tête*."

She gasped. "Oh ... oh, you are abominable. You ... you odious hypocrite! Do you mean to tell me that you feel I need protection from Louis? Why, then, do you not protect Lady Beldon from yourself? I am sure she is in need of far greater protection than I, since the Count's intentions toward me are honorable!"

The Duke was in a passion but this thrust went home. "Lady Beldon needs no protection from me, and as for my intentions toward her ... I have none!" He took a step toward Nicole. "Nicky ..."

But he had no chance to continue for Nicole, unable to control her emotions, turned on her heel and fled the room.

She sped down the long hallway and stopped, suddenly putting her hand to the wall to steady herself. She felt a large tear roll down her cheek and hastily wiped it away. *God,* she thought, *I ... I hate him. How could he say such a thing to me!"* She turned to the card room and saw that her mother was engaged with some ladies in a game of whist, while her father was at the other end of the room at another card table. Nicole steadied herself and walked sedately toward her mother. She rested one trembling hand on Lady Beaumont's shoulder, leaned toward her, and whispered, "Mama, I have the headache, but I see that you and Papa are both engaged and have no wish to interrupt your game. I will ask Harry to escort me home if you do not mind."

Lady Beaumont directed a searching look at her daughter, but merely smiled and patted her hand. "Why, of course, darling. I do hope you will feel better presently."

"Yes, I am sure I will. Thank you, Mama."

She then turned and hurried from the room in search
122

of Harry. Having finally found him at one end of the wide drawing room, she tried to get his attention with a quiet "Harry?" But as he was quite involved in a heated debate (it seems there was some question as to whether a red cock had it over a gray), she was obliged to pull at his sleeve.

"Harry, please if you do not mind, take me home now, for I am not feeling at all the thing!" she said urgently.

"But I do mind, Nick! Confound it, girl, have something to settle here, you know!"

"Please, Harry, please. I . . . I do not want to ask either Mama or Papa, as they are playing cards, and if I were to interrupt them they would think it so serious they would be bound to make a fuss over me and you know what that would mean. They'd be pushing gruel and doctors and God knows what at me. So please, Harry, help me just this once."

Harry, much struck with this aspect, as he was well aware of the type of fussing his parents could and probably would lavish on Nicole if they thought her ill, relented slightly, and finally acquiesed reluctantly. They had called for their carriage, and as it was a lovely night, decided to wait on the front steps for it to arrive.

Roth had by this time taken leave of his hostess and nearly collided with them on the steps. Nicole, after one startled moment, turned her back to him and moved down the remainder of the steps.

Harry looked surprised at his sister's rudeness and smiled apologetically at the Duke. "She's not feeling quite the thing, you know."

Roth smiled ruefully. "Yes, I see that. Harry, one moment please, I should like a word with you."

Harry looked toward his sister, who had just entered their coach, and then turned back to the Duke. "Yes, of course, Duke."

"Has Nicole ever discussed my . . . connection with Lady Beldon with you?"

Harry looked thunderstruck. "Lord, why she just asked me about her this morning. Funny thing too, wanted to know if men gave jewels to ladies they don't love. Not the type of thing you want your sister knowing about, but then Nicky is forever asking things she shouldn't."

The Duke grinned, feeling a great weight lifted. "Now don't forget, Harry, bring Arnold to me at ten tomorrow morning," he said, changing the subject abruptly.

"Lord, yes, won't let me forget. Devil take it, bound to be at my door before breakfast, and with the fidgets."

They laughed before Harry entered his coach to find his sister glaring at him furiously. "What was all that about, Harold?"

"What . . . my talk with Roth?" he asked, surprised. Something, perhaps instinct, told him he had better not divulge the subject they had just discussed and so he said lightly, "He was just reminding me to bring Arn to him in the morning!" He had a strong suspicion that Lady Beldon was behind Nicky's headache, and he had no wish to get involved in a discussion about the lively widow.

"Oh, that reminds me. I think it most infamous of all of you not to bring me along to meet . . . the lady who will be acting as Arnie's fancy piece . . ."

"Nick!" objected her brother. "Really, Nick, you shouldn't use a term like that, it is most unbecoming."

"But I heard you use it just the other day, and it seems to sound right for what I meant to say, for how shall I describe her then?"

"You can't go saying everything you hear me say. It won't do, you're a lady. If you want to describe a female of that sort—which you shouldn't, for delicately bred females shouldn't be talking about such things—however, if you find you need to, say . . . say—dash it, Nick, how am I to know!—say 'lady of that sort!' "

"Well, don't get excited! All right, then, but that doesn't help me. What I want is to be in on this part of the doings, for after all, Harry, it is my plan!"

"Well, you can't and that's that!" said her brother emphatically.

"Oh, that is really too bad of you, Harry!" objected Nicole strongly.

"No, really, Nick, you can't be meeting a girl like that. I won't have it. You've done some crazy things, but I won't allow you to do this. So don't be nagging at me."

His jaw was set in a firm line and thus the rest of the ride home was accomplished in silence, neither looking at the other.

So it was for the second time that day that Nicole threw herself down upon her bed and cried into her pillow.

Chapter Eleven

Nicole awoke the next morning, none the better for her sleep, and dressed in the black velvet habit. She drank a cup of coffee and went to the stables where she had Ginger saddled and called for Jed.

"Jed, get a pony saddled for yourself. I wish to ride, and as I need someone in attendance on me, I will take you. Will you like that?"

"Gawd, mistress, I would!" he replied, grinning.

He rushed off and within a few minutes they had left the stables for the park. Nicole thought, *Oh God, how I love him, but it's hopeless, get a hold of yourself, girl. He is not for you. You must realize it now ... now that you have seen him with Lady Beldon. But he came to help me last night—yes, and so would your brother and your papa.* She sighed but her thoughts could not be stilled. She longed to run through the park and gave Ginger her head, for it was early and there was no one about. They galloped for a minute before she slowed down, hastily looking about her. She then turned her horse round, making her way back to the stables, Jed following discreetly behind.

Nicole dismounted and handed the reins to Jed and he led the horses into their stalls to be brushed. Nicky turned to the head groom.

"Hallo, Becky, how's the parrot treating you, my friend?"

"Ha, if you don't mind my saying so, he was a filthy bird, he was, Lady Nicole."

"*Was*, Becky?"

The groom rubbed his chin and winked at his mistress.

"He ain't here anymore . . . left us, he did. Not a speck of loyalty did he 'ave."

Nicole laughed. "Well, Becky, tell me, how is my little tiger doing? Will he be ready to handle my team when I get them?"

"Well now, missy, told Master Harry he be not ready yet, but he'll be ready soon, he will. Loves the 'orses, he does."

"Good. Thank you, Becky." She turned to her phaeton, one hand went over it lovingly, and she sighed.

Jed returned and pulled at the sleeve of Nicole's jacket and she looked at the boy inquiringly.

"Mistress, I be better than he says. Learnt reel well, I did . . . for you!" He looked adoringly up at her and Nicole's heart went out to him.

"Thank you, Jed. I know you will be just wonderful with my horses and I shall always trust you with them, have no fear. You will be my groom for as long as you wish!"

The boy choked, and a tear rolled down his cheek. "Thankee, mistress."

She patted his head and went toward the house. She was removing her gloves when Grudsly presented the salver to her on which rested a note with gold gilt edging and the Duke of Lyndham's crest. She took it and ran to her room where she opened it hastily.

Dear Lady Nicole:

I should like to make my humble apologies for the unforgivable utterances I made to you last night.

I hope you will find it in your heart to forgive me and consider me, as ever, your friend,

Adam Roth

She put the note down and felt a pang of disappointment. He showed no affection, no desire . . . no love! She would have preferred him to rave at her passionately than to calmly apologize. She picked up the note and

126

ripped it to shreds. *You should have known better, Nicole Beaumont,* she told herself.

Nicole's mind would have been much relieved had she known what the Duke's exact sentiments had been when he had composed his cool note of apology.

Roth had laughed to himself as he put pen to paper. He had made up his mind to marry Nicole Beaumont ... but not quite yet. The unnerving pangs of jealousy he had experienced the evening before when he viewed Nicky ensconced in the Count's arms had brought home to him all he felt for her. He had been furious with her for turning on him until he realized Nicky's storming had something to do with Lucy Beldon. His bachelor's reign had received its death blow and the Duke of Lyndham groaned happily to himself. He decided he would court her ... first gently, and then wildly, never doubting his ability to win her. He fully believed she would accept his apology and settle back to the comfortable friendship they had been enjoying. This would enable him to woo her in his own careful and elegant fashion. The Duke, it would seem, had a bit of a surprise in store for him!

Feeling quite confident of the future, he was disposed to be amiable and sat conversing with Harry and Arnold for quite some time, carefully schooling Arnold in the part he was to play during the next few weeks. After this had been completed, he escorted them to Tilly Billings' room, which was on the other side of the city.

Nicole, pacing about in her room, was not surprised when Marcy came to her and advised her that the Count D'Agout was begging admittance. "Tell him to wait for me in the morning room, I will be right there."

She went down quickly and hesitated at the doorway. She felt a little frightened and wanted no repeat performance of the previous evening's lovemaking.

The Count made his way to her across the room and bowed low over her hand, lightly brushing it with his lips. "Please, Lady Nicole, before you speak, please allow me to offer my deepest apologies. I have my phaeton waiting outside ... would you consider taking a drive with me and letting me explain?"

Lady Beaumont had just entered the morning room and smiled at them speculatively. Nicole had no wish for this form of conversation to take place in the presence of her mother and so responded impulsively, "Very well, I will just fetch my pelisse and be back in a moment."

On the way up the stairs she thought angrily, *Why could not Roth have come? Why could he not have begged my pardon in person? Because he does not love you, you idiotic dolt!*

They drove for a few minutes in silence, until the Count reached the park. He slowed down so that he was able to turn his attention to Nicole. His voice was low, repentive. "Nicole, my dearest, what can I say? My dearest angel, it is that I adore you, want you to be my wife. I frightened you with my passion. I am sorry . . . I was an animal, but try to understand how much I love you, want you. Say you will be mine, say you will be my Countess!"

"Oh, Louis, you do me a great honor, but . . . I am afraid I cannot accept. Please, do not ask me. Let us forget this and be comfortable again."

"Comfortable . . . comfortable," he sneered. "My God, how can I be comfortable until you say that you will be mine? Nicole dearest, listen to me. You are young, and I was too bold. Only say that you forgive me. I will not press you further now."

"Oh yes, yes, I forgive you, and only want to forget it, so please let us talk of something else."

It was at that moment that Roth, cutting through the park on his gray, came upon them. Nicole looked up to find the Duke's startled gaze resting on her. She felt the heat rush to her face, burning her cheeks. She could have sworn out loud, she was so vexed at having the Duke see her here with the Count. Instead of swearing, she purposefully put her hand on the Count's arm and looked adoringly up into his face, saying softly, knowing the Duke watched her still, "Louis, I am feeling a chill and would like to return home."

The Count was disappointed but murmured that he understood and turned his horses back in the direction of Mount Street. Nicole noted with some satisfaction that the

Duke appeared to be riveted, his eyes never leaving her until she had reached the exit.

Nicole came into the house and stifled a gurgle of laughter. A thought had struck her and she was suddenly feeling her mettle. *I could not be so wrong,* she told herself. *He must care, for if that was not jealousy I saw on his face, then I am a fool—and I know I am not a fool!*

"Harry," she called as she saw her brother descend the stairs, "come into the library."

Harry raised an eyebrow, wondering *Now what,* but kept silent until she spoke.

"You have arranged everything with ... with Arnold and the girl?"

"Yes ... Arn will be taking her about in the park this afternoon, when he will be bound to see everyone and everyone will see him."

"Wonderful! Now, Harry, I have been so busy arranging the affairs of others that I have neglected my own. Can you bring Archie here ... at once, for I need him!"

"Eh? What are you up to, Nick? You've got that look in your eyes."

"I can no longer leave my fate to the care of Mother Nature. Apparently she has been down on the job. I mean to catch a fish and it cannot be had without a little bait."

"If you mean that Arch is to be the bait, I feel sorry for the poor devil. Mind, though, I shouldn't like to kick up a dust with Mother Nature!"

Nicole burst out laughing. "Oh, Harry, you are so funny! Go now and bring Archie to me, for I want to get started immediately."

"Can't ... the twins left town this morning. They will be back in a day or so. I'll bring him round then."

"Oh bother! However, there is little I can do about it!"

Harry eyed his sister with some misgiving. "What's it all about, Nick?"

"Oh no, I shan't tell you this time. You will have to wait."

He stood up, feeling exasperated. "All right, but I am not going to wait around here, I can tell you that. Keep your secrets!"

Harry marched out of the room, feeling just a little

129

hurt, and it was with much control that Nicky prevented herself from calling him back and telling him the whole. *No*, she thought, *it had better wait until Archie returns.*

She smiled to herself. *All right, your Grace! So . . . you won't be caught by a schoolroom chit! We shall see."*

Nicole then spent a good part of the afternoon lost in ruminations about bringing the wayward Duke to his knees and standing triumphantly beside him.

It was in this spirit that she proceeded to Almack's that evening, looking quite lovely. She had pulled her hair tightly back and wound it about the top of her head in a neat braid, allowing only the wisps at her forehead to curl about her face. She chose a dress of pale green that clung to her figure. She looked regal, and very womanly. There was nothing of the demure young miss about her. She stood talking with Sir James Litchfield, who was lost in admiration, when she felt rather than saw His Grace, the Duke of Lyndham arrive. Within a short while he had contrived with his usual adroitness to get through the crush of people and reach her side. He smiled down at her tenderly, taking in every detail of her appearance.

"And so, my imp, I am forgiven?"

"Is that a statement or a request, Your Grace?" She did not smile.

His Grace ignored her question and continued glibly. "I have found your team, Lady Nicole, and if you are willing, I should like to have them sent round to your stables for your approval."

A friend had in the meantime called to Sir James, who reluctantly left their side. His Grace took this opportunity to guide Lady Nicole away from the crush of people toward an empty corner.

"Oh," Nicole exclaimed, her eyes alight, "that is famous news. Thank you, Duke. I should like that very much. I suppose I cannot remain angry with you after you have been so obliging."

"No, I am afraid that would not do!" he replied amicably, looking at her intently and thinking that her dress was almost indecent. He asked her softly, "Why did you drive out with the Count today?"

"Do you not know? You seem to know all else," she answered haughtily.

"No, imp, I must confess I did not think you would allow him near you after last night . . . so I should like to hear your explanation."

My . . . *my explanation!*" she almost shouted. "Of all the abominable, odious, tyrannical—I do not have to give you any explanation at all!" she replied in outraged accents.

"No, you do not. However, I should be a happier man if you would, so do not fly up at me."

Strangely enough, Nicole felt an anxious need to explain her motives for driving out with the Count and so allowed herself to be persuaded to do so. "Well—I do not see what business it is of yours, but even *you* must admit that the Count could not apologize to me in my mother's presence."

"I will admit that. However, he could have sent you a note, as I did!"

She put up her chin. "He has far greater sensibility and would not make little of it by merely sending me a curt penance note. Besides, the Count wanted . . . wanted to . . . well, he asked me to marry him. He could not have done so in a note. Now please, Duke, I wish to forget it. Look, Harry and Arnie are with Jimmy and I am most anxious to hear how Arnie's meeting with his new lady went."

He smiled at her and led her to the little group that had gathered at the far side of the room.

Nicole tugged at Arnie's arm and looked inquiringly up at him. "Well, cuz, how did it go with you this afternoon?"

"Oh gad, Nick, it was awful."

"Why, whatever do you mean?"

He looked at Roth apologetically. "Well, you see, I . . . I took Miss Tilly . . ."

"Tilly? Oh lord, is that her name?" Nicole choked on a laugh.

"Yes. Well, I took Miss Tilly for a drive in Green Park. I will tell you that I find this is very difficult, for she is not . . . not quite in my style."

Harry leaned over to Nicole and nudged her confidingly. "Brassy blonde full of . . . shall we say, joy!"

Nicole giggled. "Well, Arnie, do go on. What happened?"

"It's rather indelicate, Nick. I do not know if you should hear."

"Good God, Arnie, how it could be indelicate when you were in public is beyond me, so please do go on."

As neither Harry nor his Grace objected, Arnie proceeded, with just a slight tinge of red in his cheeks.

"We drove in the park and Miss Tilly commanded me—for there is no other word for it—she commanded me to stop, whereby she . . . she . . . she rather snuggled me, you see."

As this appeared to cause all his listeners a great deal of mirth, Sir Arnold, understandably, became reticent, refusing to continue if they would not stop laughing. With much self-control, they managed to stifle their chuckling and he went on. "We went around the park twice, and then I escorted Miss Tilly home. I am to call for her again tomorrow morning."

"Wonderful!" exclaimed Nicole.

"*You* may think it wonderful, Nick, but I do not. I tell you Miss Tilly is not in my style. She is . . . she is rather loud, you know."

"That's even better than I could have hoped for. Aunt will go into convulsions."

"That is another thing! M'mother! Should like to come stay with you in Mount Street. Don't want to face m'mother!

"You can't do that, Arn. She's bound to know you're there and come kicking up a dust!"

"Lord, yes," replied Harry much struck. "Don't want Aunt coming over and having the vapors."

"Tell you what, Arnie, come to my lodgings," put in Sir James amicably.

"That's splendid of you, James. Thank you!"

"Now that that is settled, I have a plan. I have been itching to give Ginger a good run, and as the weather is really becoming lovely, I thought we could get up a picnic."

132

"By Jove, Nick, that's a devilish good idea!" exclaimed Harry merrily. "We'll get up a party. What do you say, Jimmy . . . Arnie?"

James readily assented, as anywhere Nicole was going was exactly where he wished to be.

Arnold also agreed happily. "Yes, to be sure, I'll be one of your set. Should like to keep away from Mama, you know," he added, lowering his voice.

Nicole put a pensive finger to her lips and added thoughtfully, "Hmmm, perhaps you should bring your Tilly along with us and really bring things to a climax."

"What?" shouted Harry, startled. "I won't have Arnie's doxy in our set, Nick. Why, good lord, girl, it wouldn't do for you to be seen in her company!"

"She is not my doxy, Harry! She's Roth's!" retorted Arnold, incensed.

"She is *not* Roth's doxy, and it is most improper for both of you to use such a term in my company!" Nicole admonished angrily.

Sir Arnold had the good grace to turn crimson, "Eh, beg pardon!"

"Yes, it is most improper for you to use that term in Lady Nicole's presence!" repeated Roth, his eyes brimful with amusement. He turned his smiling countenance to Nicole. "And for you to repeat such a word, my shameless imp!"

She felt a shiver as she very often did when he used the possessive term when he addressed her, but she stilled her heart and replied calmly, "Well, Roth, you must admit that it would not be such a bad idea for Arnie to lose his head and bring Tilly along with us."

"I will admit nothing of the kind. Your cousin is a gentleman, and he would never lose his head to the extent that he would offer *you* an insult. Miss Tilly is not respectable! She may have a fine heart—we know not—but she leads a life that . . . that is not proper for you to know about, so do forget this idea of yours."

Nicole sighed. "Oh well, I suppose you are right. However, I can never agree with that line of thinking. People are people, and but for fate—or the grace of God,

133

whichever you prefer—I might have had to take on such a life."

"Nicole!" Harry and James ejaculated in one voice.

"Oh, but Roth knows what I mean. Don't you?"

"Yes, my adorable imp, I do!"

At that moment their eyes met and held in a look that left her breathless. Nicole's eyes sought the marble floor and she felt the color rush to her cheeks.

"I say, Nick, do you think you could invite Mary to be part of our set?"

Nicole pursed her lips. "Hmmm . . . you are supposed to be in love with Miss Tilly, and you will be seen with Mary, and then how are we to convince anyone?"

"Oh well, as to that . . . you are a friend of Mary's, she is accompanying you."

"Yes, that is true. All right, I will send her a note. Only when are we to go and where shall we have our picnic?"

Harry had in the meantime turned to his Grace and said, "Will you be able to join us, Duke?"

Nicole found herself waiting breathlessly for his response and was very gratified to hear his ready assent.

Adam Roth had meant to be a part of this delightful excursion the moment he had heard the arrangements. However, he had held back, hoping to hear Nicole ask him. There was some disappointment when she did not. Still, he had no intention of refusing. They set the date for the day after the morrow.

"But where are we to go?" asked Nicole.

The Duke smiled tenderly at her. "If you will permit a suggestion, my Aunt Elizabeth had begged me to bring you out to see her. This would be the perfect occasion, as she has a country estate only a short distance from London and it is quite a lovely ride at this time of year."

"Oh, that would be delightful . . . but are we not a large group to suddenly spring on her for luncheon?" Nicole asked doubtfully.

"Not at all. Aunt Liz loves young people. She has often said that they breathe life into her."

"Good, it is all settled then," put in Harry, summing

134

up. He turned to Sir James, engaging him in conversation, while Arnie went off in search of his friends.

Roth turned to Nicole and said softly, "I could have wished James elsewhere. However, perhaps Harry will contrive to keep him occupied, while Arnie is occupied with Mary, and I, my adorable imp, will also be—occupied!"

Nicole blushed prettily, and looked up into his eyes candidly. "Duke, I should like to take leave to tell you that I think you an outrageous flirt ... a rake ... but even so, I like you well!"

His Grace, the Duke of Lyndham was momentarily taken aback, for he had not expected this. He had thought that while he remained in the somewhat dubious position of aloof admirer, she would never admit to any feeling for him. He had thought that was what he wanted, for he was willing to play a game with her for the Season. Oh yes, he wanted her—more than anything he had ever wanted in his life. At the same time, he wanted to see her grow, watch her reject others, and then accept him as her only love. This frank admission softened his resolve. Her innocent words left him feeling like a cad. *Have done, man,* he told himself angrily. *Tell her you adore her ... want her ... cherish her.* And then, *No, it is too soon, she is but a child.* I want her love, not her infatuation!"

He heard someone call his name and bowed to her before taking his leave without a word.

She watched his departing form and sighed. He would have felt less the cad had he known that the remark she had made had not been so *very* innocent.

Chapter Twelve

Miss Tilly Billings looked at Sir Arnold with some exasperation. "Here now, m'lad, it's in love with me you are, so don't be looking so shy!"

"It's just that—well, to be frank with you, Miss Tilly, I am in love with ... my ... my Mary, and I feel thoroughly ... a swine to be here with you."

Tilly laughed loudly, throwing her head back so that her white lovely neck could be seen beneath the gauzy material of her bright dress. She looked at Sir Arnold and laughed again, nearly causing her bonnet to fall off. Sir Arnold put out his hand to catch it, and her arms went around him immediately. After a moment, Sir Arnold pulled back from what had been a wild and passionate kiss. His face was red and his eyes downcast.

She laughed low this time, deep and huskily in her throat. "Look at me, m'lad, it's a talk we must have, you and I!"

Obediently, Sir Arnold raised his eyes to hers, but try as he would, he could not keep the blush from his cheeks and felt the fool. Miss Tilly paid no heed to this, other than an appreciative chuckle. "Now, the way I understood this game was that you were to take me about town as we are doing, but that you was to make love to me for all the world to see. You ain't going to get the swells' tongues a-jabbering otherwise, I can tell you that! Why, Lord love you, sir, every London buck has a light-'o-love or two and drives about with her. There's nothing in that to make the quality bat an eye. What will pop their eyes is if they was to see you all lost to a sense of their precious proprieties. So you will have to put your hand under my chin, like so. You will have to kiss me . . . like we just did . . ."

"Miss Tilly . . . Miss Tilly!" expostulated Arnie quickly.

Miss Tilly paid no heed. "Well, I declare, there's many a man that wants a kiss and more besides, and you . . . you hedge . . . and—"

"Oh please, Miss Tilly, do not misunderstand, please do not take offense. It's just that I . . . I am promised to Mary and—"

"Ay, I know all about that, and if it's Mary you want, it's me you'll have to kiss. So don't be a-naying and a-croaking about your precious sense of morality. I'll do what I've been paid to do, or I might as well give you your blunt back here and now!"

Horrified, Sir Arnie again protested. "Oh please, Miss Tilly, you must not. I . . . I will do anything you say."

136

"Then kiss me, sir!"

"Must we kiss? Could we not . . . perhaps just hug?"

"Lord love ye, sir, I sure would have liked to have a fella as loyal as you be to your darlin' Mary. Ain't I explained? Your polite world has got to carry the tale back to your mama that you are head over heels in love with me and ready to make me your *lady* . . . not your mistress."

"Miss Tilly, you must not say such things!" Sir Arnold replied, much shocked.

"What—mistress? Lord love ye, such a sweet boy you are. Now I tell you again, it's kissing we should be doing, not talking. If it helps, think of me as a conspirator . . . not a woman!"

Sir Arnold seemed to consider this and smiled. "Yes, I like that. That is precisely what I shall do." Then suddenly he pulled her into his arms quite roughly and kissed her long and ardently.

When he finally allowed Miss Tilly to come up for air, she regarded him from amused, if somewhat startled, eyes. "When you make up your mind to a thing, you do throw yourself in wholeheartedly, don't you, sir?"

He grinned at her and now, thoroughly at ease, drove on for all the Beau Monde to see. Happily, they did.

"Dear God, is that not Augusta's son with that . . . that creature?" exclaimed a lady to her companion. "Ha, shameless hussy. Why just look at them, kissing . . . in public."

The kindly lady beside her looked away and said softly, "I . . . why yes, dear, it is Sir Arnold, but pray . . . look away from them. The boy knows not what he does, and I do not think we should stare, do you?"

Mrs. Merrimount, a widow of some ten years, lived for and through the scandal of others, and so did not agree with this opinion and continued to stare. Once a pretty young thing, she had turned into an elderly woman with little to recommend her.

"No, no, but I am sure . . . why just the other day poor Augusta was crying her heart out because the match she had hoped for between her son and Sybil Seldon did not fadge. Now I see why! The boy is besotted!"

Lady Sefton had never liked Mrs. Merrimount and would not be here now with her had she not met her accidentally. She had stopped momentarily to chat, as she had no wish to be rude, but was now rapidly losing patience. "My dear Mrs. Merrimount—"

She was quickly interrupted. "Oh dear, Lady Sefton, I . . . I must excuse myself, as I feel it is my duty to repair at once to Lady Merdon's home and advise her of this . . . this terrible thing. Perhaps you would like to accompany me."

Lady Sefton put up her chin. "I do not carry gossip from door to door. Pray leave me out of your, shall we say, errand of mercy," she mocked haughtily.

"No, no, Lady Sefton, you misunderstand. Augusta is one of my oldest friends. She would wish to know what is happening, and better to hear it from a friend than from some stranger. Why, good lord, what if the boy is thinking of doing something rash? My goodness, what if he were contemplating a *mésalliance* with that creature, for I tell you frankly, he looked quite taken with her."

Lady Sefton put up her hands impatiently. "Dear me, I think you are refining too much upon what you have observed. Why, I believe all young men indulge in such . . . frolics without becoming attached."

"I hope that is all it is," Mrs. Merrimount said in tones that clearly indicated she did not think so.

Lady Sefton took her leave, feeling quite put out with the business of Mrs. Merrimount and put her down as a mischief maker. A few minutes later Mrs. Merrimount was shown in to Lady Merdon's tea room.

Lady Merdon eyed her friend speculatively, for she knew her well and had noticed that she had a look in her eye that portended trouble. After pouring out her tale to receptive ears, Mrs. Merrimount sat back to observe the reaction and was quite satisfied.

Lady Merdon went white . . . then livid. *"No!"*

Mrs. Merrimount clucked her tongue. "I know just how you must feel—just as I would feel, had my dear Jeffrey

138

done such a thing. Luckily, though, he has so much better sense."

This stung Lady Merdon into giving her a sharp reply. "Sense, what has that to say to anything? As for that, it is quite normal for a man to have a flirt of that nature, and if Jeffrey does not, well then, that is not to his credit, is it?" In defense of her son, her hackles were up and gave her strength.

Mrs. Merrimount stiffened. "I have only come to advise you of what I thought was more than just idle flirting. Augusta dearest, the way they were kissing . . . was quite serious, I assure you, or I would not be sitting here now."

"You are a fool!" replied Lady Merdon in strong accents.

Mrs. Merrimount stood up, flushing. "How dare you! I come here to warn you, for your good and the good of your son, and you insult me."

Lady Merdon retracted slightly. "Please . . . I do beg your pardon. It is perhaps because I am . . . so distracted."

Mrs. Merrimount put out her hand and patted Lady Merdon's. "I understand, dear."

"Again, I must repeat that what you saw today was certainly an indiscretion, but I assure you my son is not planning to marry the creature. He would not kiss her in public if that were the case. He was treating her as she should be treated. Not as a future wife."

"Yes, that is what I thought when I first saw them together, but that creature had a way about her. Why, when I first watched them, he was treating her with all due respect, and then suddenly, as if he couldn't control himself any longer he"—she lowered her voice—"he grabbed her quite wildly. That is why I am warning you. I fear that she would be able to persuade the poor lad to do the honorable thing by her."

"What honor when she is . . . is a . . . ! No, Arnie could not be such a fool." Her words sounded hollow, even to herself.

Mrs. Merrimount turned to leave, a look of satisfaction on her face. "Oh, I am sure you will now be able to control him, won't you, dear? I fear it has grown quite late and I must be getting back as I am having an at-home this afternoon."

Lady Merdon sank back onto her sofa after Mrs. Merrimount left. She put a lavender-scented handkerchief to her nose and let her head sink into the pillow. Then she got up, making plans in her mind. Most certainly she would talk to Arnold. Tonight without delay.

Her butler entered then and presented a note on a silver salver. She opened it to read that Sir Arnold regretted that he would not be home for a few days as he was engaged with some friends. She ground her teeth, and sank back onto her pillows.

Harry entered the library of the Beaumonts' London town house with the Wychburn twins in the rear.

"Well, I've brought them, my girl!"

"Hallo, Archie, Robby." She turned to Harry and whispered, "Didn't tell you to bring Robby, too, you know."

"Dash it, Nick, can't bring one without the other, you must see that."

She didn't, but refrained from arguing the point. "Well, I suppose I can trust you as well as Archie, perhaps better."

Robby, the more serious-natured of the twins, grinned. "Come on, Nick, what's all the secrecy. Get on with it."

She turned to Archie, who was beginning to look worried. "Arch, my friend, you are going to court me and I am going to appear to accept, or at least to prefer your wooing to that of any of my other suitors."

"What?" ejaculated Archie, much stunned. "No! I say, Nick, should love to help you out. Anything in my power. Thing is, not in my power ... to ... to woo you. No, really." He turned lamely to Harry. "Must see that, don't you? Tell her, Harry, tell her you won't have me courting her!"

Harry laughed, looked his friend over, and laughed again.

Archie, by now quite desperate, turned back to Nicole. "Nick, Nick, think I am not your type. Not the type to pay you court. Must see that."

140

"No, I don't see that. Why, you flirt with every new face presented to you, and those that aren't as well. You will be perfect for the part."

Robby had been watching all this with interest and interjected reasonably, "Bit of a problem there, Nick. You know Archie is always flirting, as you put it. Fact is most of the *Haut Ton* would put it that way. Bound to be uncomfortable for you to have Archie flirting while he is courting you. He would give it away, I'm afraid. Won't go down easy that he has dropped all his flirts and is courting a girl he has known from the cradle."

Nicole's face fell ludicrously and she sat there for a moment, quite at a loss, seeing all her neatly laid plans at death's door. Robby, ever a kind-hearted soul, laid a hand on her shoulder. "However, if you would permit, should love to assist you, dear girl. Not in the petticoat line myself, you know ... don't know how to turn off a pretty compliment. But I am heir to the title and a tidy sum. Would be more believable if you were to be interested in me, you know."

Nicole jumped up and gave her friend a fond hug. "Oh, Robby, you dear, dear friend. If this works, I shall never be able to thank you enough."

Robby looked at her thoughtfully, while his brother looked much relieved and Harry stood by searching his sister's face intently. "Will you honor us, Nick, by telling us what you have in mind."

"Must I? Can you not pay me court just because I tell you it is necessary to my plan?"

"No, Nick, I am afraid not. Come, out with it, girl."

Nicole sighed. "Well, in truth, if you were not such dear friends, I would find this most embarrassing, for I am laying a trap ... for a man, and you must swear secrecy. Swear, now!"

They did. She proceeded, with a deep intake of breath.

"You see, the Duke of Lyndham . . . well, he is the only man I could ever contemplate marriage with—that is, if I could be certain he is not carrying on with anyone else. I have felt at times that he—that he was not indifferent to me, and yet he treats me like a child. Then, other times, he treats me as if I am the only woman in the

141

world. I am a very good judge of character usually. At one time, I thought perhaps I was wrong and that he thought no more of me than . . . well, never mind. He has done certain things, acted in a certain way that leaves me free to believe he is . . . not indifferent. I mean to force his hand!"

Archie looked thunderstruck. Harry gave a low whistle. Robby regarded her thoughtfully. "Yes, Nick, I am inclined to agree with you. I have observed that his Grace does indeed have a partiality for you. How deep this is, is yet to be seen. He is not immune to your charms, but tread carefully, girl. You are not up to snuff yet. You could catch cold at this, you know. Then where will we be at?"

"Oh, Robby, that is why I need a friend, and not . . . not someone who cares like Jimmy. You see, it would not be fair to flirt outrageously with him, for he is in earnest. Even the Count—and that is why I think Roth really does have . . . a feeling for me, because when he saw the Count trying to force a kiss on me, well, he went wild with jealousy."

Harry jumped to his feet at that. "What?" he shouted. "That . . . that swine! He forced a kiss on you, do you say?" He took a turn about the room and put a hand through his fair hair. "I'll have his head for this. That . . . that—"

"Harry, please do stop your ranting before you say something I am sure I should not hear," rebuked Nicole, upset with herself for making such a slip in front of her excitable brother.

"No, this time, Nick, I will not be quiet. I am going to call him out for this. You—"

"Stop it, Harry, you will do no such thing. First of all, you will involve my name in scandal if you do such a thing. Secondly, poor Louis was only trying to . . . to ask me to marry him and got carried away. It was probably my own fault. And I only brought it up to explain why I thought Roth might be interested in me, and why I want Robby to do this for me."

Harry, still incensed over the Count's behavior, continued to pace the room, cursing beneath his breath. "Marry you, indeed, without so much as a by your leave. You have a father and a brother—one of which he should have approached first. Devil take him. Wish he had, would have landed him a facer."

"Well then, I am very glad he did not approach you, Harry, so do be quiet."

Harry was not to be put off so easily and stood fuming, his eyes glinting angrily. He picked up a book that had been reposing on his father's desk and flung it to the ground angrily. "Devil take him. Damned if I am going to forget about it, Nick. The man has insulted you—a Beaumont, my sister—and you want me to be quiet! Well, I'll not be. I have a mind to go out and pay my *respects* to the fellow right now," he said ominously.

Nicole saw that the situation called for a little diplomacy and stood up quickly, went to his side, and put her hand on his. He shrugged it off angrily. "I'll not be put off, Nick. Not this time!"

"Harry, you are being absurd and I will soon lose patience with you. Come now, sit down and listen to reason," she said coaxingly.

Harry's mild temper had been aroused, however. The thought that the Frenchie, someone he had not trusted from the first, had dared to touch his sister enraged him. The fact that obviously the Frenchie thought he had gotten away with such an outrage incensed him further. "No," he cried, "it is not to be borne."

"Harry, I think that you cannot go calling the fellow out. As Nicky says, to do so would most definitely set the tatter-mongers about, and Nick's name would be dragged into the mess," Robby said gravely.

"Hell and damnation!" expostulated Harry, beyond control. "Blast the fellow! Do you mean to tell me I am to do nothing? Are you crazy, man? Do you think I will let this pass?" He eyed them challengingly. "I'll tell you what. I'll go pick a fight with the swine. Say he has insulted me, then challenge him to a duel," he said grimly.

"No and no again! Harry, you are vexing me to the point of tears," cried Nicky, worried now.

"Really, Harry, you are disturbing your sister. Not the thing to do to go spouting off like that in her presence.

Want to fight a duel? Talk about it in private!" Archie replied reprovingly, always mindful of the conventions.

Nicole, exasperated beyond the point of endurance, stamped her foot at her brother and shouted, "Harry, if you say another word, just one more, you will force my hand, and I will . . . I will tell Father."

"What?" Harry was clearly surprised by this. "You would?"

"It is not what I should like, but to prevent you from doing something that would place you in danger—"

"Ha!" interrupted Harry, insulted.

"As I was saying—that would place you in danger, and perhaps ruin my reputation, I would go and confess to Father that I had placed myself in the position where I was alone with a man—in this case, the Count—and he, overcome with the desire to make known his love for me, tried to kiss me. Really, when you think about it, it was no great thing! Papa would censure me and that would be the end of it. Would you have me put in such a position, Harry? Would you have me humiliated before my parents?"

He eyed her angrily. "Devil take it, Nick, you know I wouldn't want such a thing, for Papa might restrict your movements, you know. But you must see that I have to pay the Count for his disrespect to you and to the name of Beaumont."

"No, I do not see that at all. In fact, the Count did me the honor of asking me to be his wife. I refused, and *you* will forgive him."

"Ha—devil, I will!" came the reply. Harry sat down, his face contorted into one of consternation.

Robby interjected softly, "If we may, I should like to get back to the matter at hand. Nicole, if you would continue, I should like to hear what you expect of me."

She smiled at Robby and looked directly at him. "It is this, Rob—I am going to flirt with you and appear to accept your court. I will show the world, and his Grace, that I am not averse to your addresses. I will lead him to believe that while I am not in love with you, I am willing to marry you . . . one day, and then watch his reaction."

Robby frowned. "You know, I am not well acquainted

with Roth. Not a part of his set. However, he appears a proud man. If he thinks you are taken with me, he might draw back. Might not make a push to engage your affections."

Nicole gave him a superior smile. "Robby, do listen. I have said that I will allow him to know that I am *not* in love with you. It is also my opinion that his Grace is a proud man and thinks quite a lot of his consequence and his ability to get what he wants. I believe the Duke is playing a waiting game. He sees that I have rejected all the boys who have asked for my hand. In fact, the only time I thought he might speak was when he feared I was involved with the Count. When he quickly saw that I did not care for Louis, he retracted and became aloof. If he thinks that I have flung away my ideals and decided to marry someone I would be comfortable with instead of someone I love—do you not think he would make a push for me then?" she ended, looking at Robby appealingly. He grinned and pinched her cheek. "To tell the truth, Nick, I don't know how he is to resist you if you ever look at him like that."

She laughed. "Why, Robby, and you said you didn't know how to pay a compliment. You just have, and very nicely done! You, my dear friend, must do just that type of thing whenever you are within the Duke's hearing, and leave the rest to me."

He sighed, made his bow, and turned to his brother and Harry. As Harry and Archie also rose to take their leave, Nicole put out her hand to her brother and said softly, "Harry, I beg of you, if you love me . . . you will not do anything foolish!"

He looked at her for a while, blue eyes meeting green, and his expression relaxed. He patted her hand. "Nicole, I will promise you this, and this only. When I pay the Count back—and I must, you know, perhaps not violently, but in some way, I have not yet decided how—it will not involve you. I promise you, Nick, so do not look so very worried. Trust me to do what is best in this regard."

This in no way relaxed her and she would have detained him had he not turned resolutely away and walked out with the Wychburn twins.

Chapter Thirteen

This particular problem was forgotten in the excitement of the following morning's excursion. The party assembled outside Mount Street at the reasonable hour of ten, and all appeared to be in high spirits. The morning was a fine April day. Brisk, sunny, and almost windless.

Harry leaned over to Sir James Litchfield and beamed. "Devilish fine day. Too bad the twins couldn't make it. We could have had a splendid kick-up together. Daresay we shall anyway!"

"Bound to, Harry," responded Sir James merrily.

Mary walked her gentle mare and pulled up aside Nick's spirited Ginger. "Nicole, I do want to thank you for inviting me today. It was very thoughtful of you."

"Oh, silly Mary. Do not thank me. I invited you at Arnie's insistence. I thought it would be much better if he had Miss Tilly here today."

Mary, much affronted, answered in shocked accents, "Indeed!"

"Oh, there is no need to take a pet, dear. I did not mean that I preferred that creature's company. Why, how could I when I have never met her? I meant only that I had thought it would help the 'cause' if Arnie were to bring her along. But everyone thought it would not do. At any rate, this is just as good a plan, I suppose, for by now Aunt has heard about Tilly and it is just as well that you are here and being introduced to him. I shall be able to use it later."

Mary still felt aggrieved but inclined her head. "I hope so, for Papa is giving me a very hard time, and would not have let me go today. He wishes to make it very hard for me at home, you see. But Mama advised me that it would not do for him to appear to forbid me your company, for you are a Beaumont and he does not wish to insult your father, you know."

Nicole laughed gaily. "Oh no, that would never do!" She then motioned her horse forward easily. Ginger's ears twitched. The mare seemed to sense her mistress's excited spirits and responded to them in kind. Roth, on his gray, came up beside her and smiled. "You look eager, imp."

"I am eager! How I have missed an open run. I can barely wait till we are out of this traffic."

"London does not seem to hold too dear a place in your heart."

"Oh, as to that, I like London—the excitement of London, the parties and plays. However, there are things I miss, such as a wild gallop. The freedom of country ways and country hours. I really could be happy living in the country for the better part of the year, for although I enjoy the gaiety of London, there is much that depresses me here, and when I cannot change something, cannot get involved, it saddens me. Perhaps that is why I prefer the country. There, it is so much easier, if one has a little wealth and power, to implement them for the good."

He frowned. "What do you mean, Nicole, for you have lost me."

"Well, here in London, one cannot help but see all the suffering, all the poverty. Oh, the gentry close their eyes and pretend it does not exist. But it does. For example, take our Miss Tilly. Now while she is young and still has her looks, she will be able to make money in the only trade she can, but will she be able to do so when she is old and her looks have faded? What about orphans, and cripples, and . . . oh, I suppose it is useless, for I could go on and on. Here I am helpless to do anything. If I help one, two, it is nothing. But in the country, one could set up an institution for orphans, set up a fund of some kind for the old and helpless of that particular county, and hope, pray, that the gentry of other counties would do the same for the people of their villages. Do you see?"

The Duke saw very well. His face was inscrutable as he replied, "Have you ever thought that when you married, you might organize the ladies of the Beau Monde to set up the type of institutions here in London, where they are most needed?"

"Yes, in fact, if I do not marry for love, then I will marry someone who will be in a position to give me free rein to do so."

He stiffened. "Have you anyone in mind?"

She smiled to herself, she couldn't have planned it better had she tried. "Strange that you should mention it, for I have often thought that if I did not meet someone I could love, I would marry Robert Wychburn. He is heir to the title and a considerable fortune. He is a dear, dear friend and someone I could be extremely comfortable with and push toward politics, for his ideals match my own. Yes, if I do not marry for love, I will marry him."

The Duke relaxed and chuckled. Nicole stole a glance in his direction and felt satisfied. They had reached the edge of town, and she suddenly broke into a gallop. She heard the boys laugh behind her and felt the ground rumble as they followed her lead. After they had ridden for some time, Nicole slowed down to an easy gait, with his Grace beside her. She giggled. "You know, I was just thinking how much I miss my breeches."

Roth laughed. "Even still? Do you not like your splendid feathers?"

"Oh, in truth, I must admit that I do. It is very comforting to know that one is dressed in the first style of elegance. But I miss the freedom of being a . . . girl in breeches, without the complications of town life."

He looked at her steadily. "Are you unhappy, imp?"

She returned his gaze forthrightly. "Unhappy? No, no. Please pay no heed to me. It is just that . . . life does not really hold the type of adventure one reads about in novels. Things are so much more matter-of-fact in real life."

"No, Nicky, there is no such thing as 'happily ever after,' for nothing remains the same. Life is full of bends and twists and one must learn to adapt if one is to survive."

She glanced at him, but said nothing more, as the others had caught up to them. They all stopped their horses and stood about letting their animals rest awhile.

"How much further, Roth?" questioned Harry.

"We are nearly there. Another two miles or so. Shall we proceed?"

They all agreed and continued down the road at a sedate pace.

A few minutes later they stopped again and Roth motioned with his head. "There."

Harry gave a low whistle. "So this is Walden House? Heard your aunt was as rich as a nabob!"

"Harry!" admonished his sister.

Roth smiled ruefully. "It was not always so. Poor Aunt Liz had a time of it when she was young."

They gathered round him, for he was about to tell them a story apparently, and all were quite eager to here the account.

"Aunt Liz had been promised to someone else, then she met my uncle. He was penniless, untitled, and with little prospect. He was a second son, you see—perfectly respectable, but with nothing to offer—and my Aunt Liz was the only daughter of proud parents, wanting a brilliant match for her. They forbade him her hand. They sent her away to a cousin in hopes of keeping them apart. Aunt Liz, however, was not one to be put down so easily and they managed to see one another. They ran off to Gretna Green—"

Mary uttered a shocked exclamation and then bit her lip as his cold stare came to rest on her.

"Bravo, Adam, do go on," said Nicky approvingly.

"They continued together to India, where they remained for the next five years, and my uncle came back as rich as a nabob, as you put it Harry. He bought my aunt this house—Walden House." His hands made an expressive gesture. "And they were reconciled with her parents. So you see, Nicole, some real-life stories do have happy endings."

"I always thought they did . . . Adam," she said softly, their eyes meeting.

"By Jove, imagine that!" exclaimed Harry, much impressed.

"It is the most romantic thing I have heard, and it happened in real life. I thought your aunt had a great deal of spirit," Nicole said warmly.

149

"Do you approve of defying your relations, Nicky? It was not an easy thing then . . . or now! She was ostracized from them, and as such, had a difficult time entering society."

"Oh, as to that, if one is so unlucky as to have parents who do not support one in one's decisions, then it is one's duty to defy them!"

Mary was much shocked by this very radical opinion. "Oh no, Nicole, I am persuaded you do not mean it!"

"Oh, but I do! What sort of creature do you think I am? Marriage without love is . . . is a desecration of the soul! Love without fidelity, loyalty . . . is not love! If one falls in love with a man, one must take a stand . . . beside him, and he beside her!" Then meeting Roth's quizzical look, she bit her lip.

He said softly, for her ears alone, "And what of marriage to execute high ideals?"

She turned and met his look squarely, saying equally softly, "If one finds no love, then one must settle!"

He frowned, and said nothing.

Sir James Litchfield laughed. "You are very romantic, Nick, but it does not always work out so well. If his aunt had returned with Mr. Dowling a pauper—well, who knows what misery they might have endured?"

"Perhaps when there is real love, it forces one to make a good life in spite of the obstacles in one's path!"

Sir James smilingly shook his head. "Not so, Nick. Life is not so cut-and-dried!"

She put up her chin. "If you are to laugh and make light of my very deep beliefs, I shall not voice them, James." She turned her head to look at Roth. "And you, Roth, you have not commented. Do you also think what I have said is foolish?"

"Not I, Nick. I applaud what you have said, and what you have left unsaid," he answered quietly.

James scowled. Harry looked pensive, his mind straying to a pair of large brown eyes . . . lost to him. Arnie reached out and touched Mary's hand, causing her to blush.

Nicole, suddenly shy, put up her hand as if to ward off the sun and take in her surroundings. They walked their horses onto the drive that led to the house and stopped again to take in the spectacle. The drive was lined on both sides with towering rhododendrons, budding but not yet bursting with color. However, farther up to the left was a field alive with color. Rows and rows of flower beds crammed full with daffodils and crocuses met their eyes. There was white and yellow everywhere, peeping through the green.

Nicole exclaimed appreciatively, "Why, Adam, this is exquisite. The flowers . . . are just lovely. I have never seen such an extensive arrangement."

He nodded. "I have always found Walden House to be breathtakingly lovely at this time of year. I am pleased to see that you agree, for I have spent many a happy day here and have grown to think of it as my real home. I was never overfond of Lyndham Hall—which, by the way, is not far from here."

They had reached the end of the drive and a stable boy came running up to help them with the horses. Nicole turned her attention back to the yellow and brown Tudor mansion, with its bay windows, and ivy creeping sedately and regally up the stones. Here was a home, not just a house, but something that two people had poured their souls into, put themselves into. The green lawns leading off into different paths lent mystery to the house. She found that she already had a feeling for the place, without having been inside its walls.

Roth and Litchfield had already dismounted. Nicole was still gazing about her rapturously when she realized that both men stood patiently at her heel in the hopes of helping her dismount. She gurgled good-naturedly, more amused with the situation than pleased. "Shall I give you each an arm and settle the matter?"

Roth grinned at Sir James, and then tilted his head to Nicky, giving her a slight smirk. "Ah, as *I* do not care for *divided favors,* I will step aside and allow Sir James the honor."

Sir James was quick to take his chance and held Nicole's small waist in his hands a moment longer than necessary after he had lowered her to the ground. He said urgently, "Nicky, Nicky, I have hardly had a minute alone with you. Please, dearest, do not avoid me. I could not bear it if I were to lose your friendship as well. I have promised not to tease you with . . . with my hopes. Do not be forever turning away from me. I could not bear it!"

She was touched at once, for she had indeed been avoiding him with the fear of encouraging him. She liked him too well to hurt him and did not at this point know how to act. She had thought that perhaps a cool aloofness was needed to put his "hopes," as he phrased it, to rest. It was obvious that instead it had only served to fan his desire, for nothing was more desirable, it seemed, than the unobtainable. She sighed heavily and looked at his melancholy expression. She had no wish to end a friendship that she had cherished for so many years. She patted his hand indulgently. "Come along, Jimmy, for the others are already at the door."

They were all met at the front door by an elderly butler who appeared, at first glance, to be somewhat frigid. He thawed considerably when his gaze rested on the Duke and bowed them into the house, announcing that Lady Elizabeth was awaiting their arrival in the salon. He bowed again and led the way, as they followed in subdued and awed silence.

The salon was a lovely room, if somewhat overfurnished. There were many objects and pieces of furniture that were clearly Oriental, and these held the attention of Lady Elizabeth's guests until she herself, looking quite small and thin, called attention to her presence. She was sitting on a cushioned sofa beside the fire, a book of poems—*Childe Harold*—was beside her. "Bah . . . lot of nonsense. Can't see why all the world is raving about the fellow. He ain't mealy-mouthed like most of your generation, Adam, but he's an impudent dog. Well, what are you all gaping at? Come here and make my acquaintance."

Nicole, already acquainted with her, stifled a giggle. Sir James Litchfield, came forward with Harry beside him, Sir Arnold Merdon lagging behind, and Mary, blushing hotly, making up the rear, while Roth and Nicky stood to the side. After the necessary introductions were made, Aunt Liz sniffed and with a pointing finger said in an imperious manner, "Sir James, I know already. Young Beaumont seems a nice lad, his cousin seems a fool, and this young lady—too shy for my liking. Take them off with you, Roth, and show them the gardens. Leave Nicole with me."

Happy to make their escape from their brisk hostess, the young people left through a garden door at the rear of the salon, and Nicole, strangely at ease with this odd old woman, sank down without ceremony beside her, unbuttoning her jacket. Her hat and gloves she had already removed and placed on a nearby table.

She smiled at the aged woman beside her and thought it strange that she should feel so fond of her. Perhaps it was because the woman had shown a preference for her. "How glad I am to be visiting with you, Lady Elizabeth, and what a lovely day to be here. Your gardens are the loveliest I have ever seen."

"Thank you, my dear. Daniel and I put quite a lot of planning into those beds. He was overfond of flowers and we would work together always."

Nicole regarded her hostess from twinkling eyes. "His Grace said that he loves this place even more than he does his own home." Nicole had a lively curiosity about the Duke. Today was the first time he had ever mentioned anything of a personal nature, and she found a need within herself to know more—to know everything he had done and felt when he was growing up.

His Aunt Liz smiled kindly. "Well, my dear, the poor boy never knew his mother, for she died giving him life. My poor Adam suffered by it, much more than others do."

Nicole frowned and leaned closer. "Why? Why should he suffer more by it? What of his father?"

Aunt Liz sighed. "My brother was a cold, somber gentleman. Then he met Davinia. She was a breath of fresh air. I loved her well. She was delicate, though—beautiful, soft, and delicate." She sighed again. "For a few short years she made him live, and then they found she was with child, he was wonderously proud. They laughed and planned, and then . . . she died. He saw not his son, and by that time I was away in India and so I was not here for Adam when he needed me most. My brother went into a blind rage. From what I was told, they feared for his sanity. He drank for months. When finally he emerged from his grief, he was hard. There was no love left in him. Not for a soul, not even for the little boy that so needed him. When I returned, Adam was about five or six. Don't imagine that he was running around neglected. No, his father saw to it that he was taught well, dressed well, fed well, but he paid him no heed. My brother had never been so much against my marriage, and so when we returned, we came to Lyndham Hall. My parents were staying in the London town house and still refused to see me. You see, I married without their consent. Why they never bothered with Adam shall always be a mystery, unless they did not realize my brother's antagonism toward the boy. It was during those months that I grew to love Adam . . . to care for him as I would have cared for my own. It hurt to see my brother turn so cold against the boy, and when we settled at Walden House, we brought little Adam back with us. I was never able to have children, and Adam filled this gap for me. Thomas, my brother, was quite content to allow the boy to remain with me for a few years and I think that Adam grew to love Daniel and myself as much as we loved him.

"Suddenly, Thomas turned to religion and decided to take Adam back under his wing and give him religious training. Thomas had become a cold self-righteous man, and Adam was even then a rebellious boy. They did not get along. Adam went away to school and spent his holidays, whenever his father permitted, with us. He more and more became a boy very different from his father and he grew mature before his time.

"When he went up to Oxford, he became involved with everything a young man becomes intrigued with in kicking up larks, but he went a step further . . . he made sure his father was *aware!* He wanted to hurt Thomas as much as *he* had been hurt. When he left school, he became a notorious friend of the Prince, he drank heavily . . . too heavily. The final break came when Thomas was given his notice to quit, and knowing he had not long, called Adam to his side.

"Thomas advised him, since Adam was the last of their name, to marry a suitable lady and produce an heir. When Adam refused, his father, for the first time, almost begged. He said that Adam's mother had died in giving him an heir to carry on the line, and he would not let it be in vain. An heir there must be! Adam refused staunchly. They never saw one another again, and then Thomas died.

"That was almost two years ago ... perhaps less ... and it left Adam cynical. My Daniel, just before I lost him last year, took things into his hands and called Adam in for a talk. The boy had gone wild ... committing every kind of excess imaginable. Yet for Daniel, Adam came to grips with himself and found his way into politics." She sighed. "There is still a bitterness in the boy." She looked away and mumbled, "Do not let it ruin him ... and you."

Nicole regarded her thoughtfully; here was something new, something she had never suspected.

Lady Elizabeth looked fondly across at Nicole and one old, yet surprisingly elegant, hand touched Nicole's arm. "Now go, child. I wanted you to know about him. Thought it might help you to understand. If I have overstepped, then you will forgive the whims of an old woman!" she said softly. Then she added with a mischievous smile, "Lord, child, if you don't have my boy eating out of your hands, it's more than half surprised I'll be."

"Why, Lady Elizabeth, do not talk so, for although I have listened to you with a great deal of interest, I must confess, do not imagine that I wish to have your 'boy' eat out of my hands," retorted Nicky.

She received a rap across her fingers and a grin. "You wicked girl, lying to an old woman! Be off now and let me rest."

Nicole suddenly took Aunt Liz's hand and kissed it gently, before taking her leave.

Nicole went out the door toward the direction she had seen her friends take, and then changed her mind. She turned toward her left instead and found a maze of evergreen hedges. She walked into the maze and sank down upon a cold stone bench. She wanted to think, needed to think about all she had learned. She was lost in thought and did not hear the rustle of branches as someone approached.

"And why does Lady Nicole sit here alone, when she has engineered an outing and should be at the head of that party, presiding over us?"

She looked up, startled to find Roth towering above her, a gentle smile hovering about his mouth and eyes. She thought once again that he was the most attractive, virile man she had ever been acquainted with. Her heart fluttered, leaving her feeling breathless, and she was conscious of a wild desire within herself. She longed to feel his arms about her . . . his lips. . . . She turned away hastily lest he read her thoughts.

"I have just left your aunt and I must tell you that I like her very much."

"It pleases me to hear you say so, for I love her dearly. However, that does not explain what you are doing here alone. Is there something wrong?"

There was concern in his voice and his eyes searched her face intently. She smiled brightly up at him, not knowing what to answer. She had come here to think . . . about him, his youth. She answered quietly, "No, there is nothing wrong. It is such a lovely day, I had wanted to be by myself for a moment to drink it all in."

He raised an eyebrow doubtfully. "No doubt you find being secluded here, surrounded by evergreens, the epitome of spring beauty."

His tone mocked her and she flared at him instantly. "Well, I certainly would not have been able to enjoy the peacefulness of the day if I had joined everyone in the garden!"

Roth's eyes grew hard, he made a stiff bow, and said coldly, "Clearly, I am intruding. Your serv—"

Nicole impulsively put out her hand and caught his own, interrupting him. She trembled at his touch and managed to say, "Please, Adam, do not go."

He held her hand tightly before releasing it and then sat down on the opposite side of the bench, with his body turned to face hers.

They said nothing as they sat looking at each other there in the cool stillness. Nicole put her hand to her heart, for it was beating so hard she thought he would hear its severe palpitations. Her voice, breaking the stillness of the moment, sounded strange to her ears.

"Your aunt told me about your childhood. Do you know that when she was telling me about you, I had a great urge to have known you then? We would have been great friends, I think."

He laughed. "You never cease to delight me, darling imp. How could we have been great friends? When you were ten, I was already twenty, with my youth quite irrevocably behind me." His face took on a sneer and for the moment he seemed not to see her, as he remembered things long past.

"No, you do not understand. I mean if we had been friends when I was a girl, and if you weren't so very much older then, for it is strange that while you were so much older when I was ten, you are not so much older than I am now . . . are you?" This sounded garbled, even to her own ears, but surprisingly enough, the Duke smiled and then chuckled appreciatively. "Splendid, I am losing years instead of gaining them. What strange thing will you say next, dearest imp?"

"Well, perhaps you will not like it, but I should like to ask you something which you will think impertinent, but I should like to know. When your mother died and your . . . your father became so . . . so cold-mannered toward you, did you hate her—your mother I mean—did you hate her for dying and leaving you?"

Roth was at first taken aback, then angry. He stood up, and then once again in control, sat down, this time not turning to face her. His answer came quietly, his voice hard. "Yes, I suppose I did hate her at first. I was too young to know anything but that she had gone and left me with . . . with him. Then, as I became older, I realized my father was dying—not with an illness, for he was not ill yet. I watched him shrink away . . . into himself. I heard him call her name night after night. I suppose it was then I made up my mind never to love anyone so completely . . . that I would lose myself if I lost her." He

157

squared his shoulders, shrugging off a bad memory, and sighed deeply.

"Did you never love your father?"

"Thank God, no. I hated him. He was not—at least not in all the years I knew him—a good man. He was self-righteous, pious, but not good. I had no respect for him. Perhaps that saved me. You see, it is much easier to do without the love of someone you do not care for, and I had Aunt Liz and Uncle Daniel."

"Then did you not give all your love to your aunt and uncle?"

"I loved them dearly, but I made a life for myself apart from them. You see, I had made up my mind not to allow my feelings to go too deep, so I . . . always held back!"

"How sad, how very sad. I am sorry for you. How can you be complete without the fulfillment of loving someone? And it needn't be a woman—although I think it must, for love of a friend is different. No, Adam, you will not lose yourself because if you do not fall in love, you never really find yourself. You have nothing to give or to lose."

"Those are pretty words, Lady Nicole, but life is not like the books you have been reading, and which have apparently gone to your head. I hope you will not have too long a tumble, for I have no wish to see you hurt."

She sucked in her breath. What was this, was he telling her that she might get hurt if she cared for him? Was he warning her off? She felt a constriction within her breast, but continued bravely, "Say what you will, but I have not got those pretty words from novels, Duke. I have learned them from life . . . the life of my parents."

"They are very lucky . . . perhaps you will be too!"

She sighed. "I think now we should go join the others, Duke." He stood up immediately and came round the bench, offering his hand. She placed her small white hand in his large bronzed one and stood up. As she did so, her ankle gave way and she fell against him. His other arm went around to steady her.

"Oh, I am sorry, my ankle." She looked up to find his face near her own, his eyes filled with emotion, and she thought that she would swoon with the suffocating feeling that was threatening to overcome her. She could not move and closed her eyes. Then suddenly she was standing on her own two feet, free of him. He had released her and had stood aside. "Can you walk now, Lady Nicole?" His voice was cool, aloof.

She flushed. "Oh yes, yes. I am so sorry my ankle gave way."

He led her back to their party and all was forgotten . . . or seemed so in the gaiety of the luncheon party. She was never alone with the Duke after that, as Sir James Litchfield kept her fully occupied.

When she reached home and flung herself down on her bed, she felt the day was not all she had expected and hoped for, and burying her face into her pillow, she sobbed.

Chapter Fourteen

Adam Roth leaned back against the cushions of his sofa and mused deeply. When Nicky had fallen into his arms the day before, he had thought all was at an end. He had wanted her—wanted her in a way he had never known was possible. The touch of her in his arms had driven him to distraction, but he was an experienced man, well able to control himself, and he did. He was now feeling the after-effects of regret. Deuce take you, Adam Roth, for a fool, he told himself bitterly. *You will lose her if you keep this up. But what of it? She is merely a woman, there will always be others.* The vision of her smile mocked him. *There is no other like Nicky!* he said vehemently to himself and heard the words echoed in the quiet of his study. *Tonight, tonight perhaps I will tell her, tell her she is mine.* He thought again and shook his head. *No, not yet, the time is not right.*

Nicole accepted to see only one person that morning, young Dereck. She wore his gift of yellow hothouse roses, and smiled sweetly at him as he declared his love

159

and devotion. After seeing him off, she retired to her room, where she remained in deep thought; she had been despondent after yesterday's episode, for nothing else but Roth's rejection of her in the garden could have shown that he thought her still a child, not to be touched. *The Duke is not for you,* she told herself fervently, wishing it were not true.

Nicole was made of a strong will, and this despondency did not last. She went to her closet and pulled out a red velvet dress she had been saving. Saving for a night like this. It was a full-skirted gown, tight-waisted, which she knew would accentuate the smallness of her waist. The dress was sleeveless, off the shoulder, with a swag of velvet that went over the arms and hung low over her breast. *Yes, I will wear this tonight.* She laid it on the bed and turned to the window, which overlooked the small garden in the rear of the house. *You wanted me, Adam Roth, I saw your eyes. You shall want me more, but I will have none of you, only Robby will fill my eyes . . . I will allow only Robby to attend me, be at my side, touch my hand. So you want none of my love. All right, your Grace, you shall not have any, until you beg . . . no, no, I never want you to beg, my sweet life, I love you too well. And you, Duke, shall love me!*

Tilly turned to Sir Arnold and gave him a sly look. "Look 'ere, m'darling, just look at that bonnet. Let's go in and buy it."

He patted her hand fondly. "Yes, of course, but wouldn't you prefer some jewelry?"

"No reason for you to put up so much blunt. Enough ladies will know you are buying me clothes. That's good enough." She kissed his cheek and whispered for him to do the same, which he did promptly. Unfortunately, Miss Mary Melville happened to be passing down Bond Street just at that moment and froze in her tracks. Sir Arnold saw her and turned hastily away and led Miss Tilly into the shop. It was some few minutes before Mary, almost in tears, was able to move, and then she nearly ran in the direction of her home, to fall sobbing upon her bed.

Harry went happily upon his errand to inform Robby

Wychburn that he was required to attend Lady Sefton's rout party that evening, and attend his sister as planned.

Things were now in full swing.

Nicole entered the rout party that evening on her brother's arm. They were extremely late, and when people turned their attention toward the newly arrived guests, there was almost a uniform gasp, and Nicole was certainly aware of the silent applause. Her red velvet dress looked fiery, catching the lights of the candles and shining them against the whiteness of her skin. She wore her black hair—glinting now with a star brooch made up of diamonds—piled in curls at the top of her head, with some of the curls falling toward her left ear. A red feather, caught by the diamond pin, twirled round the top of her head and curled under round the same ear. She wore a diamond star in each ear and one around her neck. Long white gloves were pulled over her bare arms. Her eyes sparkled coldly.

Much to his annoyance, Roth found that he was unable to keep his eyes away from her as she moved away from the drawing room door and into the room. He had arrived late himself, and when his eyes scanned the room, he was surprised and disappointed not to see Lady Nicole Beaumont there. It was with relief that he heard her name announced, and then with a gasp that he saw her. This dress was in no way maidenly or modest. It was quite low, and he felt a strong inclination to drape a shawl about her. *Really,* he thought, *your jealousy over the chit is getting out of proportion.* Her gaze met his admiring eyes and he raised his wine glass to her. She looked haughtily away.

Devil take her, what's wrong now? he thought angrily.

Mr. Robert Wychburn, true to his word, made his way to her and murmured in her ear, "You were magnificent, Nick. What an entrance! Damn if I don't marry you myself!"

She looked up at him coquettishly. "Remember now, you are not to believe all the outrageous things I will be saying to you. I promise you, Robby, I am going to be a devil." She smiled saucily up at him.

He groaned. "Dash it, Nick, said I wasn't in the petticoat line, but I will try—though if you insist on looking at

161

me the way you are now, I will be hard put to it not to laugh at you."

"But I must look at you just so. Can't you see I am flirting with you, Robby?" she said, surprised.

"No? Are you really? I was wondering why you were batting those lashes of yours. Oh, oh, here comes the Count. Don't let Harry see you with the fellow, he's apt to start something, you know."

He led her away, and as the music started up again, he would have led her onto the floor, had not Mr. Dereck claimed her hand. When the country dance was at an end, Robby once again came to her side and led her away to a secluded corner, where they could clearly be seen, lost in deep conversation.

Sir James Litchfield had been trying to engage the elusive Lady Nicole's attention, but found her both unwilling and unresponsive. He retired to an empty chair, a glass of brandy in his hand. Roth pulled up a chair beside him. "Who is this whippersnapper, James?" asked Roth, as he was himself out of temper.

"Robert Wychburn. Never would have thought she'd—well, look at her, Adam. Dash it, she seems taken with him, don't she? Known him even longer than she's known me, and there she is looking at him as if no one else existed!"

The Duke said nothing, he seemed to remember that Nicky had mentioned Robert Wychburn the day of the picnic, said something foolish about marrying him if she couldn't marry for love. He felt suddenly incensed. His black brows drew together in a severe frown. He looked across at Nicole and managed to catch her eye. She could not help but give him a lingering look, for she dearly wanted him by her side and her resolve was beginning to crack. He stood up, sucking in his breath, and thought, *Devil take it, the chit is flirting with me from across the room. Where did she learn to use her eyes like that!*

He strode over to her quickly, and ignoring Robert Wychburn, who watched him from her side, took hold of her bare arm. "Come along, Nicole, I want a word with you!" It was a demand and he was in no mood for interference.

162

"Not now, Duke." She smiled saucily.

"*Now!* Nicole, you will soon learn that you cannot look across a room at a man as you just did, and not get exactly what you asked for."

"Oh?" she elongated the word. "What did I ask for, Duke?"

He looked at her and cupped her chin with his hand. "Your eyes called me to your side. Did they lie?"

She looked back at him, she had to play a part. It was vital, and yet, she did not want to lie to him. "No, Duke, I did want you. The horses were sent round this morning, and they are indeed magnificent creatures. Just what I wanted."

"I am glad that they met with your approval. However, I do not wish to discuss horseflesh with you at the moment." His hand guided her away, and they found themselves walking down the hallway. He stopped and turned her to face him. "James seems to think you have lost your heart to your friend over there." His chin indicated Robert Wychburn, now conversing with Harry.

Nicole eyed him speculatively. "Does he?"

"Well?" He had an urge to shake her.

"Well what, Roth? You indicated that Jimmy seems to think I have lost my heart to Robby. Did you require confirmation or denial, or were you just imparting Jimmy's opinion?" she replied coolly.

"Devil take it, Nick. Answer me, do you love the boy?"

"Love? I am very fond of Robby. He is a dear, sweet friend, and I will probably be his wife one day. It will be comfortable to be *his* wife, for he will always adore me and be *faithful* to me, and if one cannot have love, that is the next best thing!" She answered him calmly, still in full control.

He looked at her searchingly, thinking that he was not hearing correctly, that his was not the same girl. Here was a woman, cold and calculating, and he did not like it. *Damn you,* he cursed himself, thinking that this was the result of *his* game. He was angry now, and gave her small bare shoulders a shake. "Devil a bit! What new kick-up is this, Nicky, for I do not find it amusing!"

She pulled away from him and glared. He grabbed her

163

arm and pulled her roughly into the empty room at the end of the hall, closing the door behind him. He stood leaning against it, his arms folded.

"You will tell me, my girl, what the devil you are up to," he said grimly, staring her down.

She looked aside and moved away from him, saying, her voice light and carefree (so very different from her feelings), "I am not up to anything, Duke. It is simply that I am not in love with any of the *boys* I have met. I must marry someday, so I suppose it will have to be Robby. We are the best of friends, you know!"

He strode across the room angrily and turned her round to face him, his hands tightly gripping her shoulders. "Do not speak such fustian to me, girl! It will not fadge. You will not marry him or anyone else, Nick. Do you hear me?"

She looked up at the Duke's angry face, her eyes invited him, her lips were close to his own. If he would not kiss her, then she would kiss him, she thought, then suddenly she changed her mind. *No,* she thought, *he has not said one word of love.* She pulled away just as Roth's mouth sought her own. One small hand pushed at his chest. "Do I need someone to protect me from *you?*" Her voice cut at him, and he released her immediately and turned round, walking quickly toward the door. He hesitated as his hand touched the knob—fleetingly, so it seemed—for in a moment he had opened the door and was gone, without looking back at her. Nicky stood for a few moments, staring at the door, hoping he would come back, tell her he loved her, wanted her.

When she returned to the drawing room, she scanned the room, instinctively knowing he would not be there. Roth had left the party, taking with him all her hopes of pleasure.

The next few days and nights were wildly busy ones. She went riding with Robby, shopping and walking with him. All of London was chatting about them, smiling at what was thought would be a charming match. Lady Beaumont looked anxiously at her daughter, knowing in her heart that Nicole was not the carefree, happy creature

164

she was pretending to be. Harry had seemed to forget his grievance against the Count, until one night when they were at Vauxhall Gardens. Nicky was standing beside Robby, chatting vivaciously, when the Count spied her and weaved his way toward her. Harry eyed him, flushed darkly, picked up a glass of wine and intercepted the Count, bumping into him and neatly spilling the wine onto the Count's ivory-colored waistcoat. The Count clenched his teeth, but composed himself and said silkily, "It's quite all right, Harry. Think no more about it!"

Harry's eyes glinted at him, challengingly. "I don't intend to, and my name, Count D'Agout, is Viscount Beaumont!" His voice was hard.

Robby moved away from Nicole, who stood frozen with fear lest a quarrel start up, but she needn't have worried, for the Count had no intention of picking up the gauntlet—*not* with *her* brother. He bowed and moved away without another word. Harry cursed beneath his breath.

"He won't fight with you, Harry. Must see that. Wants your sister. Knows he won't get her by fighting with you. Forget him!" Robby urged.

Nicole's eyes searched the crowds for the Duke, but in vain. He was not present.

The next morning Nicole had her phaeton brought to her and went out, with her tiger perched proudly behind, for her first solitary ride in Hyde Park. She saw the Duke astride his gray and hailed him. His Grace rode up to her immediately.

"They look famous, imp. Are you happy with them?"

"Oh, Adam, I am so much in your debt. There are not a finer pair of horses in all of England, with the exception of your bays! Indeed, I am very pleased with them, how could it be otherwise?"

He smiled at her tenderly. "They are, in fact, better than my bays. I am convinced that I should marry you and thereby settle the matter."

She flushed hotly, the tears started to her eyes, for she could not bear for him to joke about a matter that meant

165

so much to her. She could not keep the hurt from her voice when she answered him.

"No, Roth, for while I fancy our horses would, *we* would not suit! Thank you again, and I promise not to bother you with such errands in the future."

She was about to leave, but his hand reached across and held her arm, restraining her. "What is it, imp? Why do you look so and say such things to me? Do you not realize that I want always to be doing your errands?"

She gasped, for surely his tone was sincere, caressing. "I must go, Adam, please excuse me." She looked resolutely ahead.

The Duke had no other choice but to release her arm and stare thoughtfully after her. Nicky continued in the park for a few minutes when she was hailed by Beau Brummell. She leaned over, giving that elegant gentleman her hand.

He smiled warmly up at her. "Your phaeton, Lady Nicole, is most exceptional."

"Please Mr. Brummell, allow me to take you up for a drive."

He assented readily and she drove on at a sedate pace.

"I am so pleased that you approve of my phaeton, for I do feel so comfortable with it, although some of the dowagers have raised their eyebrows. I am sure they think it too sporting for a female."

"That is nothing! It is important that you *be* what you are. For, my dear Lady Nicole, who would have heard of me if I had been anything but what I am? It is my folly that is the making of me. If I did not impertinently stare Duchesses out of countenance and nod over my shoulder to a Prince, I should be forgotten in a week. And if the world is so silly as to admire my absurdities, you and I may know better, but what does that signify?"

She sighed. "It is very sad, but true."

He flicked open the lid of his snuff box with his left thumb, and took a pinch of snuff, and then without looking at her, he said softly, "How goes it, Lady Nicole?"

She looked surprised. "Whatever do you mean?"

"Rumor has it that you are soon to wed a certain

young man by the name of Wychburn. I was very much surprised by this, as you must realize it will not do."

She was momentarily diverted and nearly lost control of the reins. "How you manage to keep so well informed when you have been out of town these past few weeks is beyond me, sir, but if you promise to keep a secret, I will tell you the truth."

"That is rash of you, my dear. You musn't be so trusting. However, I will try to keep your secret."

"Well, I do not intend to marry Robby Wychburn at all. It is someone else, someone entirely different."

"Poor Mr. Wychburn, alas—but I thought you a different sort of maid."

"Silly Mr. Brummell, you know full well that Mr. Wychburn plays a game with me, I can tell by the look in your eyes. I don't know how you know, but you do."

He grinned broadly at her, pleased with her reaction. "So you and this boy—Robby, did you say, yes?—well, you are playing a game to catch . . . *who*, my dear?"

"No, that I will not tell you, for you will think me a . . . a mercenary female like all the others, while it is nothing of the sort. It is for love and not position that I am trying to . . . to win this man."

He looked at her gravely. "I could never think you anything of the sort. I am an excellent judge of character, Lady Nicole, and I wish you luck with Roth."

"Huh! she gasped. "You know?"

"I am only surprised that the fool has not snapped you up yet. I must bid you farewell now, Lady Nicole, for I have an errand I must discharge and this would be an appropriate place to put me down."

He made his leisurely way toward Brook Street and was shown into the Duke's study.

Roth stood up and strode across the room, extending his hand with a welcoming smile. "George, how are you. We have missed you at the club. How is the Regent?"

"Returned last evening. I do not know how our illustrious Regent fares, as I have not been with him. You have been misinformed. I spent the last few weeks at Oatlands. Had a marvelous time, would have remained longer, but those dogs of hers finally got to me. Do you know that she has now at least forty of the beasts roaming at will about the house?"

The Duke laughed. The Duchess of York was universally liked by the Beau Monde, and in spite of the drawback of the dogs, nearly everyone jumped at the chance of spending time at Oatlands where one was bound to find an informal atmosphere and the finest of England's wits gathered.

"Met Lady Nicole Beaumont in the park this morning. Drove with her a bit. By gad, she's a lovely creature. Had a funny idea you'd be tied up in strings by now, Adam." He searched his friend's face openly.

Roth returned his gaze, and grinned. "Will be soon, if I'm not careful."

"Why be careful? Marriage wouldn't do for me, you know, but it's just the thing *you* need. She will do you a world of good, that little lovely. It's not her face, you know, it's her soul. There is a depth there."

"I know, I know, she is just what I need. I am fast beginning to realize that I cannot live without her, but she is leading me a strange dance, George."

"How fatiguing for you. That is precisely why I avoid just such a girl as that. A life of leisure is a most difficult art. Bring a woman into it, and there is no rest." He then made a quick decision. "Come on then, Adam, I have a horse running at Ascot. Let's go for a few days."

Roth hesitated, for he did not want to leave Nicole. In this strange mood of hers, there was no telling what she might do. However, instinct told him perhaps it was what was needed to bring things to a head. "Yes, I think I will go with you. In fact, we will leave immediately. Pick up James before we go. The boy needs a change as well."

Brummell rose languidly and bade him farewell. "Come for me at Watier's, I shall await you there after I have my man pack a few things."

"Devil take you, George, I want to go in my curricle, but if you insist on bringing a lot of luggage, it will have to be the coach."

"We cannot sit comfortably in your phaeton—all three of us at any rate—so let it be the coach. And if you wish

James to accompany us, you had better repair to his lodgings immediately. He has been drinking deep, Adam."

"What, when did you see him?"

"I stopped by earlier before going to the park and he was already into the brandy."

"My poor James. All right, Beau, in two hours."

They parted and Roth called for his coach to be prepared, ordered his valet to pack and be ready to leave within the given time. He then walked the short distance to Sir James Litchfield's bachelor rooms. He was greeted warmly by the butler, advised him that he would announce himself, and went quickly to James' bedroom. He was shocked to find his friend stretched out in a chair, a bottle of brandy in one hand, his clothes askew, and his eyes red.

"Jimmy, what the devil is this?"

"Hallo, Roth. We've lost her, you know. She'll have none of me. Don't seem to want you either. For a while there, thought she did. Wouldn't mind losing to you, but to that puppy! It doesn't bear thinking of."

Roth strode impatiently into the hallway and called for Sir James' valet. He curtly gave the man orders to pack a portmanteau for his master and to be ready to leave in two hours' time. He then turned to James, held him up, called for the butler to perform this office for him while he proceeded to straighten his friend's tie, waistcoat, and cutaway coat. He then called for Sir James' greatcoat, which he draped about his shoulders.

"Come on, my friend, let's walk back to my place and have some lunch before we go."

"Go? Go where? Why are you pushing and prodding me, Adam? Really, there's no need to do that!"

Roth linked his arm in his friend's and maneuvered him toward the door.

Outside, they walked along in silence while Sir James drank in the cool air. He sighed suddenly. "Oh, Adam, remember now what I wanted to tell you. Saw Barnaby last night at Cribb's Parlor. Went with Alvanley to blow a cloud. He was sitting with some brute of a fellow. When he saw us, he turned white, and ran out without even a nod. Thought it strange."

169

"Barnaby will be taken care of very shortly. We have arranged a little surprise for him."

"Something else ... oh yes, now I remember. The Count—the one always following Nick about—he was there. Just as Barnaby was leaving, he walks in and grabs him by the throat. Then Frenchie looks up, sees us watching him, and throws Barnaby away from him. Looked too smoky by half!"

The Duke's expression changed, his eyes narrowed. "The Count—Count D'Agout? Of course, of course. Good God, have I been blind?" He looked at his friend. "Thank you, James, I will leave little to chance, I promise you, for what you have just told me explains much!"

Mary Melville entered Nicole's bedroom in a huff and threw herself on the bed. Nicole, startled, went to her immediately, putting her hand to her head and stroking it gently.

"Why, Mary, my poor dear, whatever ails you?

"Nicole, oh, Nicole, I have been so miserable. I knew this would happen. I do not say it is your fault, for you thought you were doing the right thing, but ... but the worst has happened."

Harry opened the door to Nicole's bedroom in time to see Mary throw herself once again against Nicky's bed in a fit of tears, and hastily retreated, but Nicky called him back and bade him sit down with them. He grimaced at her, but as his curiosity was aroused and he had nothing better to do, he sat down, looking interested. Mary eyed him doubtfully, but Nicole admonished her gently and she continued. "I saw Arnie, my Arnie, a few days ago on Bond Street with that ... that woman," she exploded, her small face flushed.

Nicole became immediately exasperated, as her own temper was easily aroused these days. "Oh the devil, Mary! What the deuce do you think he was supposed to be doing these last days and more? I explained how it would be!"

"Did you? Did you, Nicole? I do not remember your saying they would exchange kisses ... and in public!"

Nicole looked surprised, even somewhat shocked, for

she did not know anything about this and was at a loss to explain. Harry, however, after clearing his throat, ventured to say that he knew all about it. Two pairs of eyes turned on him.

"Well?" questioned his sister.

"It was decided that Arnie must make love to her in public, buy her a few trinkets and such, and give the overall impression that he was about to make her Lady Merdon!"

"It was decided that they would kiss?" Nicole was still surprised.

"Devil take it, I shouldn't be here explaining such bold matters to you," replied Harry testily.

"Well, I am afraid you will have to, Harry," replied Nicky calmly.

"All right, all right then. Most men have bits—I mean, they have young females under their protection—and there is nothing uncommon in taking them about and furbishing them up. But if a fellow was to lose all sense of the proprieties, and show that she was leading him about on a string, then they'd say the girl had him in her pocket. If he was known, as Arnie is, to have a domineering mama, and he still went about with her—kissing her for all the Beau Monde to see and report—it would appear that he intended to do what he wished, despite his mother. So there you have it!"

"Well, I won't . . . I won't have it, I won't! If he kisses her again, I'll . . . I'll marry Sudley!"

"Never say you would!" exclaimed Harry, much struck. "Wouldn't think that would serve at all, but there's a female for you."

"Listen now, Mary, I cannot say that I care for this type of thing either—in fact, I fully sympathize with you, I would not be able to bear it if I knew that someone I . . . I loved were kissing another female. However, I have already heard Mama say that Arnie and my aunt are coming to dinner tonight. *You* will, too. You will go home to change and return here and join us for dinner. We will start bringing you to my aunt's notice now." She turned to her brother. "Better go and warn Arnie what's afoot."

"Lord, yes." Harry stood up quickly and left in search of his cousin.

Mary departed soon afterward, promising to return in the evening. Nicole sat back on her bed, her thoughts returning once again to her own problems. She dosed off, dreaming that she was being held by the Duke . . . and just as their lips met, his father pulled him away. She woke with a start and then quietly started to cry.

Chapter Fifteen

Nicole was not looking forward to the evening. A bout of tears had done nothing for her looks. It was with little attention that she chose a dress of pale blue silk and allowed Marcy to dress her hair. Her mind ached with wishing . . . wanting . . . wondering. What was he thinking? How could his eyes, his voice, caress her, and yet not claim her? Why did she love a man who had sworn never to fall in love, she chided herself, over and over again until she felt she could think no longer. She got up and moved about her room listlessly, with her maid watching her.

Marcy frowned. "Go downstairs, Lady Nicole. Your young friend will be here soon and you'll be wanting a word with her before your aunt arrives."

"Yes, yes, you are right, Marcy." She turned and walked slowly downstairs, just as Miss Melville entered the house. She had been accompanied by her family's groom and turned to bid him good night, saying that Viscount Beaumont would see her home, so he needn't return for her. She turned and the two girls' eyes met, both solemn. Nicky floated rather than walked (for she felt as if she were not really there), and took Mary's hand in hers and led her to the library. "Hallo, Mary. Do not fidget, I promise all will go well."

"Yes, I . . . I have a feeling it will, but do you know I just noticed, Nicole, you are not looking well. I mean, you are as beautiful as ever, but you look . . . pale, withdrawn.

I was so wrapped up in my own worries, I didn't notice. Are you ill?"

Her voice held concern, and Nicky, never one to confide, felt a strange urge to do so, but said merely, "No . . . no, just a slight headache, it will pass!"

Harry strode into the library, a grin covering his handsome face. "Hallo, are you here already, Mary?" He looked around hastily then. "Oh good, Aunt's not here yet. Arn will be bringing her, no doubt."

"Remember, Mary, you have no real acquaintance with my cousin. My aunt does not know that you were with us the other day at Lady Elizabeth's. You have seen him at the assemblies, but you have never been properly introduced."

There was no chance for her to answer or for the admonishment to continue, for Lord and Lady Beaumont entered just then, and were joined shortly thereafter by Sir Arnold Merdon and Lady Merdon. Lady Beaumont made the necessary introductions between Mary and the Merdons, and Nick gave Arnie a nudge to move toward Mary and engage her in conversation. Nicky then took the opportunity to sit beside her aunt.

"Dear Aunt Augusta, I have been wanting to speak with you."

Her aunt sighed deeply. "Oh, is it about Arnold? I have been so worried about the boy lately."

"With good cause!" Nicole said deliberately.

"What do you mean? What do you know?"

"Aunt, I do not believe in carrying tales. However, you know how fond of Arnie we are—after all he is my cousin —and I would never think of . . . of betraying him to you, except this time"—she lowered her eyes and her voice— "this time he has gotten himself into a scrape that is far more serious than ever before. There is a girl, a simply awful girl, and we—Harry and I—have reason to believe that she has convinced him to elope with her to Gretna Green!"

Her aunt looked faint and Nicky knew a moment of guilt, but reminded herself it was for a good cause.

"No! Oh no, Nicole! Harry . . . your father will not allow him! He is not yet twenty-one."

"He will be soon, and then there will be nothing to stop him."

"No, no, he could not be so foolish! Yet I have heard such tales about him lately, his behavior in public!"

"Just so! Arnie is befuddled with this . . . this hussy" —*Forgive me, Tilly,* she thought—"and there is no saying what he might do. That is why I asked my dear friend Mary to dinner tonight. She is such a fine girl . . . all the makings of a lady. Her manners are excellent, her nature sweet. I thought if he were to be thrown with someone of his own class, he could not help but draw comparisons, don't you think?"

Her aunt regarded her with eyes that were filled with hope. "Oh, Nicole, do you really think so? Why, my dear girl, that would be marvelous. Yes, yes, she is just what we need to divert his mind."

"So then, Aunt Augusta, you approve?"

"Approve . . . approve . . . I applaud you, dear!"

Nicole eyed her aunt and felt a tendency to feel smug. She rose, excusing herself, and went to Harry, giving his sleeve a pinch.

"All goes well, my brother."

"She fell for it?"

"Totally . . . applauds our good sense."

"Ha, that's jolly. Ha!" He grinned at her.

"Well, don't look too complacent, we're not over the mountain yet, just a small hill!"

"You think so, do you? Just look at the way Aunt is looking at Mary! She loves her already."

Nicky laughed and moved away to join Mary and Arnie.

They enjoyed dinner, and when the ladies rose to leave the men to linger over their port, his Lordship stood up as well, advising them that this was a family meal and therefore he would not be banished from their presence. They retired, laughing, to the library where Lady Beaumont took a seat beside her sister-in-law and Nicole and Harry engaged their papa in conversation. Sir Arnold was content to be left to converse with his Mary. However, she seemed not to want his company and turned her eyes away from him.

"What is it, Mary my love?" he whispered.

"Ha . . . your love? How many loves have you, Arnold?" she whispered back. Her voice sounded angry.

Sir Arnold looked startled. "Why, Mary, whatever do you mean?"

"I saw you, Arnold Merdon, with that . . . that woman and you . . . you kissed her!"

Arnie blanched. "But . . . but . . . that was nothing!"

"Nothing?!" Her voice had a hysterical note to it and was louder than it should have been.

Arnie looked around hastily and told her, "Ssh! Not so loud, dearest!"

She dropped her voice immediately. *"Nothing you say! Ha!"*

"Beloved, believe me. Oh, at first I did not want to kiss Miss Tilly—I insisted that we should merely hug . . . but!"

"What? You insisted that you hug? Oh, Arnie!"

"You don't understand. I didn't want to kiss her, but she insisted that I must. Said I must think of her as a conspirator, not a woman, and I agreed. It worked! Kiss her all the time now and doesn't mean a thing!"

"You kiss her all the time? You kiss . . . oh, Arnold, I never want to see you again." Her voice had risen again and she turned from him. "Never, do you hear? You . . . you *rake!*" She marched off to Nicole, but as her last words were heard by all present, Arnie viewed his audience in much discomfort. His mama glared at him, Lord and Lady Beaumont regarded their nephew wonderingly (for they would have never thought it in their chubby, sweet nephew to be a *rake*), Nicole looked disconcerted, and only Harry broke up the stillness by bursting out with a bubble of mirth that kept him rollicking.

Lady Merdon rose and beckoned her son to her side. "We will leave now, Arnold, for I am exhausted." She turned and bade her brother and sister-in-law good night. For Mary she had a kind word, and for Nicole a pleading look. For Harold she had a militant sparkle, and for her son a glint of steel.

When they had left, Nicole turned to Mary and said anxiously, "You will spend the night here. I will have my

175

tiger take a note to your family and say you are not feeling quite the thing and we are keeping you with us tonight." She then sped out into the hall and caught the sleeve of Arnold's greatcoat and whispered hurriedly, "You be here at nine tomorrow morning, Arnie."

"Can't. Escorting Miss Tilly to—"

"Arnold, you be here. Send a note to Tilly."

"Oh, all right, but Mary don't want me now!"

"Don't be a fool Arnie. Do you still love Mary?"

"You know I do," he responded fervently. "But she said—"

"Be here!" She gave him no chance to reply and ran back to the library. Harry had bade them good night, as he was engaged with his friends at the club, and then Nicole, following suit, bade her parents good night, leading Mary up to her room. She went through her draws and pulled out some night things, which she gave to her friend, and then dropped onto her bed with a sigh. "Now, child, you will tell me what that . . . that scene was all about!"

"Your cousin . . . had the . . . the nerve to tell me that he has been kissing that woman on a regular basis!"

"No, has he?" Nicole was clearly astonished. "And the fool told you? Really, sometimes I wonder how he could be part of our family, the idiot!"

"What does that signify? I do not count it foolish to be honest, and after all, Nicole, he *was* being honest."

"You say he was being honest. Does that mean you believe everything he said?"

"Of course. Arnold would never lie, especially to me!"

"Then what else did he say? Did he enjoy kissing Miss Tilly?"

Mary's face contorted and a tear dropped down her cheek. "He said it meant nothing."

"Well, then, it did not!"

"But how do I know that he hasn't done . . . hasn't taken her to be . . . hasn't made love to her?

"Because if he did, the fool would have told you. Didn't you just say he was honest with you? What else did he say?"

"That he hadn't wanted to kiss her, only hug her—can you imagine his saying *that* to me."

Nicole grimaced. "Oh God, can I! Well, never mind. It means nothing, and he *is* coming here to see you in the morning, before you leave."

"Is he? Oh, I am so relieved, I couldn't bear to leave things as we did. One says all the wrong things when one is upset."

Nicole looked thoughtful. "Yes, especially if one is in love. Well, good night, Mary." She got up and called for Marcy, who showed Mary to her room. Nicole then scribbled a hasty note and ran to the front stairs and called Grudsly to her. "Dear Grud, please give this to my little tiger Jed and have him take it to Miss Melville's home immediately. Also give him the direction. Thank you, and good night."

Nicole rose from her chair and smiled at Arnie as he entered the morning room. "Hallo, Arnie, how are you this morning? Please excuse me, Mama has been wanting to see me this morning. I will be back in a few moments." She left him staring at Mary, who was sitting in a cushioned chair by the large bay window.

"Mary, my sweet love, please look at me," he begged.

Mary turned her head and regarded her swain. "I am looking!"

This seemed to disconcert Arnie and he put a finger to his cravat and gulped, "Yes, so you are. Please, Mary, do not be angry. After all, I am only doing what I have been told, and I am doing it for you—for us!"

"You are kissing Miss Tilly for me?" she asked sweetly. Her eyes, which usually held little sparkle, were now glinting dangerously.

"Yes, deuce take it! You know I am. So do not look like that and speak in that cattish way. I am surprised at you, Mary!" He was annoyed now.

Mary thought she had never seen him look so masterful, and blushed.

"Oh!" was all she could think to say, and he pulled her up into his arms, kissing her possessively and then releasing her. "I have never kissed Miss Tilly like that, ma'am, nor will I ever."

"Oh!" was all she could think to say, and as he pulled her into his arms once again, that was all she had time to say.

Nicole reentered the morning room to find them thus, and with a hand to her smiling lips she coughed demurely. The couple sprang guiltily apart, and then looked with relief at Nicole.

"I take it all is well?" said Nicole with a soft chuckle.

Mary's eyelashes brushed her pink cheeks. "Yes, all is well."

"Good, now take yourself off, Arnold, and find Harry, as it will not do for you to become too interested in Mary too soon. It would make Aunt suspicious. Actually, the scene you made last night was quite good, as Aunt will think that Mary has heard about your . . . your affair with Miss Tilly and objected to any advance you made toward her. Yes, the more I think about it, the better I feel about it."

Nicole then went off for a ride on Ginger, in much better spirits than she had been the day before. She had been thinking that her handsome Duke was in love with her, that she could not be wrong about the way he looked at her, spoke to her. It needed only careful planning to bring about his downfall. He was determined not to marry, and he was in control of his emotions. *Well, Roth, I will drive you mad . . . wild . . . you will not have any control when I am finished.* It was in this state of mind that she attended the soiree that evening, flirting with Robby and dazzling every man who came within her scope. Her eyes flew to the door constantly, on the lookout for the Duke, but he did not come. Nor did he attend the Venetian breakfast on the following morn. By the time three days had passed, Nicole had worked herself into a state of frenzied agitation. She kept wondering, *Where the devil is he?* It was beginning to appear that her flirtation with her willing friend was in vain. She became restless, her smile was stilted, and her nerves were on end. It was in this frame of mind that she finally succumbed to the Count's

178

begging and pleading and walked to a private corner of the room to listen, without hearing, to his protestations of love for her.

She felt heartily sick of flirting with Robby, and while the Count's attentions were flattering, they did little to soothe her agitated soul. Count D'Agout bent his shining black head over her hand and kissed her fingers lovingly. "Nicole, my bird, do please look at me!" She obeyed mechanically and he continued, "Let us leave this room, that puppy"—his head bent toward Robby hovering in the background—"and stroll about outside."

"No, Louis, and you are *not* to call my dear sweet Robby a puppy!" she retorted angrily, her small foot stamping at him.

The Duke of Lyndham walked into the drawing room in time to catch sight of Lady Nicole Beaumont, looking ravishing in a yellow muslin gown, stamping her foot at the Count. He smiled to himself. He had found that running off to Ascot to forget the chit had only intensified his feelings for her. His Grace made his way across the room to Nicole.

All at once she saw him coming. Everyone else seemed to vanish. She saw only him. Felt his presence. Their eyes met and locked. She wanted him, wanted to feel his lips touch hers, wanted to hear his voice in her ears. Then at last he was there, taking her hands into his and holding them both to his lips. Neither was aware of the surroundings, nor did either care.

He led her away and she could not resist, did not protest. Somewhere, it sounded like a long way off, she heard the Count protesting and noticed that the Duke somehow disposed of him. She could not take her eyes from his face.

Suddenly she pulled herself together. *Did you not hear that he was off on some wild party with Cyprians and their like, and if he wasn't, where was he? Papa did not know, so it was not department business.* Every inch of her yearned to know where he had been, wanted her doubts eased, but she refrained from asking and refrained from showing him that she was aware he had been missing.

The Duke had made up his mind that his bachelor days

179

were at an end. He had never had any doubt that when and if he should want to marry this chit, he could do so. He wanted her, and he had returned with the express purpose of having her! He said not a word as he led her past the terrace gardens to a stone bench secluded in the shrubbery. His eyes took in every detail of her hair, her face, her gown. He was hungry for her and it showed, exciting a response within her. He sat down, pulling her gently down beside him. All at once she was wrapped tightly in his arms and he was kissing her as she had never been kissed before. She had no will to resist, nor did she want to. She responded passionately and then suddenly remembered the rumors, remembered he had been away without explanation, remembered he had not yet said he loved her. She pulled away hastily.

He laughed at her lightly and held her shoulders in his large strong hands. His shining locks fell across his forehead and she was acutely aware of his magnetism.

He loved her, with all his heart. She delighted him, amused him, stirred every need and desire within him. His face was gentle as he regarded her, but his tone was self-assured, *too* self-assured. "Nicole, this game we have played must come to an end! You will be a beautiful bride and do me credit. I should be most happy if you would set a date for the wedding as soon as possible. Of course, I shall ask your father for your hand tonight, but I first wanted to tell you! We shall settle on an early date, for I am impatient to make you my Duchess!"

She gasped. Surely this is what she had wanted, to marry this proud, handsome man. Then why did this proposal fill her with fury and indignation? All she could think, respond, was, *How dare he? He disappears for days, comes back suddenly, and announces that I will be his Duchess and do him credit! He thinks all he need do is flick one proud finger and I will be his. Of all the vain, autocratic. . . .* She answered between clenched teeth, "I am sorry, Roth, I fear I cannot accept your flattering proposal. I do not think we should suit!"

He looked astonished. "What new flight is this? I have just kissed you, imp, and you allowed me—in fact, responded to my kiss. How can you say we would not suit?"

She blushed hotly, remembering how she had responded to his kiss, how she had wantonly pressed herself against his hard, masculine body, her arms around his neck, and it was a moment before she could answer, and then only by not looking at him. "Do not speak to me of marriage, Roth. If . . . if I seemed to respond to your kiss, it is because I am a romantic female and you are a . . . a handsome rake that I found at that particular moment irresistible. But I take leave to tell you that I would not put up with your . . . your women, your disappearing for days on end . . . your . . . all your oddities! No and no again! You have had so many caps thrown at you, you think all you need do is pick the one up of your choice, and *voilà,* she is yours! In case it is not clear, *I* did not throw a cap in your direction. *I* am not yours for the taking. No, Roth, I would not make you a good wife! I am not at all comfortable. I should not be pleased to bear your name, your children, and look the other way at your indiscretions! I have told you that I will probably marry Robby, for I am fond of him and he adores me and would be just the sort of husband I should have. I have not changed my mind! *No,* I will not marry *you!"*

In her agitation she had jumped to her feet and would have now run from him had he not reached out and pulled her roughly down beside him. His arms went round her in a crushing embrace as his lips once again found hers. She felt that surely if he did not let her go, she would betray her feelings for him, for she found it impossible to resist his lips, his arms. Then all at once he had released her. She gasped, brought her hand to his face with a resounding slap, and ran from him.

She reentered the drawing room to find Robby standing to one side talking with a friend. She tugged at his sleeve. "Robby, would you take me home? I do not wish to disturb my parents, as they are in the card room, and Harry left earlier this evening with Archie."

Robby looked searchingly at her face. "Fact is, Nick, should like to see you home. Engaged to meet your brother and mine, and was hoping you would excuse me early tonight—but do calm down a bit, girl, don't want all the dowagers eyeing askance at us, now do we?" He steadied her with his eyes.

"Yes, yes, Rob you are right, of course. I will be calm in just a moment. Please, my friend, may I have your hand."

He took her hand in his at once, placing it to his lips and looking firmly into her eyes.

Roth entered the drawing room just in time to find his beloved in this position and he scowled across the room at them. Happily, she was unaware that he stood at the garden entrance watching her. Robby led her to their hostess, they bade her good night, and he called for Nicole's wrap. "I will go tell your parents I am escorting you home, Nick. Steady, girl!"

The Duke called for his own greatcoat and followed them into the hallway a few minutes later, just in time to observe Nicole leaning heavily on Mr. Wychburn's arm. He cursed beneath his breath, and ordered his carriage to go home without him. He walked out into the brisk night air, a growing rage within him, and made his way to White's. The Duke gambled heavily, lost heavily, and drank heavily.

His Grace then went home, none the better for his excesses, and planted himself in a comfortable chair by the fire in his study. A glass of brandy, held with both hands beneath his chin, relaxed on his broad chest. His thoughts tumbled, one on top of the other. *The little vixen, kissing me one moment, rejecting me the next! What was she about, talking to me like that? I never asked her to put up with my women ... what women? The little fool. I did her the honor of asking her to become my wife and she spit fire at me! Damnation!* Nicole had stunned him with her rebuff. He felt at a loss. The vision of her little face came to his mind. He saw her eyes, full to the brim with unshed tears. *No, devil take it, I won't live without you, imp! I will not allow you to marry that boy, poor chap!* Nicole was his, why could she not see that, he told himself angrily. *You have made love to the most experienced women in the whole of England, and you cannot find the right words to win the only woman you love.* He remembered her lips, her soft, full little body pressed up against him, and he stirred. "You are mine, Nick, you will be mine, make no mistake!" he said out loud in the darkness of his study.

His Grace called in Mount Street the next morning only to receive word via Grudsly that Lady Nicole was indisposed and could not receive visitors. Nicole went to her window and watched him descend the steps to the street and his waiting phaeton. She felt all chance of happiness for her was at an end. Like the fool she was, she had rejected the only man she wanted. *"Fool, you fool, could you not take him, even on his terms, would that not be better than not having him at all?* She shook her head furiously. *No. I will not share him. He must be mine and mine alone!*

Later that morning, Nicole did accept to see her aunt and walked into the morning room, one hand outstretched in welcome. "Good morning, Aunt Augusta. I am so sorry, but Mama went out a short while ago with Lady Jersey."

"I know, your man told me—what's his name? Gruddy?"

"Um, I think you mean Grudsly, ma'am. Really Aunt, you should learn his name after twenty years."

"You have always been too pert, Nicole. Learn to curb your tongue. That is no tone to take with your aunt!"

Nicole controlled her mouth and managed to look repentent. "I am sorry, Aunt."

"To be sure. Now, yes, I remember, it was to you I really wanted to speak, Nicky, so come sit beside me."

Nicole did as she was bid and waited expectantly.

"Something terrible has happened!"

As Nicole had been behind the "happening," so to speak, and had, in fact, put all the words into her cousin's mouth that she knew he had said to his mama on the previous evening, she was not at all surprised. However, she managed to look so. "Oh, what has happened, Aunt!"

"Your cousin, that loathsome boy, has advised me that he is planning to marry that creature as soon as he becomes of age."

"I was afraid of that. I had hoped that he would take a liking to Mary. In fact"—she lowered her voice—"he did take a liking to my friend and . . . was too precipitate in showing it. He quite startled her the other night."

"Aah, so that is why she called him a rake and ran from him. The odious boy. He has learned bad manners from that woman already."

"It would seem so. However, I have asked Mary and Arnie to accompany Harry and myself to Wellesly Court the day after the morrow. I have already had a talk with Arnold, and he did seem taken with her. I am hoping that by throwing him in Mary's way, she will revise her opinion of him and perhaps change his mind about that woman he is seeing."

"Oh, I hope so, for there isn't much time, is there? In a few months he will become of age and can do what he wishes."

"Let us hope that he will not wish at that time to marry a woman so far beneath him," Nicole said blandly, finding it extremely difficult not to giggle.

"Oh, my dear, my dear, you have no idea what a trial this is to me. To think that Arnold could be so brazen with me. He said that he cared not a wit for his inheritance, that he would live with . . . that creature anywhere in the world until he had control of his money, and that she was more than willing to wait."

"There is another way, Aunt," Nicole said slowly, hesitating, as she was not sure this was a good idea, but wanted it voiced and rejected before her aunt had time to think of it and try it out.

"Oh, what is it? Please tell me at once."

"She could be bought off!" said Nicole, eyeing her Aunt narrowly.

Lady Merdon went white, then purple, and then white again. She put a hand to her head and leaned back against her chair. "How much do you think it would take?"

"Quite a lot. After all, this creature sees herself becoming Lady Merdon as well as having money for the rest of her life. Oh, I would say no less than twenty thousand pounds."

"Good God. No, no, we would never be able to get that much from the trustees, and I do not have that much capital. He will have to become interested in your friend. Oh please, Nicole, do bring that about if you can. It is vital!"

"I will certainly try, but it will not be easy. Mary's father intends her to become engaged to Sudley, for it seems Sir Thomas has promised to make a very attractive settlement for her hand in marriage."

Lady Merdon was shocked, for she had liked the sweet child she had met and the thought of her being forced into a marriage with an old rogue like Thomas Sudley was infamous, and she said so in strong accents. "Why, child, I am very well acquainted with Sir Thomas. He had, many a time, tried to catch my eye when I was first widowed and still had my looks. He is a libertine!"

"Nevertheless, Melville intends Mary to be his, for he has five daughters to establish and is not willing to pass up such an offer as Sir Thomas Sudley has made."

"And what of the girl, what has she to say?"

"Poor Mary has said quite a lot, but her father says that within one month's time, if no better offer is forthcoming, he will make her engagement announcement!"

"Dear God, he is heartless!"

Nicole was hard put to keep from sneering. However, Harry entered the room just then, almost cursing beneath his breath when he realized his Aunt Augusta was present. His worries were without cause, though, for his aunt rose and bade them a hasty farewell, reminding Nicole that she depended on her.

Harry let out a relieved sound and sank into the sofa beside his sister, exclaiming, "Thought I was walking right into the middle of one of her swoons. Glad she's gone!"

"You may very well be, but I've been closeted with her nearly an hour and I'm quite done in."

"You look it, Nick. What's ailing you these last few days? You are not yourself!"

"Oh, Harry, I am . . . I am so miserable!" she cried.

She looked up and a large tear rolled down her pale cheek. "I wanted Roth to propose to me . . . and then he

185

disappeared for three days. It made me wild . . . furious! I couldn't think, I just acted out my emotions. Then he came last night and he did propose—if that is what you can call it. He didn't say he loved me, he said instead that I would make a beautiful bride and be a marvelous Duchess, and demanded I should set a date!" she said miserably.

"Did he, by Jove?" exclaimed Harry. "Well, then, girl, why are you unhappy, you have what you want!"

"No, Harry, I have not. The Duke told me we were to be married. He said nothing about loving me. In fact, not very long ago he advised me that he would never love one person completely . . . give himself completely. How could I marry him knowing that he merely wants a Duchess who will do him credit?"

Harry pursed his lips and looked thoughtful. Brother and sister sat quietly for a while.

"What makes you think he don't love you, Nick?"

"I have told you he went away for three days. I have heard he was at some wild party. Then, when he returns, he offers no explanation, which confirms my belief that he has been with a woman—or women."

"But he has never before asked any female to be his wife, you know. That must mean something."

"Yes, perhaps he wants me. In fact, I believe he does. As I am the respectable daughter of an Earl—his friend's daughter—the only way he can get me is through marriage. So he is willing to marry me, for . . . for lust! Perhaps he thought I would conform, as other wives do, and look the other way at his infidelities."

Harry shook his head. "Don't see how he could think that. You ain't a biddable female, anyone could see that, and the Duke ain't blind. I think you're out on this one, Nick!"

"I wish you were right . . . but I do not think so."

"Well, we will see. He is coming here tonight you know!"

"What, Roth is coming here . . . why?" exclaimed Nicole, jumping up.

Harry frowned. "That's what I have been trying to discover, but Papa has been tight-lipped about this. Something's afoot, something to do with Sir Charles Barnaby. Roth's coming for dinner, but it's because of some trap they are setting up."

Nicole's interest was caught, her curiosity whetted. "What trap for Sir Charles? How . . . why?"

"Stap me if I know!"

"Oh, this is most vexing, what has Sir Charles done?"

"Well, I don't know for sure, but I have heard something about his having given information to the Frogs!"

"By God, treason? He has committed treason?"

"Lord, Nick, I ain't sure, but yes, I think so. They have to catch him in the act, and it seems it all falls together tonight."

"Here? They are setting it up here?"

"No, I don't think so. Lord, Nick, how should I know. Now, *you* know as much as I do."

He got up to leave her, and flicking one of her black curls, said, "Chin up, girl, you're bound to come through this!"

She sniffed, but said nothing as she watched his retreating form.

Chapter Sixteen

Nicole entered the library that evening, fully aware that the Duke was already there with her parents and brother. She knew not how she was to face him. She had been crying a good part of the day and her eyes showed evidence of this. She had decided to wear a gown of peacock blue velvet, high-waisted, sleeveless, with a demurely scooped bodice. Her hair was brushed so that the thick black locks fell down her shoulders and back in luxurious waves (she had not wanted to put it up that evening) and she wore a modest set of pearls at her throat and wrists. She walked into the library and swept a smile at the group assembled there as a whole, singling no one out, and went near her father, whose protective arm went round her shoulder in a fond embrace.

"Hallo, Nick, so you haven't forgotten your poor papa. With all the young men surrounding you these days, I've barely had a chance to speak with you."

"Oh, Papa, best of my beaus, there will always be time for you. Always!"

Lady Beaumont frowned. She was fully aware of what her daughter was going through and knew not what to do about it. She had felt it best to wait and see.

His Grace looked at Nicole, trying to catch her eye. *God she is lovely,* he thought. *Devil take it, why won't she look at me!* Her father released her and she moved away toward Harry, but Roth stepped adroitly in her path and she was forced to look up at him.

"Your hair becomes you in that fashion. It reminds me of how you looked in your breeches!"

"Thank you, Duke. I myself have always preferred to wear it down, but it would not do at the assemblies." She barely heard herself; her lashes fluttered against her cheeks, veiling her eyes.

Dinner was announced and they filed out; Nicole was again forced to look at the Duke as he offered his arm to lead her in. He was placed beside her at the dinner table, and she soon discovered she could hardly breathe. Eating was impossible. Conversation came mechanically, and only when she was addressed. She prayed that no one would notice her anguish. When this harrowing experience was at an end, Lady Beaumont led her daughter back into the library where they would wait for the men, who would linger over their port.

Harry excused himself as he was engaged with friends that evening, and left the house. The Earl poured Roth another glass, and sat back in his chair, eyeing him thoughtfully.

At last the Duke spoke. "I think, sir, that I should advise you that I have asked your daughter to do me the honor of becoming my wife! Although she has refused me, I think you should know, as I am still hopeful of changing her mind."

"She refused, you say?" The Earl made a clicking sound with his tongue and frowned. "Silly chit of mine,
188

what is she up to now? Tell me, Adam, are you asking my permission—for you have a strange way of doing it, after you have already asked my daughter for her hand without my leave. Take a lot for granted, don't you?" The words were said gently, no tone of rebuke in them or intended.

The Duke of Lyndham smiled, looking very much the young man he was. "I mean you no disrespect, sir, nor have I any wish to go against you in this matter, but if Nicole would have me, I would marry her in a minute, letting no one stand in my way."

"I see," the Earl of Sutland said gravely. "Is this because you want her and are used to getting what you want, Adam, or is it because you think you can make her happier than any other could!"

The Duke hesitated. "Make no mistake, I am what I am, and I am used to getting what I want, as you have said. I want your daughter, but I love her. If I thought she could be happier with another, I would step aside— though it would kill me, I would step aside. I intend to make her happy if she will let me. I would put her above all else and all others. I love her!" He said it fervently, challengingly.

The Earl of Sutland's face relaxed. "Splendid. Now let us see what we can do to bring this about. First, let me tell you, Adam, that I firmly believe that girl is very deeply in love with you."

"I must confess I did not think she was averse to me. However, she has refused me most . . . most heatedly and—"

"Never mind that." The Earl's hand waived this bit of information as insignificant. "What I want to know is, how did you ask her?"

"I told her that she would be a beautiful bride and wanted her to set a date for the wedding as soon as possible."

"Aah, I begin to see. You, in fact, told her that she would be a perfect little Duchess."

"Why . . . er, yes."

"Young fool! Have you been in my daughter's company these two months and not known you don't *tell* her
189

things. Good God, man, surprised she didn't box your ears!"

The Duke looked chagrined. "She . . . er . . . did, sir."

"Ha! Serves you right! You have gone about the thing all wrong. If you want her, Adam, win her! Convince her that she is the only woman in your life . . . convince her, Adam, that you love her. For she'll not have you any other way!"

"Thank you, sir, I will most certainly try!"

"Fact is, I think you are just the man my spitfire needs. Don't make a muff of it this time! Remember, she needs gentle handling . . . gets into a miff easily. Sensitive chit, you know!"

They joined the waiting ladies in the library and sat chatting in front of the blazing fire until Lady Beaumont rescued her long-suffering daughter and led her upstairs for the night. Later that evening Nicole, not being able to sleep, went and sat beside her window, which overlooked the street. She was surprised to see the arrival of a gentleman and recognized him to be John Wellesly, Arabella's husband. *Why, whatever is he doing here?* she thought, puzzled.

The next day Nicky was caught up in the frenzy of preparing for dinner with the Prince Regent at Carlton House. In her fervor, she forgot all about John Wellesly's mysterious midnight visit . . . and she put from her mind, almost successfully, her dilemma with the Duke. It was Wednesday, and although it was usually the night for Almack's, a change had been hastily arranged, for their father had come in that morning and announced that they were to have dinner with the Regent. Lady Beaumont was immediately sent off into a wild bustle, for she had not expected to go to Carlton House until the following week. She sent a lackey to Madame Bertin's with a stern message that their dresses should be delivered by the afternoon. Lady Beaumont's hairdresser was sent for and he worked first on her Ladyship's coiffure of silken dusky curls before arranging Nicole's gleaming black hair.

Nicole surveyed her mama's reflection in the large

looking glass. "Oh, Mama, that red feather is just perfect twirling around like that! You are so beautiful!"

Indeed, Lady Beaumont did look quite lovely in her gown of red velvet. Her neck was adorned with a simple but exquisite setting of diamonds. Her dark eyes shone with happiness and pleasure over her daughter's compliment. She swished about the room, collecting her bracelets and fastening them round her long white gloves. She stood for a moment, slipping on a large diamond ring, and appraised her daughter silently.

"Nicole, turn to me, darling, I want a good look at you!"

Nicky turned about and stopped with her hands on her slender hips. She wore a soft gown of emerald green velvet. It was high-waisted, form-fitted, as was the style, falling in a straight line to the ankles. The hem was swagged, and each peak was embroidered with bouquets of daisies, as were the swagged shoulders. The gown was sleeveless and she carried a white silk shawl. Her only jewels were a small cluster of pearls at her ears, a choker of pearls at her throat, and a few random pearl clusters peeping through her long black curls. Her eyes matched her gown . . . but tonight, her mother noted with a frown, they lacked their usual shine, and Nicky's mouth drooped in a way that was not like her! Lady Beaumont shook her head gently, for the natural glow of her daughter's cheeks was no longer prevalent. She thought ruefully that Nicole was *not* looking her best.

Lord Beaumont stuck his head in the doorway of his lady's dressing room and observed his two girls with a warm smile. "Ready, my loves?" His wife nodded, caught Nicole by the hand, and gently pulled her along to the stairs. Harry, waiting at the head of the stairs, gave a low whistle. "By Jove! You two look grand!"

It took less than twenty minutes to span the distance between their home and Carlton House, and a few minutes later they were shown into the Gothic Conservatory. The Prince Regent, resplendent in the style Beau Brummell had made famous, came forward at once, Lady Hertford at his side.

Nicole gazed raptly about while her parents exchanged

warm greetings and made their bows to the Prince Regent. She had never seen so much magnificence all gathered in the same place at the same time. The ceilings, the columns, the gold-upon-gold engravings. The intricacies of art were indeed overpowering and stupendously dazzling. She was overwhelmed and too innocent to hide her awe. The Prince was quick to note this and took it as a compliment, and as he was partial to compliments, he was well disposed to approve of the new beauty. Nicole appraised the Regent with wide-open eyes, observing that he was much the same age as her own father . . . yet, in spite of his boyish mannerisms, he seemed older. Her father would never need the stays that creaked with every move the Regent made. Moreover, she noticed, too, that while her father dressed with elegance and fashion, his attire was suitable to his age and position, while the Prince's raiments served only to emphasize his growing portliness. She was surprised by this, for she had often heard that the Regent had been quite a Corinthian in his youth! She sighed sadly, for the dissipation was all too apparent.

His light protruding eyes glistened as he greeted Nicole. She rose from her graceful bow and found his full lips upon her gloved hands. "Charming, my dear," he said softly.

She was then startled considerably, for before releasing her hand, he tickled her palm. She looked up at him and it was with a supreme effort that she refrained from requesting to know why he had done such a thing. Nicole then dismissed it from her mind, advising herself that perhaps it had been an accident. She heard the Prince speaking jovially and quite amicably to her parents and brother. "Lovely . . . lovely . . . so this is the new beauty the Beau has raved about?"

Nicole then found herself presented to the woman at his side, Lady Hertford, who was evidently playing hostess for the Regent this evening. Nicole had heard much about the Hertfords. She had heard the woman's name linked with the Regent's, but Harry had said that theirs was a friendship. Observing the frigid beauty now, she had no doubt of this. Lady Hertford was extraordinarily lovely. She was elegantly gowned, a bit too tall, but most certainly a "Juno." She murmured some pleasantries to the lady, who was bearly civil, Nicole thought, and then turned her head toward Harry, who was by her side and in just as much awe. "Lord, Harry," she whispered, "how we shall brush through this night is beyond me."

Harry nodded vigorously, for he was just as uncomfortable, and then suddenly, from almost nowhere, the Duke of Lyndham appeared at their side. Foolishly she had an inclination to throw herself into his arms. He looked so handsome—wondrously so—and so sure of himself. She noted the way his black hair fell in long waves about his head, the way part of it fell upon his forehead, fringing it. She was attracted by his gray piercing eyes, his quiet assurance, his proud, arrogant walk. She sighed and put a stop to such nonsensical thoughts.

He chuckled. "You look overwhelmed, my imp!"

"That is precisely how I feel, Duke," she said with deep feeling. "I shall be relieved when this night is at end."

"I take it you don't care for all this splendor," he said, his gray eyes twinkling.

"Well, while it is magnificent . . . it is really—and I can see some excellent works of art—but it is just . . . just . . . well, look about you, can you find one spot without finery upon it, for I cannot! It is so overdone, really woefully so." Nicky frowned over it.

The Duke laughed and pursued. "And our Regent?"

Nicky lowered her voice. "Do you know, I think it very odd, but he . . . he tickled my palm! Why would he do such a thing?"

The Duke burst out laughing. "Impudent old dog! Don't go off alone with him, imp!" he added, suddenly turning more serious.

"Shh . . . what a thing to say about his Royal Highness, though I assure you, I have no intention of going off alone with him!" she ended caustically.

Their attention was then caught by the new arrivals, and they watched Lord and Lady Boothe enter. Rather, Roth was watching them, and Nicole was watching him, speculatively. This was indeed an odd gathering tonight she thought, and so hurriedly assembled. Something is afoot. She glanced at the Boothes.

His Lordship was of average height, balding, and had a tremendous paunch. He wore his clothes (which Nicole grimaced over) quite carelessly on his heavy person. He took snuff, dropping huge amounts over his jacket and not bothering to brush it away. He moved toward Lady Hertford, a distant relation, and took up conversation with her, while Sir Charles Barnaby attended to Lady Boothe. His lady was as thin as he was fat. She wore a dress of puce satin. Her gray hair was cropped short and looked as if it had not been brushed. Over this she wore a strange headdress of satin and feathers. Her cousin, Sir Charles, sat beside her, and Nicole noted the strong resemblance. For he, too, was quite thin, and he had the same hook nose. His clothes were cut elegantly and worn elegantly, though his figure could never do them justice.

Suddenly Roth was guiding Nicole by the arm in their direction—to which she protested fervently in a low voice. "Deuce take it, Roth, I don't want to talk to Lady Boothe . . . she proses on and on forever!"

"Nevertheless, you will engage her in conversation, for I wish to speak to Barnaby without interruption." He was grave, and Nicole looked sharply at him. They stopped in front of Lady Boothe and Roth bowed, taking her hand and brushing it lightly with a cavalier kiss. Lady Boothe then immediately pounced on Nicole. "My dear child, how enchanting you look . . . though a bit pale, I think." Nicole sighed and sat down beside the woman.

Barnaby looked nervously at Roth and began to fidget. His watery brown eyes darted to and fro. His mouth was thin, and his tongue was serpentine in nature, with the constant habit of licking his lower lip. He smiled nervously and offered by way of conversation, "Splendid gathering tonight, eh, Roth?"

"Devil a bit!" replied the Duke testily. "I'd rather be home catching up on some sleep . . . like John!"

Barnaby raised his brows. "Oh . . . why is that?"

Roth lowered his voice impressibly. "Up late last night . . . with the Earl and John. Thing is, John is off for Portsmouth on Friday . . . mind though, must keep it quiet—

we were up all night over the affair and I'm burned to the socket!"

Barnaby's brows drew together and he lowered his voice as well. "Eh . . . dispatch going out?"

"Why do you ask?" retorted the Duke suspiciously.

"I . . . I mean . . . I was just curious, since you mentioned it," said Barnaby falteringly.

"All right, it's just that we can't be too careful, you know," said the Duke conspiratorily. "Oh, please do excuse me, I see Lady Beaumont wants her daughter." With which the Duke picked up Nicole's hand and led her away.

Nicky eyed him inquiringly, noting the soft self-satisfied smile hovering about his mouth. "What was *all* that about, for I did manage to hear snatches of what you were saying! It sounded to me like you were baiting the man."

"My, my, was it that transparent? Let us hope Barnaby does not have your powers of observation, my bright little imp."

She said nothing to this but looked sadly away. After a moment she said in a low voice, "Papa mentioned that you were going away on Friday. Will you be gone long?"

He looked at her tenderly. "Why, will you miss me?"

She put up her chin at once. "Heavens, what a silly thing to ask. Oh, there is Harry!" She called her brother's name and abruptly hurried away.

He watched her hurry off and chuckled to himself, and then turned his attention to the immediate problem. He approached the Prince and said quietly to his ear alone, "Your Royal Highness, walk with me a bit."

The Regent looked at him and laughed. "Roth, you rogue! Ordering your Regent about, are you? Oh, and by the by, what the devil do you mean absenting yourself from Carlton House these past weeks? Are we not good enough company for you any longer?" he asked testily.

"Ah, your Royal Highness, but you had been away, and then when you returned, I was busily employed in your service."

"Eh, well, come on, come on, out with it, man!" ordered the Regent peevishly.

"Well, Prinny, you are not going to like this, but Barnaby has been involved in treason. As he is connected to Boothe, and Boothe is connected to you, there is only one way out of the mess. You must order Lord Boothe out of the country . . . by the end of next week. Make him ambassador to some country or other, but get him out by the end of next week. For on Friday there is a trap laid out for Barnaby and his henchmen, and once we have Barnaby—who is too stupid to be behind all this—we will have the main man, and it will probably blow sky high!"

"What the devil do you mean . . . what have you planned? I can't have any scandal at this time," the Prince blustered, for he was at present involved in hearings with his wife, whom he had been separated from for some ten years and was trying desperately to be rid of.

"Calm yourself, Prinny. You shall immediately be rid of Boothe, who will sail and be forgotten. When Barnaby and his leader are caught, it will be due to your foresight and competent action."

The Prince stopped his restless movements and regarded the Duke from narrowed eyes. "Yes . . . good . . . very good, Adam. I shall arrange for his . . . er, departure from England immediately."

The Duke sighed. "Good. You see, as I have said, catching Barnaby will not take place on Friday. We plan to allow him to overtake John Wellsely on the road to Portsmouth, steal a list of our agents in Napoleon's army, and deliver this to his man. He will, of course, be followed. We will allow the list to be delivered to its destination before we close in on Barnaby. When we do bring him in, our case will be iron-clad, for we will have ample witnesses. However, in order to avoid being attacked in the press—though there is bound to be some outrage—we will minimize it by perhaps deporting Barnaby instead of executing him."

"Not execute? Confound it, Adam! He and that other scoundrel deserve to be hanged. They have committed treason against England . . . against me!"

"And what better punishment than for them to be deported to France, where Napoleon will discover they have given him the wrong information? We will allow Boney to eliminate them."

Again the Prince Regent's eyes narrowed. "Yes . . . yes . . . I like that. Splendid . . . splendid! Indeed, Adam, that is precisely what we shall do. Now come along, we must get back to my guests."

"One other thing, Sir. Those documents you gave us yesterday . . . no one else knows that you have signed such papers?"

"Of course not. Now do come along, Adam." The Prince was anxious to drop business and attend to pleasure, and the Duke followed in his wake.

Sir Charles Barnaby had turned to Lady Boothe after the Duke had departed. He listened to her endless rattling without giving her his full attention until he heard her say, " 'Tis terrible really!"

"What is?" said Barnaby absently.

"That poor young thing Lady Wellesly is with child, and her husband has to run off to Portsmouth. He has been running about quite a bit lately for the department, it seems. What I find strange is why Roth should have to go off to Dover and Wellesly to Portsmouth all in one day?"

"What? What do you mean?"

"Boothe was very angry. Seems they won't tell him anything . . . but he heard a special guard being arranged for the Duke's trip to Dover. Oh my, you can imagine the row he had with the Earl of Sutland. Demanded to know why he had been kept in the dark."

"Well, what did the Earl say to it?" asked Barnaby, his eyes popping.

"I really don't know actually. Oliver was very tight-lipped about their conversation. All I do know is that something must be afoot if both Wellesly and Roth are off on the same day!"

The evening did not pass soon enough for Sir Charles. He was in a tither to be off, but it was past midnight before he was finally able to go. He dismissed his own carriage and walked across the Mall to Picadilly, where he hailed a hackney. A few minutes later he was deposited outside the elegant, if somewhat meager, bachelor lodgings of Count D'Agout.

Barnaby pushed roughly past a sleepy-eyed gentleman's gentleman and demanded to be taken to the master of the house. The cold rebuff he was about to receive was clipped by the Count's frigid welcome.

"What the devil are you doing here?" Then, without waiting for an answer, he dismissed his servant curtly and stepped back into the room he had been occupying. "Come in . . . don't let us speak in the hall!"

"I . . . I had to see you," said Barnaby nervously.

"Are you mad, coming here yourself? Why not send me a message? All right, it is too late now. What is it?"

"I fear a trap is being laid for me. I think that I am suspected," replied Barnaby, trembling.

"*Mon Dieu . . .* ! How did I manage to appoint such an idiot? Tell me everything at once."

Sir Charles sank into a cushioned wing chair and proceeded to advise him of the night's events.

Chapter Seventeen

The Earl of Sutland bade his children and their friends a fond farewell before taking his leave of them the next afternoon. The cosy group was assembled about Nicky's phaeton, and all were in high spirits for they were off for an afternoon's frolic with Lady Arabella Wellesly, at Wellesly Court. Sir Arnold handed Mary into the phaeton, where she sat demurely beside Nicole, arranging her skirts, her youthful cheeks flushed with excitement at the prospect of one *entire* afternoon spent in the company of her darling Arnold. The thought that there would be virtually *no* chaperone brought heaven to Mary's mind and she smiled amicably at Nicky.

Nicole looked stunning in her black velvet riding habit. Her hair was tied to one side and swooped across her shoulder in a cluster of curls. The curly-brimmed velvet top hat was banded with white silk, which floated down her back. Her green eyes sparkled appreciatively as she appraised the horses Roth had chosen for her ... and then she thought of Roth and her smile faded.

Harry, too, stopped to admire the pair that led his sister's phaeton. He clicked his tongue admiringly. "Stap me, Nick, if those aren't the finest pair of tits in all of London! I tell you what, that Roth is a splendid fellow!"

He mounted his own horse and led them into the traffic while Arnold brought up the rear. Nicole's tiger Jed sat proudly on his perch in the back of the phaeton, pleased to be a part of the group and listening to their lively conversation with interest. They made quite a set wheedling their way through the London hubub, which was dangerously thick at this hour.

After a few minutes the city's bustle was left behind and they were on the open road. Arnold had ridden up so that his horse was abreast the carriage and he was alongside his Mary, who sat shyly looking up at him. Harry held back and came up alongside Nicole whenever the road allowed, and it was not long before a ballad was struck up. The journey was accomplished with much singing and jesting. Mary's reserve had quite vanished under such comradeship, and Nicole found that she liked the shy creature's company after all. She watched Mary and Arnold conversing and it struck her that they were perfect for each other.

The party reined in before turning onto the drive that led to Arabella's estate. Wellesly Court was vast and quite beautiful. The house was surrounded by large evergreens, many of which hid some of the lower windows from view. The lawns were already beginning to show spring's greenness and flowed in wavy patterns into the dark woods that flanked the estate. There was a lily pond that could be seen from the drive, but was hidden from the house by a profusion of budding birch trees.

Crocuses were in full bloom and the ladies went into raptures over the purple and white flowers. After they all agreed that Wellesly Court was quite worthy of their visitation, they laughed and proceeded down the drive.

Nicole raised an eyebrow when the small party reached the front of the white-columned brick house. She was surprised, for she had felt sure her volatile friend would have been waiting at the door for their arrival. She looked about her, slightly troubled, and for no apparent reason felt a chill run down her spine. *Surely, the place seems quite deserted,* she thought to herself.

Harry looked about and stifled an oath as he brought his questioning gaze to his sister. "I say, Nick, are you sure Bella was expecting us today?"

"Yes, quite sure, Harry. I received a letter from her only yesterday confirming it all! Today is Thursday ... and we were to come for tea. There can be no mistake!"

"Well, then, I can't say much for Wellesly's staff! Dashed improper! Here, sis, let me help you off and—ah, there is one of the stable boys now!"

They all turned to see a young lad running toward them. He darted a frightened look and apologized for his tardiness. Nicole and Mary were helped down by the gentlemen and the stable boy made as if to lead the phaeton off, but Jed cut him off with a gruff admonishment.

Harry took his sister's arm as they watched the carriage taken off to the stables and led her to the front mahogany door. Surprisingly enough, the door was opened immediately. A rather frigid gentleman stood in the opening, barring their way. After being told that they were expected, he replied that they must have confused the dates because his mistress was away. He would then have closed the door in their faces, had not Harry put his foot in the man's way, sweeping past him. The others quickly followed suit and stood upon the dark oak planking staring disbelievingly at the rude retainer.

Nicole put up her chin and demanded austerely to be shown into the parlor, for the least that could be done was to allow them to rest and take some sort of refreshment after their journey! Harry agreed to this, advising the retainer that some show of common courtesy was called for.

Mary seemed a bit reluctant and hid behind Arnold, clutching his sleeve, while he patted her hand.

The butler repeated his speech and requested them to leave. Nicole opened her mouth and was about to fling some of her best when a voice bellowed out at them. They turned their heads to find a tall heavy man dressed much in the way of a seaman. He had a beard that was black, but the hair that hung about his ears was steel gray. The gray cap he wore covered a bald head and his eyes were dark and sunken. "Tried to warn ye off, but ye quality always got to 'ave yer own way. All right then, 'ave it! In with ye!"

Four pairs of eyes stared at this grisled-looking man, and then followed the line of his arm to the pistol now being leveled at them. Harry stepped forward, putting himself between the pistol and the ladies, and Arnold followed suit, so that they both faced the man with the gun.

It was Harry who found his voice first and spoke in a menacing tone. "I'll thank you to lower that weapon, my good man, for you have nothing to gain by this behavior and quite a bit to lose." It was a good bluff and Harry was rewarded by a smile from his sister.

"Ha, will you listen to the lad! Eh now, govn'r, it's you that's got somethin' to lose—if you don't go nice and quiet like into that there parlor—for Cap will know what to do with the likes of you!" The smile that had been hovering about the beard had vanished and there was a cruel twist to the mouth. "Now *move!*"

As there was little else they could do, the party turned back toward the parlor. When they entered the room, they were presented with the vision of Arabella Wellesly, sitting bolt upright on the couch with her hands clenched together in her lap. Nicole ran to her immediately, ignoring the man with the gun who blustered to her to stand still. She embraced her friend and inquired anxiously, "Bella, love, what is this? Who are these dreadful men?"

Arabella returned her embrace and sniffed remorsefully. "Oh, Nicky, I am so terribly sorry. To think that you, too, are now prisonors of these ... these beasts ... well, it quite sinks my spirits. I don't know what we are to do, for I believe they mean to do us harm!"

Upon hearing these appalling words, Mary promptly fainted, which brought Arnie hastily down to his knees beside her.

Harry had been clenching and unclenching his fists, while he stood staunchly between the gun and his sister.

He looked at the man that had been referred to as Cap and said between clenched teeth, "I warn you, gentlemen, that while you may now have the advantage of weapons, we have a party of friends joining us here shortly, and I assure you we will then have the advantage of numbers. So if you are wise, you will leave now—while you still can." Again it was a good bluff, but the man called Cap barely hesitated at his work—which was the ransacking of the room—to let out a laugh, harsh and angry. "Lord love ye, govn'r, we know who's coming and who's not, so don't ye be fretting and threatening!" He then turned to his accomplice and jerked his head toward the door. "Bo, show the ladies up to their room and put the gents in the cellar with the butler and the rest of them."

Nicky walked slowly toward where Mary lay on the floor and helped Arnie rouse her. "Mary, love, do get up, and please, child, stop whimpering. We must go upstairs."

Arabella joined them, taking Mary's other arm, but suddenly Mary turned to the man called Bo and sobbed, "Please, oh please, sir, can you not take what you want and leave us alone? Can't you see this lady is with child . . . and I am not feeling too well. . . ."

This caused a momentary diversion, and Harry, seeing his chance, dove at Bo, landing him a flush hit, which caused the gun to fall backward and slide out of reach. Harry then plunged after the gun. A china vase came crashing over his head, which left him sprawled out on the floor.

Arnie had been too taken by surprise to act quickly enough, but he had seen Cap pick up the vase and this brought him back to life. He dove at him with a strangled call to Harry . . . and was immediately knocked senseless by a third man, who had entered the room during all the commotion and quickly and forcefully brought the butt of his pistol down on Arnold's head.

Nicole dropped Mary's arm and went down beside her brother. She was close to tears now, for there was blood gushing from a cut just above his hairline. She was allowed to wipe the blood with some cloth from one of the nearby tables and tried unsuccessfully to revive him.

In the meantime, Mary had gone to her knees beside

her swain, and then, once again, fainted. It was left to Bella to put the smelling salts to Mary's nose and to chide her gently, "Do, Mary, sit here quietly, for I must attend to Arnold."

However, she was not allowed to do so, for the man called Cap ordered Bo and the new man to throw the lads into the cellar.

Nicky stifled a sob and turned on their assailants. "You cannot do that. They are hurt. Please allow us first to revive them."

"Get *them* upstairs ... *now*. Can't abide fainting wenches. Come on, Bo ... now."

Nicole had been too distracted by this sudden turn of events to notice the new man who had come into the room and laid Arnold low. She now glanced at him, for he looked familiar. He turned his face in an effort to avoid her eye. She looked at him intently as Bo led them out of the room and gasped audibly, "My God!" but then quickly looked away. However, she had been heard ... and the look of recognition had been seen. Barney Hookum, she thought wildly, the man she and Harry had taken Jed away from!

Hookum looked hard at Cap. "She knows me!" he said angrily.

"No matter. You won't be around after today's work "

"I tell you, Cap, she knows me ... knows my name. I won't be able to come back into the country if I needs to. Don't know that I want to stay out of England always. It's me home ... should like to come back someday ... and this wench knows me."

"Well, listen to me, Barney. It can't be helped. You won't need to come back, I tell you. This is going to fix us up for life. We'll have a nice time of it overseas in the New World, and no one will be the wiser."

"I'd rather finish her, I would!" he grumbled, casting a look of hate toward Nicole.

"Forget it. Are you daft, man? She's quality. Hurt her and you'll have every gent in the entire country after our hide. What you waiting for, Bo, get 'em upstairs."

Bo led them up the winding staircase and Nicole put a hand to Bella's arm and practically had to pull Mary with

203

her free hand. *So, they do not mean to kill us,* she thought. She rarely panicked, but with Harry lying in the cellar bleeding and poor Arnold also unconscious, she was beginning to feel desperate. *What am I to do? How will I get to Harry? How can we escape?* she asked herself, and then systematically answered herself: *Harry will be attended to by the servants, for I heard them say they were locked up together. I will have to make my plans when I see where we are to be placed.*

They were pushed roughly into a small room, which turned out to be Bella's fitting room. She waited until she heard Bo's receding footsteps.

"When will John be back, Bella?" she asked in a hushed voice.

Bella wrung her hands. "Nicky, oh, Nicky, he will not be here until tonight. He has gone to Dorset to see his uncle."

Nicky sighed. "I see!" She turned then and made a grimace. "Mary, do for the love of God stop your whining. It cannot help you . . . and it is most certainly distracting my thoughts and I need to think."

Mary sniffled, "But poor Arnold—and Harry, too—lying downstairs in a cold, damp, awful cellar—and maybe they are dead." With which thought she resumed her whimpering.

Nicole threw up her hands and raised her eyes heavenward. "Mary, I will not ask you again. Stop crying! Arnold and Harry are being attended to by the servants who are locked up with them in the cellar. As to it's being cold and damp, it cannot be helped."

However, Bella had sat down beside Mary and she, too, began to sniff. As a sob escaped her, Mary, finding a sympathetic comrade, went off into another bout.

Nicole regarded her two friends through angry eyes. "Stop it, both of you! How am I to think with you, Bella, crying, and Mary fainting and whimpering all over the house, and I half-crazed with worry for Harry and Arnie? You must stop it, both of you, or I shall break down myself."

Strangely enough, this seemed to bring them to their

senses and they sat quietly, a sniff escaping every now and then, until Nicole broke the silence.

"Confound it, Bella, I cannot imagine why they are here. Who are they, and why are they searching your house?"

Bella sat up and regarded her friend with a frown. "I . . . I had assumed they just wanted to rob us, but I can see that cannot possibly be their purpose now, for they would have finished and been off."

"When did they get here? Tell me all you know, from the beginning, Bella."

"Well, now, let me see. It was just about half an hour or so before you arrived. There are four of them, Nicole! One is in the stables. They forced their way past poor Trundle, my butler, and before I knew what had happened, they had everyone gathered about and sent down to the cellar." Then with finger pressed to her head, she frowned. "There is something—yes, I know, they said something about looking for a paper of some sort. John does not discuss state affairs with me, but I seem to remember his saying something about taking a document, or documents, to the Coast tomorrow. Why, Nick, Nick, could it be they are searching for that?"

Nicky walked to her friend slowly. She patted Arabella's arm reassuringly and gave her her back. Finding a corner chair she sank down and buried her face in her hands. Coming out of her thoughts, she said softly, "Of course, but how did they know John would be away today? Well, that doesn't matter, does it? Somehow they knew. Listen to me, Bella. Those men are looking for something they must not have. It has something to do with the War . . . I am sure of it. Did John hide anything in the house on Tuesday night? He must have come in very late, for I saw him at our house near midnight. Did he come in and hide anything?"

Arabella Wellesly opened her eyes wide. "So, he *was* at your house. That is what he told me . . . we had a bit of a row over it. Oh, I am so glad—"

"Never mind that now, Bella. Did he hide anything?"

"Yes, yes, I remember he came in close to two in the morning. I was quite incensed with him and didn't pay much attention, but he did slip some sort of envelope beneath the mattress. I . . . I think it must still be there."

"Good Lord!" ejaculated Nicole. "Those men will be up here any moment to search the bedrooms . . . and will be sure to discover it. We can't let that happen!"

She then surprised her companions by walking briskly to the door, bending over the doorknob, and peering through the keyhole. She gave a satisfied but contemptuous snort, and without speaking, went back across the room to the sewing table and pulled out a long swatch of silk. She then proceeded to shove the material beneath the door, saying quietly as she did so, "Harry and I once spent an entire month at Arnie's, you know. He had a totally unreasonable governess who took it upon herself to lock us up for the slightest provocation. Well . . . that would never do. 'Twas then that Harry showed me this trick . . . now watch!" After she had inserted the folds of material beneath the door, she went back to the sewing table, produced a long and sturdy hat pin, and prodded it through the keyhole. A second later the brass key fell heavily onto the material, which was then drawn slowly and carefully back into the room. Nicole clutched the key and felt her heart throb dangerously. Swiftly she opened the door and looked outside, motioning with her arm toward Arabella. "Do hurry, Bella . . . lead me to your bedroom," she whispered.

It seemed as though an age and a tremendous amount of exertion passed before the envelope was found and shoved into Nicky's boot. She smoothed her skirts over her legs, and this time followed by Arabella, made her path back to the fitting room, sadly aware that there was no escape down the staircase.

Then all at once, Nicole felt the beating of her heart make its pulsating way to her throat as she gazed directly into the hard eyes of one of their jailors.

"Trying to tip us a double, are ye?" sneered Bo, grabbing Nicky's arm with one large hand and pushing Arabella with his other. He flung open the door and shoved the ladies roughly into the room.

At sight of this mean handling, Mary stood up, gasped

her objections, was told to keep her mummer shut, and promptly fainted.

Bella and Nicole looked at each other as the situation suddenly struck them as ludicrous. They fell upon each other with the sort of laughter born of tension. Bo shook his head, but said no more as he closed the door, turned the key in the lock, removed and placed it on the hall table outside their reach.

Nicole wiped the tears of laughter from her cheeks and sighed heavily. She looked at Mary's limp form and pulled a face, leaving her to Bella's soothing.

Nicole's head tilted as she gazed out the window. "What room are we above, Bella?"

"Why . . . the pantry storage room, off the kitchen."

"Are there any windows in the storage room?" asked Nicky, her eyes narrowing.

"No. Why, Nicky? What are you planning?" asked Bella anxiously.

Nicole did not return an answer, but turned her attention toward Mary, who was now conscious and sprawled across the bed. "Mary, do get off the bed, dear."

Mary groaned, "But, Nicole, I am not feeling—"

"Please, Mary, there is no time to consider your sensibilities. Sit over there, until I am finished."

Mary heaved a sigh, but obeyed without further objection. Then both Bella and Mary exclaimed in unison as Nicky began pulling off the linens.

"Hush, please! Whatever are you about, you stupid things . . . screaming like that!" scolded Nicole, incensed at their thoughtlessness. "Now, Bella, hand me the scissors . . . quickly!"

However, Bella stood her ground, a horrified expression covering her countenance. "Nicole, what are you planning? No, no, please, Nicky, it is far too dangerous. I won't . . . can't be a party to it!"

With an angry oath (one that caused Mary to put her hands to her ears and called down a strong reprove from Arabella), Nicole jumped up and obtained the scissors. Her eyes glinted angrily at them as she began cutting the sheets into long strips. This kept her occupied for some time. A few more minutes were wasted in convincing her friends to help her by tying the lengths of linen strips together.

Jed had entered the stables beside the stable boy in charge of their phaeton, and found himself hurled to the ground. He looked up to find his old tormentor standing above him, with a pistol leveled at his head. Jed gulped and watched silently as another man proceeded to bind and gag the stable boy. The same action was taken with him, and he was flung roughly into a stall. Suddenly he felt his face being smashed into the straw beneath him and he heard Hookum's harsh laugh.

"So now, noddlehead, where's your quality to help ye?" sneered Hookum, kicking at Jed's thigh before turning away.

Jed lay there on the straw without moving, his thoughts a whirlwind. He knew he had to escape. He knew he had to save Lady Nicole, whom he adored, and whom he knew would be at Barney Hookum's mercy ... for surely Barney was here to seek his revenge upon her. He struggled to free the bonds that held him and managed to turn over so that he was on his back. He slid deeper into the stall, and with the help of the wall, managed to work himself into a sitting position. He looked down at his feet and smiled to himself, for in their haste they had tied the rope around his ankles without taking off his boots ... the boots he had just bought the other day that were too large for him. But before he had a chance to go any further with these thoughts, he stiffened, for Barney had come back into the stable. Jed listened intently while Barney described the position of the two swell coves now sleeping it off in the cellar. "Yes, turning out just fine, it is. Locked up the ladies so they won't be giving us no trouble."

The two men laughed over this and then the guard asked Barney to fetch him some food and drink. Barney departed, promising to return with it soon. The man left behind in the stables sat down on a clump of straw in the doorway.

Jed slid out of his boots with very little trouble and stood up, looking over the stall into the next one. There he saw an older man, evidently the head groom, also tied and gagged, but with eyes as fierce as the devil. Jed had never before worried about anyone but himself, and he fell into the old habit of wondering what was to become of him when he noticed his mistress's phaeton standing in the open space. *No,* he thought, *I can't let them harm her . . . not her . . . nor Master Harry.* He had to do something. Quietly he made his way to the older man. The fierce dark eyes motioned him to a hook in the wall of the stall, and Jed, quick to comprehend, went to work on his ropes. They were loosened in a matter of moments, and he took off the old man's gag.

"Ssh, lad, out the window—there." His head motioned to an open window at the back of the stables.

Jed nodded and patted the old man's shoulder. Without saying a word, he ran quietly to the window and climbed out. Looking around, he saw there was nothing for it. He would have to make a mad dash for the woods, as there was a clearing between the stables and the woods that could clearly be seen from the house. His heart turned over and thumped hard in his chest. He gulped and then ran, ran as he had never run before. He didn't stop . . . couldn't stop . . . until he was in the very thicket of the woods. He fell upon his knees and breathed hard, trying to recoup his breath and his strength. He looked about him. "Gawd!" he said out loud, wondering where he could go from here. He made his way through the thicket until he came across a path and took it. Ten minutes later he found himself at a farmhouse.

Barney Hookum had returned to the house and started to make his way to the kitchen when a thought struck him and he changed his mind. He went upstairs and stopped in front of the room that held the ladies. Nicole had taken the precaution of barring the doorway by putting the heavy dark oak chest in front of it. Barney tried opening the door and found it would not budge more than an inch. He heard a scrambled movement inside and bellowed, "Eh, what ye doing in there? Open up this door."

"Please, sir, do go away. Our little friend is ill and we are trying to calm her," replied Bella sternly.

"Well, get this furniture out of the way and let me have a go at it," replied Barney, with a sneer.

"Go away!" It was a command now. "You are upsetting us all."

"I am going away ... far away after today's work ... and want to see my friend in there. Now if you don't move this furniture, I will!"

As he gave every indication of breaking down the door—and was large enough to do it—Nicole slid the chest slightly away from the door, picking up the scissors and shoving them up the sleeve of her riding jacket.

Nicky's closeness with her brother had thrown her into a lively and happy friendship with his friends as well. She had grown up in a boyish atmosphere, listening to their discussions of duels, wars, hunts, boxing, and women. She had become so much a part of their gatherings that they quite often forgot to guard their tongues, forgetting altogether that she was a female. She had listened intently, raptly, about their tales regarding the "muslin set." She was aware of many things young maidens her age had little knowledge of, and therefore it was not strange that she should know at once how this man meant to seek his revenge upon her. She winced at the thought, and was quite ready to use the scissors to protect herself.

Arabella saw the expression on Nicole's face and worried, but then she saw the man's eyes and stood at once between him and her friend.

"Please go away!" she cried.

Nicky pulled Bella away from the doorway and motioned her to the bed, saying gently, "Bella, calm yourself." She then turned her attention back to Barney, who had made his way into the doorway. "You wish to have words with me?" she asked haughtily.

"Oh, more than a word or two, missy, for I want to get to know you better, so I can take *proper* leave of ye when I do leave."

"Certainly, whatever you wish, but I believe in giving you fair warning. There is no distance you could travel that will hide you from my father, and when he does find you, I promise you it will not seem worth it, sir!"

His ugly laugh filled the room.

"Come along, missy. It's privacy we be a-needin' for our little talk." One grease-stained hand reached out and she prepared herself.

He would never know what he was saved from, for then the man called Bo shouted up to him that Jed had escaped from the stables. He cursed, gave Nicole a darkling look, and said, "I'll be back, don't you fret now . . . we'll get together, my pretty wench. You just wait here for me."

Quickly Nicole ran to the window and pulled up the length of sheets that had been lowered earlier, just as one of the men came round the garden, evidently looking for Jed.

"We'll have to wait till they settle down," Nicky cried in exasperation.

Mary whimpered, but said nothing. Bella, a new worry taking hold of her, came to Nick and put her arms about her. "Nick, you will have to get away. That man . . . he means to . . . to . . . oh, Nick, you have to get away." Nicole gave her a long look of understanding. "Yes, I know, Bella."

Down in the parlor Mr. Hookum was receiving a dressing down from the man called Cap. He looked at Hookum with a sneer. "So, you have given the lady a scare. Leave it at that, or I'll have to send you on your way, for there has been too much trouble over this and we still ain't got what we came for."

Barney looked angry, but he said nothing to this and went outside to search for Jed.

Down in the cellar, Arnold had been brought to some time ago, for the servants were indeed all gathered together and had managed to find a few candles and accessories to make their sojourn bearable. They had soaked a rag in a puddle of rainwater and applied this to Arnold's bruised head. He awoke to discover that he had a large lump on the back of his head and that it ached terribly. He immediately went beside Harry, who was still lying unconscious with his head snuggled in the lap of a

211

young serving girl. He called his cousin's name several times but Harry lay inert.

It was sometime later, during the commotion of Jed's escape, that Harry opened his eyes, upon which he immediately closed them again and groaned.

Arnie was beside him at once. "Hallo, ole boy . . . that's it, Harry, come on now," he urged.

Harry reopened his eyes and said, his voice low, "What . . . what has happened?" Then with a wince, "Oh God, yes, I remember now." Upon which he tried to sit up, which made him feel quite sick, so he sank back onto the lap of the obliging girl. He smiled tremulously at her and thanked her in his gentle way. After a few moments he sat up resolutely, holding two hands to his aching head.

"Dear God, Arnie, we've made a botch of it, and Nick up there worrying. Well, I don't suppose Nick will worry, though—calm sort of girl—but she won't like this, and Lord knows I don't like it. How we are to get out of this mess is beyond me." He looked about him and groaned.

"I have been thinking, Harry," said Arnie, his face lighting up.

"Good Lord, Arnie, don't we have enough problems?"

Not in the least affronted, Arnie continued. "I have been thinking that places like this old house have secret panels—secret rooms—so why not secret escape routes?"

Harry eyed his cousin narrowly. "Hmmm." He turned to one of the servants. "How old is this house?"

Trundle, the butler, a stolid individual, answered this query. "I am sorry, Viscount, but the house is but fifty or so years old. It has no hidden avenues of any sort."

Arnold looked stricken. Harry's eyes roamed about the room, and then found the puddle of water the servants had been using to revive them with. "What is that?" he pointed.

Trundle answered gravely, his eyes holding concern for the poor young man who had evidently been hurt much more than it seemed, "It is water, Viscount!"

"Damnation, man, of course, it's water. I mean where did it come from?"

"It is rainwater, my Lord," answered Trundle, feint but pursuing.

Harry eyed the group assembled and they eyed him back. He put up his hands, exasperated. "You bunch of fools! We have been down here all this while and none of you has realized that where there is water, there must be a leaky window, for it cannot have seeped in through the walls, the walls do not appear to be wet!"

They looked at one another and it was Trundle who answered, only a slight crack at the opening of his mouth betraying the fact that he was pleased. "Why, yes, I do remember there is a window. We boarded it up many years ago because of the leak." He walked to the wall and pointed some four feet above him to planks of wood.

Harry stood up, excited, and swerved, still not steady. "Good God, come on then, Arn, find me something to stand on."

They found some old pieces of furniture, one of which was high enough. Harry, being the tallest, proceeded to remove the planks of wood that had been concealing their means of escape.

Jed had reached the farmhouse, some forty minutes before, and had been relieved to find that not only did the farmer's wife believe him, she was more than willing to lend their best riding horse, apologizing that her husband was away. "For if he were 'ere, laddy, he'd finish off those villains." Jed thanked her and jumped upon the mount she showed him, pleased to find that it was a roan horse and well able to carry him swiftly to London. His weight was light, and they maintained a spanking pace until he reached the hub of the city. He was well pleased with himself, sure that the trip that had taken them an hour this morning had now not taken him more than half that time. He was bowling down the streets of London when he was caught in traffic at Brook Street. He breathed a string of oaths at the people and carriages that blocked his way.

Roth saw the boy as he stepped down from his front door to the sidewalk. He frowned and hailed him, wondering what the devil Nicky's tiger was doing astride that horse, here, when he had thought she had taken him with her to Wellesly Court. The frown deepened when Jed jumped down from the roan and ran breathlessly to him, for here was a man he knew could help. "Thank Gawd, your Grace!" he cried with relief. He had dragged the horse along by the reins and Roth could see both horse and rider appeared to be winded.

Suddenly Roth felt a twinge of apprehension. Something was wrong, dreadfully wrong! He looked penetratingly at the boy. "What is it, boy?" he asked harshly, but Jed was still sucking in air, trying to get things clear in his own mind. Roth was worried now. "Tell me at once."

"Your Grace, they have got Lady Nicole, and the Viscount, too! They have 'em all, and I don't know what they be doing to them!" cried the boy desperately.

The Duke felt something cold plunge into his heart. His eyes narrowed, and the aspect of his face was grim. Jed looked at him and thought he would never want to become this man's enemy.

"Who has your mistress and where?" he asked harshly.

"At Wellesly Court. They tied me in the stables and I heard that my mistress is locked upstairs ... but poor Master Harry and Sir Arnold Merdon be in a bad way in the cellars. It's my ole guardian. Means her harm, he does. I knows it, I just knows it!"

The boy began to bluster, but Roth had no time to comfort him. His own heart and mind were in a frenzy of agitation. He turned back toward his waiting curricle and called to his groom Duffy in a harsh, hard voice. "Duff, go round and saddle my gray. Saddle the bay for yourself, for I mean to ride hard and need you to keep up—and Duff, pack a pistol and one for me!"

He went off hurriedly to do this bidding, as the Duke turned back toward Jed and said, "Now, you will tell me everything—how many men are involved . . . why they should want to harm your mistress . . . and why they have invaded Wellesly Court."

"I don't know, your Grace. I was kept in the stables. I did hear snatches of what they said, though, but not enough to tell you why they all be there. I know Barney—he was my guardian till Mistress and Master took me up—and I know he means revenge against her. Should I fetch Lord Beaumont?" he asked anxiously.

"No, he is away from home. You will go to my lodgings and stay there, as I do not want Lady Beaumont disturbed with these tidings while she is alone and unable to do anything."

Nicole was in danger, he thought ... and the word *danger*, linked with her name, caused him to tremble. He felt something in the pit of his gut twist and turn. *My God ... Nick ... oh, my little love ... please God, do not let any harm come to her. Let me be in time,* he cried furiously to himself. He mounted his horse and with Duffy beside him rode out of the city and made his wild pace toward Wellesly Court.

Harry had found that taking off the planks of wood was no easy task with his bare hands. He was forced to give it up and then with the help of Arnie and Trundle began a somewhat unsystematic search for tools. This took considerable time, but at last Trundle came upon an old brass lamp that had a long thin stem. Harry remounted the table and proceeded as quietly as possible to pry loose the wood that hid their means of escape.

Nicole waited three-quarters of an hour before deciding it was safe enough to lower the sheets again. She heard them searching desperately throughout the second floor and patted her boot, happily aware that they would not find what they were after. She lowered the sheets, and then was forced to pull them up again, as Barney Hookum came round the corner, checking the shrubbery for signs of Jed. A few minutes later he came to the conclusion that the lad was well away from the estate and went into the house to give this piece of intelligence to Cap.

Once more, Nicole lowered the sheets out the window and made certain the end was securely tied to the legs of the brass bed. Having satisfied herself that everything was set right and tight, she gave Bella a hug, went to do the same to Mary, who promptly fell into a bout of tears. Nicky threw up her hands to God with exasperation, gathered up her skirts, and proceeded to make good her escape. It was no easy task, hampered as she was by her dress, but she managed in spite of the heavy material, which hung about her, to keep a strong grip. Placing her feet against the brick wall, and using the ivy to her benefit, Nicole lowered herself carefully and slowly down the lengths of sheet. However, she found she was not quite strong enough to maintain the tight hold she had initially begun with, and her hands began slipping under her own weight. She slid down the remainder of the six feet of linen, and then, barely holding on, looked down at the ground that seemed still quite a distance. Her hold was giving way, and resolutely making up her mind, Nicky jumped, landing squarely on her ankles, and with a stifled cry of pain, collapsed to the ground. She closed her eyes as the pain shot through her ankles, and prayed she hadn't sprained them. Steadying herself, she got slowly up, the pain causing her to wince, but she managed a smile to Bella, who was waiting anxiously above her, and watched as Bella pulled the linen back into the room.

Nicky walked a few feet and then leaned against the brick wall, not really knowing what she should do—or where she should go—and deathly afraid of meeting Hookum somewhere on the grounds, for in her haste she had forgotten to bring the scissors, and so was weaponless.

Harry exclaimed with delight as the last board creaked away from the wall, and then his face fell sadly as he gazed at the window that would have to be their escape route. It was not wide, and had little to recommend it. Arnie would never fit through this slit (for it was no more than that), and it was doubtful that, slim as he was, even Harry could. However, Harry began to try a series of positions, with exasperated suggestions to Trundle and Arnie as to pushing and prodding, until these suggestions became quite painful protests! Harry found himself with one shoulder in and one shoulder out and evidently quite thoroughly stuck. Arnie sat down, overcome with sudden mirth, while Harry cursed the window, the scoundrels above stairs, the cellar, consigning them all to "Dante's Inferno."

The Duke rode his gray hard. Duffy was keeping fairly close on the Duke's spirited bay. It took less than thirty minutes to reach the drive at Wellesly Court, though it seemed much longer to Roth. They tethered their horses in the woods and made their quiet way, unobserved, to the stables. There they encountered an astonished individual too surprised to give them any trouble. He was quickly eliminated by the harsh but effective method of bringing down the butt of the Duke's pistol on his head. Having disposed of the first of the four villains, they released the stable boy and groom and left them to stand guard. The groom, whom Jed had encountered earlier, took this job rather enthusiastically by picking up a pitchfork and standing over the unconscious brute with every intention of putting the fellow out if he tried anything.

Nicole, still quite shaky from her fall, pressed against the brick wall and made her silent way round the chimney, which divided the wall in half and protruded some three feet from the building. She then caught her breath and almost simultaneously began to laugh. She was overcome with mirthful emotion at finding her brother up and apparently well, as he was releasing a string of angry oaths.

"Harry ... oh, Harry ... how glad I am to see you! Here, darling, let me help you," she said convulsively between gulps of laughter. She pulled as Arnie and Trundle pushed, and by hunching his shoulders Harry found that he was able to get through the open slit— though, to be sure, he received a bruise or two as the wood tore off a good part of his coat sleeve.

"Hell and damnation!" he exclaimed angrily. "Just had this made by Davidson." However, finding that he was now free of the cellar, he grinned broadly and advised his sister that he was quite ready for action.

They sat beside each other on the warm grass and Nicky's hand went to his head where a dry crust of blood had stained his fair hair. She frowned over this and he caught her hand, giving it a squeeze. " 'Tis nothing, ole girl, nothing at all, though I must say I have a terrible headache."

"Harry . . . those men, I know why they are here!" she said portentously.

"Well . . . what is it? We can't sit here all day and chat, you know. Speak up, girl!" he said.

"It has something to do with an important state paper of some sort, and Harry I have it here in my boot! These men must be spies!" she said, ending on a note of hushed horror.

Her brother looked at first thunderstruck. "By Jove, yes, that's it, Nick . . . it all makes sense now. But never say you have whatever it is they want safe on you!" He laughed, struck by the absurdity of this advice, then suddenly his aspect grew serious. "Give it to me, Nick."

"No—not now. I have it safe, Harry. If we were to be caught, they would never think to search me . . . and oh, Harry, I forgot to tell you, Jed has escaped . . . quite some time ago. I am sure that he went for help and should be back soon."

Harry regarded her again, this time doubtfully. "It is possible, Nick, that Jed escaped and simply ran away, afraid to get involved."

"Oh no, Jed would never let us be hurt. He went for help, depend upon it! I know . . . I just know!"

He shrugged his shoulders. "Well . . . that is neither here nor there. I want you to make your way out of here. Toward the woods, and through them to that farmhouse we saw on our way here this morning."

"No, Harry. I have thought it all out. We must capture these brutes!" she said with determination.

Harry regarded her with no little admiration. "Pluck to the backbone! Always said you were, but never thought you were foolish. Now listen to me, Nick, you will be in my way. I'll be worrying about your safety, and not watching out for mine—and not being able to watch out for mine, I won't be in the best of positions . . . must see that!"

"Harry," objected Nicole, insulted, "I have never been in your way! I resent your stating so. I will help you, Harry . . . only do listen. If we can find a weapon of some sort . . . perhaps a pitchfork. . . ."

"Oooh, bloodthirsty, ain't you?" Her brother grinned.

"Yes, but listen now! You could use me as a diversion. I can lure one man out at a time, and then . . . *plunk*"— she motioned emphatically with her arm, so that there could be no question as to the word's meaning—"you could put him out!"

"Rather, run him through, you mean. After all Nick, pitchforks don't *plunk* . . . they *pink!*" teased Harry.

"Don't humor me, Harold!"

"But, Nick, do be serious! If you run off now and go to the farm, you could bring back some help. Perhaps the farmer has a few sturdy sons—"

"No! I have already explained that Jed escaped. If there had been any help at the farm, he would have brought it!" Then suddenly she put up her hand. "Sssh!"

They sat silently and listened to the shouting that came to their ears from the room at the end of the wall. Harry moved to his knees and Nicky picked up her skirts and followed suit. They crawled along the grass, hugging the wall, until they were within earshot.

Three of their assailants had gathered in the parlor and were involved in a heated debate. Clearly there was dissension amongst them.

Bo put one hairy large hand out and grabbed at Cap's arm. "I'm for loping off now, Cap! The boy has been gone close to a couple of hours—maybe more. He's likely bringing down every Redbreast in the area upon us! Here we are, just waiting for 'em. The papers ain't here. Govn'r got his noddle all messed up!"

Cap shook off his grip and then turned to look at his accomplices, stroking his chin reflectively. "I disremember when we've been in such a fix, lads. They're going to have double guards with him on the morrow . . . there is no getting at it then. Gawd! Govn'r's waiting on us at Tall Oaks . . . and us empty-handed! We've got to keep on looking."

Barney Hookum shook his head. "Ay, look 'ere now, Cap, Bo is right. We'd better try our luck tomorrow with the swell cove. I ain't been a bridle-cull all these years without knowing the ins and outs of it on the road!"

Cap sneered derisively. "Bridle-cull, is it? Stupid fool, that's all you've been and that's all you'll ever be. We

219

ain't pound dealing, for mercy's sake! What d'ye think I've been jabbering about? There's a trap laid out for us tomorrow . . . or so says our *man*. Said the blasted paper must be here, and we've got to find it!"

Hookum shook his head angrily and started to turn his back. "You find it then! I'm loping off now!"

The sound of Cap's voice brought Hookum's head round, and he found Cap's pistol aimed grimly at his skull. "Ah now, Barney m'friend, I wouldn't be a-rushing off like that. 'Tain't polite, you know!"

Bo started to blubber. "Cap . . . Cap . . . listen. . . ."

"No! You listen, you two fools. We don't get our pockets lined till we produce that document. I need that blunt . . . *you* need it!"

"Ain't likely I'll get to spend it from Newgate!" retorted Barney.

Cap mulled this about, his eyes squinting and his tongue darting in a manner that always exhibited his busy mind. He hesitated. "All right, all right then, we'll finish up this room—tear everything apart—and if it ain't 'ere, we'll lope off!"

It was at this precise moment that a shot sent Cap's loosely held pistol flying out of his hand, leaving that hand bleeding and useless. A hard quiet voice came from the doorway. "You will oblige me, gentlemen, by putting your hands above your heads. Yes, that's it. Now face the wall and spread your legs . . . quite! Duffy, kindly relieve these men of any hidden weapons. Check their boots as well!"

Roth stood there like a magnificent god, staring hard at the backs of the men his groom was now searching. His eyes never wavered from their object until he heard a squeak emitted from the window. Roth watched wide-eyed as he saw what he thought was the loveliest vision his eyes had ever beheld clamber hurriedly through the open window and run across to him. "Adam . . . Adam . . ."

His strong arm encircled her shoulders as she buried her face against his hard chest.

Harry dropped nimbly into the room, via the same route, ejaculating as he did so, "By Jove, your Grace!

Sewed it up right and tight . . . though 'tis a bit of a sad case, you know . . . wanted to have at 'em myself!" He then picked up one of the pistols Duffy had discovered. Thus armed, he sat upon the desk, swinging his foot and aiming his gun with a gleeful glint in his blue eyes.

Observing that both Duff and Harry had the situation in hand, Adam turned his attention to the little bundle now sobbing incoherent sentences into his waistcoat.

"You have come . . . you have come."

"Did you ever doubt it? Lord, Nicky . . . my darling imp . . . I have been out of my mind with worry," he said, hugging her to him fiercely.

Harry leaned his head toward Adam's groom. "I say, do you think you can manage here? I just recalled that my cousin is still stuck in the cellar and the ladies are locked in above stairs."

Duffy nodded grimly. A few moments later found Arnie running up the flight of stairs to Mary's woebegone state. Understandably Mary sank into Arnie's arms.

"Er . . . better have her lie down a bit . . . till we dispose of those scoundrels, you know," whispered Harry into his cousin's ears.

Mary made no objection to this. However, Arabella accompanied the young men downstairs.

Trundle had by this time produced a rope and proceeded to tie the prisoners. Harry grinned over the butler's ferocious grunting and assisted him in the job, so that the captives were tied to one another in such a way as to defy escape.

Arabella sank down upon her Chippendale sofa and put a hand to her bemused head. Roth eyed her a moment and led Nicole toward the sofa, where he motioned for her to sit, still retaining a hold upon her hand.

"Lady Wellesly, I regret that under the circumstances I must put a few questions to you. I know that you have suffered under the ordeal of the day, but there are a few things I must know!"

"Of course," replied Bella, frowning.

"You must by now be aware that this incident involves your husband's affairs with the department he is associated with."

"Yes ... er ... Nicky has already made me realize that."

"Very well ... where is your husband?"

"He received an urgent message from his uncle in Dorset—"

"Convenient, wouldn't you say, gentlemen?" asked his Grace of his prisoners, who squirmed within their bindings.

"Do you mean they sent the message?" asked Nicole incredulously.

"They don't have the type of intellect to produce such a plan, but the man who pays them evidently does." Roth frowned darkly and pulled up a chair. "But ... but, your Grace," said Arabella hesitatingly, "Nicky and I discussed this earlier ... and she thought that perhaps the Boothes have something to do with it. You see, I had mentioned to Lady Boothe that my husband would be away today, and then again tomorrow."

"No, no, Bella, I didn't precisely think the Boothes were behind this," objected Nicole.

"Unwittingly, I am afraid they were. You see, Lady Boothe is related to Sir Charles Barnaby, and it is Barnaby who is involved in this mess."

"Oh, bless me! I nearly forgot!" exclaimed Nicole, lifting her skirts before the Duke's astonished gaze and pulling out an impressive-looking envelope. Triumphantly she slapped it into his hand. "There ... if we had not retrieved this from beneath the bed, those villains would have had it and been gone hours ago!"

The Duke sighed heavily, which immediately brought down a strong rebuke upon his head. "I must say, Adam Roth, you could at least say thank you!

"I do thank you, darling, for the thought. However, it would have been far simpler—though we had not planned it that way—if you had allowed them to find it and whisk it off. We wanted this to get into Barnaby's hands, for he, in turn, would have—hold a moment. Harry, better put those men in another room until we have finished our talk."

"Eh, by Jove, you're right there! Come on, then!" ordered Harry as he watched Arnold and Duffy lead the men out.

"Now, then—and I trust both of you will remember the type of confidence you are receiving?" He received quick nods and continued. "This document," he said, patting it gently, "is a contrived production. I need not tell you *what* it is, or *why* it is. I will tell you that it is imperative that Napoleon receive it in the near future. We had hoped that it would have been in Barnaby's hands tomorrow ... and from there into a certain Count's—"

"Count, which Count?" demanded Nicole.

"Never mind that, Nicole. What I'd like to know is how did you know of this document's existence?" asked the Duke curiously.

"I am not stupid, Adam! As soon as I realized those brutes were not ordinary thieves, I knew that they must have something to do with all the secrecy you and Papa have been at pains about. I asked Bella if John had hidden anything on Tuesday night, for I saw him come to the house late that night, when *you* were with Papa ... do you remember? Well, Bella showed me ... for it was under the bed ... that was after I got the key out of the lock ... but then we were captured again ... but I had it hidden in my boot, you see!" she said as she slipped the sealed envelope once again into its prior resting place.

"Remarkable!" said his Grace.

Nicole accepted this tribute and then sank back against the sofa, her green eyes veiled. After a moment she looked up at the Duke, who was regarding her tenderly. "Adam, how are you going to get the document to Barnaby now?"

"That is going to be a problem, imp. However, there are a few questions I would like to put to those fellows we have caught, so if you will excuse me ladies. . . ."

They nodded their dismissal, and Bella exclaimed that she was hungry.

"Yes, love, in your condition, too ... poor thing. Food! That's it!" exclaimed Nicole as though a great dawn had lit itself before her eyes. "You rest here, love. I'll go to the kitchen and have them send you all some refreshments." And Nicky sprang up and rushed out of the room. Her mind was a turmoil. She had heard the men speaking when she and Harry were outside the window. They had said that "the govn'r" was waiting for them at Tall Oaks. She knew what she had to do.

Nicole rushed into the kitchen, which was in lively disorder, and commanded the servants to quiet down and get some sort of hot nourishment to their mistress and some substantial refreshment to the gentlemen. She then slipped out to the stables, where she found the stable boys conversing excitedly.

"Saddle your lady's mare at once."

The lad was quick to note the tone of authority and did not question this order. She swung up into the sidesaddle easily and adjusted her skirts. "In twenty minutes' time—if no one comes to inquire after me—you shall go to the house and ask for the Duke of Lyndham. Tell him I have gone to Tall Oaks."

"Yes, m'lady," said the baffled boy to Nicole's retreating form.

It was already quite dark, but the sky was lit with a glowing moon and a burst of stars. Nicole was nervous with the excitement that filled her, exhilarated by the thought that she was assisting her love and her country.

Chapter Eighteen

A darkly clad figure approached the Tall Oaks Inn, but pulled up his horse just before the stables had been reached and waited. He would have to be careful and bide his time.

Inside the small country inn, Barnaby fidgeted nervously. His hirelings were long overdue. He wanted to bolt . . . yet he was fearful of doing so. He waited another half-hour and then his sweat poured over his brow. He could not take it any longer. He nearly ran from the inn, and in his haste tipped over a chair. He shouted for the stable boy and demanded his horse. The animal was brought to him and the boy snickered as he watched Barnaby's clumsy attempts to mount him.

"Your hand, fool!" shouted Barnaby in a frenzy.

The dark figure watched from the shadows of the trees and felt a loathing contempt fill him. He wondered how he had ever connected himself with such a creature.

Barnaby rode out of the inn and followed the main road at a moderate pace, for he was not a good rider when he had the benefit of daylight and he was fearful at night. Suddenly he heard a call from behind and slowed his pace.

"Ho there, Barnaby," said the Count sweetly.

"Louis? What . . . what are you doing here?"

"I expected you many, many hours ago, my friend."

"Something has gone wrong, Louis. They never arrived . . . we haven't got it. You'll have to think of something else."

"I already have. Stop a moment and we will discuss it."

Barnaby brought his horse to a halt. His eyes wandered nervously to the Count's left hand, which gripped the roan's bridle. However, Barnaby never noticed the small pistol clutched in the Frenchman's right hand, so quick, so complete, was the movement that brought that weapon to Barnaby's head. In a moment it was over.

The Count grimaced at the lifeless figure sprawled on the ground. Barnaby's horse had moved nervously at the sound of the gunshot, but the Count had retained a strong hold.

He dismounted, bent over the bloody figure, located the ends of Barnaby's greatcoat, and threw them round the limp figure. He then dragged the body deep into the woods and tethered Barnaby's roan not far away. He emptied Barnaby's purse into his own. "Poor chap, the victim of a highwayman, no doubt!"

The Count then started to lead his own horse out of the woods and toward the road when he caught himself up short.

Nicole did not notice the lone figure walking decorously out of the forest. She was too intent on her destination, too involved with her plans. However, the Count had a very good vision of her face alight in the moonglow. He mounted his horse and followed her swiftly to Tall Oaks.

Nicky reached the small stone inn, riding, she thought,

to an inch. She scanned her surroundings, peering in through the large front window of the lodge for signs of Barnaby, when a voice from behind her made her suck in her breath.

"My dearest child, whatever are you doing here alone at this time of night?" said the Count, his face betraying all the concern he felt he should feel under ordinary circumstances.

Nicole regarded the Count and she felt her heart stop and then beat furiously. Adam had said a Count was involved . . . and here was Louis . . . oh God! Well, there was only one way of knowing and that was by following through with her scheme. "Oh, Louis, such terrible things have happened today at poor Lady Wellesly's, but . . . but I can't go into them. I left in such a haste that I had forgotten that I haven't had a bite to eat."

"Mon Dieu! Come, love, let me help you down and I shall fetch you something at once."

Nicole felt herself tremble as he lifted her from her horse. A stable boy came up for their horses, but Nicky shook her head. "No, just tether him here. I shall be leaving immediately."

The Count held Nicky's arm and walked her into the inn. "A glass of madeira and—"

"That will be sufficient . . . I have not time, you see. I must get to my papa at once."

"How is this?"

"Oh, Louis, I know I can trust you not to let any of this leak out. Today some terrible men came and tried to steal"—she bent and produced the sealed envelope from her boot—"this. My brother Harry captured them and said I must take this to Papa."

"You . . . you were at Lady Wellesly's today?" asked the Count, his eye on the envelope.

"Yes, yes, my brother and myself." She sipped the wine and then stood up to go. She lifted her skirt and made as though to slip the envelope into her boot. However, the envelope went sliding to the floor. Nicole hurried from the room, too much in haste to note that the envelope had been swiftly scooped up and inserted into the Count's inner coat pocket. She turned to wave, and only the glint in her eyes betrayed the fact that she was aware the Count was now in possession of the document.

The Count took a few quick strides and put his hand upon Nicole's arm.

"I cannot let you go unescorted, Nicole. I shall accompany you."

Oh, hang it, thought Nicky, and said, "That is not necessary, Count."

"I insist, Nicole," said the Count, for his mind had worked fast. Here was a chance to get to Dover and then across to France without hindrance. He would take Nicole as hostage.

Nicole saw nothing she could do to shake him off at the moment, and so mounted her horse. He followed suit and they rode at a slow pace until the inn was out of sight.

"There is a better way—a shortcut I am very familiar with, my dove. If you will permit me, I will take your reins," said the Count, reaching out.

"Certainly not! I guide my own horse, Louis, and I do not take shortcuts with gentlemen at this time of night. It would not be seemly."

"I am afraid, my pretty one, that you have no choice in the matter," said the Count, grabbing hold of her bridle strings.

Nicole brought down her riding whip across his arm. This made him laugh as the whip did little against the folds of material. However, she then brought it flashing across his cheeks, and while it did not lacerate the skin, it left it feeling the sting, and more important, it startled him.

She spurred her horse and made off back in the direction of the inn. Lady Wellesly's horse had unfortunately been bred for gentleness, not speed, and the Count gained on her swiftly. He grabbed hold of her horse's bridle, slowing her to a complete stop.

"Let me go, you . . . you brute . . . you swine . . . how dare you!" Once again, she had broken free, but the commotion had worried her mare and the horse reared unexpectedly.

Nicole held her seat expertly, but for a moment the

227

horse bolted uncontrollably toward the thick of the woods.

The Count was beside her at once, and this time succeeded in not only stopping her horse but in pulling her off as well.

He had slipped off his horse and then swiftly pulled her down into his arms. *"Mon Dieu*, little one, you put up a gallant fight! I see that I shall have to hire a chaise for our journey to Paris. In the meantime, my hell and fire, I shall have to dispense with your mare and settle you before me on mine."

For answer, Nicky softened unexpectantly. "Please, Louis, if that is what you wish . . . then it is my wish, too. But you said Paris, and not Gretna Green."

He laughed and his hold relaxed. He had no time for more, for as soon as his hold softened, Nicole was out of it and rushing madly away, hoping for time . . . time to be found. She ran unseeing into the woods and suddenly tripped over something and went sprawling to the ground. She screamed then, for she had stumbled across Sir Charles Barnaby's lifeless form.

The Count was there almost at once and pulled her to her feet. "Ah, my poor child, I had not wished for you to see such an ugly thing. But perhaps it is well . . . then you will believe I am in earnest!"

"You . . . you killed Sir Charles . . . ?" Her voice came hushed, her eyes were wide.

"Necessary . . . and really, my dove, no loss to your people or mine. Please dearest, I mean you no harm. In fact, though I take you to Paris and not Gretna Green, I do intend to marry you. Your money and my lands will work well together. And so, I trust, shall we, *enfin!"*

"No, no! I . . . I shall scream. Wherever we go, I will tell everyone you have abducted me," shouted Nicole, terrified now.

"I think not. You will spend the night in my company . . . yes . . . and after that, even your parents will wish you to marry me. You could never return to England without my name, for then, no one else would have you. Even in our gay times, my dear, there are some things that can ruin!"

"I . . . I will seek protection at every watering place—"

"Again, I think not! You see this?" He waved his pistol at her. "You would not endanger the life of some poor wretch foolish enough to try and give you aid. Ah, I see at last you comprehend and resign yourself."

"It is a rare quality in a woman, don't you think, Count D'Agout?" came a hard voice from the darkness.

Adam Roth had been quick to note Nicky's absence and even quicker to follow. He had been advised that Nicky had departed astride Lady Wellesly's mare in the company of a gentleman she had met at the inn.

The Duke had hurriedly ridden in the direction the couple had taken, in time to see Nicky being chased into the woods by the Count. The Duke cursed savagely, dismounted, and spanned the distance between the Count and himself in a thrice.

Count d'Agout turned astonished eyes to the Duke, allowing himself to be caught off guard by Nicole, who immediately took the opportunity to slap the pistol out of his hand.

The Count made a dive for it, but was intercepted by the Duke's fist, which made a dent in his chin. The Duke then followed through by bringing a solid blow to the Count's breadbox. Another flush hit tipped the Frenchman a settler, and he lay on the ground, apparently unconscious.

Nicole once again dove into the Duke's arms and allowed him to hold her tightly. "Adam, I am so excessively pleased that you have come, for you do have a very satisfying way of rescuing me."

"Nicole, *you* deserve a severe scold." He spotted the limp form some twenty feet away. "Hold, what is this?" he said, walking toward Sir Charles.

" 'Tis Barnaby . . . the Count has killed him, Adam."

"I see. We had better leave the area. He will be found and it will be put round that he was set upon by a highwayman. The Count has done us a favor actually. Save a good deal of scandal from spouting off."

"How cold-blooded, Adam . . . but I suppose you are right."

Their heads both came round at the sound of horse's

Hoofs receding in the night, for the Count had made good his escape.

"Won't he think it strange if you don't follow?" asked Nicole.

"Perhaps ... but then, he will think that I had no choice. Couldn't leave you here alone, you know."

"He has the envelope, Adam."

"I rather thought he might."

"How could you think so, you horrid knowing creature?"

"The moment you disappeared with the envelope in your possession, I knew what you were about. Harry had mentioned to me while we were questioning the prisoners that they had an accomplice waiting at Tall Oaks. It then occurred to me that you had retained the envelope. When I found you gone—well, I'd have to be a bit thick not to realize what you were about."

"I ... I am so tired, Duke. May we go home now?"

"Duke? Hang it, Nicole, that is doing it rather too brown! You have been calling me Adam this past hour and more and I will not let you go back to formalities!"

"When I am really formal, I call you 'your Grace' ... at any rate, it was most improper of me to call you Adam," she said, blushing, remembering how she had flung herself upon him. "It was that I was so relieved to see you. I had been so ... so worried all afternoon. First with Harry and Arnie being knocked about and thrown into the cellar, and then Mary fainting every two minutes ... and that ... that beast Hookum. How could I not be relieved to see you charge in and take command? But, of course, I should have realized you would come ... after all, it is *department* business. ..."

He took her shoulders in a strong grip and she saw his eyes flash before his lips came down hard and uncompromisingly upon hers. She didn't struggle but relaxed in his embrace, a hand fluttering to his cheek and stroking it softly. She heard him whisper in her ears, "You little fool!" Which piqued her at once and caused her to stiffen. This, in turn, brought forth his full hearty chuckle. He released her, and brought up her hand to his lips. "My glorious, brave little imp! Always so ready to take up the cudgels! Don't you realize how very much I love you?"

"Adam . . . oh, you do, don't you?"

For answer, his Grace gathered her up in his arms and it was a considerable time before she was able to speak.

"Do you know, Adam, I have loved you from the start . . . from the very first moment I saw you. I didn't want to . . . I forced myself to . . . to put you out of my mind. . . ."

"Lord, Nicky, when I thought that you wouldn't have me, I was wild with misery. I knew that I couldn't be happy without you prancing about and disarraying my orderly life. *You* are the only woman I could ever love."

"The *only* one?" she asked demurely.

He laughed. "You don't believe me?"

"I want to know where you were for three entire days. Here I was, flirting all over town for your sole benefit, with poor Robby, and you not even present to notice. Dastardly, I say!"

He laughed again and held her tighter, putting his forefinger beneath her chin and tilting it upward. "And I so furious with you that night—do you remember?—the night you said you would marry Robby! Then I had a visit from the Beau and we took poor James and went off to the races; but I found that I was miserable without you . . . driving myself to distraction wondering what you were doing . . . who you were with. I came back without them, determined to put an end to my game and make you my wife . . . but you refused me," he said reproachfully.

"You see, I had heard rumors about you. They said you were with Lord Byron at his country estate drinking wine from skulls and cavorting with Cyprians!"

"Heigh-ho!" he said, pinching her cheek. "Even Byron ain't in the country . . . er, cavorting with the wenches. The truth is he is hiding out from Lady Caroline Lamb."

"Oh," she said in a small voice and snuggled up against him. "Adam, what is being done with those men?"

"Ah, Harry will go along with Duffy and they will be taken care of!"

Nicole pulled away from him suddenly. "I warn you, Adam Roth, I will not be treated like a child . . . or

231

thought of as a mere woman! I will not be kept out of your affairs—state or otherwise! Do you realize that poor Bella knows naught of all this? I ... I will not be like other wives, content to sit home with needlepoint, talk about the latest on dit or the upcoming routs! No, Adam! Today I could have killed a man! All Mary could do was whimper and faint ... more times than I can remember ... even Bella who was always such a reliable sort ... but then, she is with child ... but my point is that *I* formed a plan and carried it through. I cut up the linen, tied it to the bed, and escaped through the window ... skirts and all. ..."

"Did you, by God?" interpolated the Duke admiringly.

"Yes I did. Didn't you wonder how I happened to be outside?"

"It had flitted across my mind that it was a bit strange considering you were supposed to be a prisoner. However—"

"Never mind that now! Adam, that man ... Hookum ... he came up to our room and he would have ... he wanted to ... to take me off ... alone ... and I knew why, so I slipped a pair of scissors into the sleeve of my jacket. I was prepared to *kill* him, Adam! It would not have been easy, for he is rather large and it is rather ... bloody to thrust a pair of dull scissors into a man's heart—" She broke off on a sob and felt the tears pour out.

The Duke's eyes had narrowed as he listened to this. He held her tightly and stroked her head, whispering her name, soothing her with soft enchanting words of love. A cold vice had encircled his being as he had listened to her and pictured her earlier predicament. A deadly resolve took hold of him and he knew a surge of revengeful determination. Hookum would be repaid for today's work, he told himself. For the moment, he had to bring his love back into spirits.

"Ah, so you are not a mere female. And evidently you think I go about asking mere females to marry me and accept my kisses! Not I! Only the best would do for me," he said playfully.

She blushed rosily. "That is not what I meant. What I

am trying to say is . . . if I am to carry your name . . . receive your . . . kisses . . . then I must share your life. That means no secrets—departmental or otherwise!"

"Are you saying that you won't marry me unless I confide things that I have sworn by duty and honor not to betray!" he asked gravely.

"No . . . no, my dearest," she said sweetly. "I will marry you . . . but I want you to understand that life will go easier for you if we make a pact to share our joys, our griefs, and our secrets! If I do not have your trust, then I can never have your love."

He laughed and pressed his lips against hers. She felt a fire leap through him to her. Something stirred deep within her and she trembled beneath him. He had aroused a flame within her and she responded to his passionate embrace.

"Soon, my darling, this marriage of ours will have to be soon," he said huskily, keeping himself in check.

"Oh, Adam, there is another thing . . . I . . . I will not allow you any . . . any . . . bits of muslins, *widows,* or fancy pieces!"

He roared with mirth, and snapped his fingers in the air. "Away with them all . . . they are nothing to me. You silly madcap, you precious beauty, you are all I want." He sighed, and took up her hand, leading her to her horse. "I had better be getting you home."

"What about Bella and Mary? What has been arranged?"

He helped her to mount, went to his own horse, and nimbly jumped into his saddle before answering her.

"Mary will be taken home by Arnold, who has announced that he will advise Mary's papa tonight that Mary is to be the next Lady Merdon. John Wellesly will be home soon enough, and Bella will be amply taken care of until that time—"

"Never say Arnie is going to drive my phaeton?" exploded Nicky, horrified.

"I am afraid so. However, he will be taking the journey quite slowly and I doubt that he can do any damage to the team or the vehicle."

"Oh, dear, I do hope you are right. Now, Adam, do please tell me what that document was all about."

He grimaced and shook his head. "It started a while back, when we noticed a file, a top-security file, had been tampered with. Then another had been rifled at the Horse Guards. We were then certain of something we had suspected for quite some time. Someone in our department was feeding information to Napoleon Bonaparte. Wellington has planned an important campaign—it includes the taking of Salamanca, for without the capture of that city we can't take Madrid, and without Madrid we won't have Spain! Unfortunately, General Marmont became aware that we had agents in his army, and he set out to discover who those English agents were. A friend of mine was slaughtered as a result. In the meantime, our men have not been able to get any information through to us and General Hill and Wellington seem to be stymied. The English campaign will stagnate until our agents can move about freely again.

"We want to know what Marmont's next maneuvers will be. Therefore, we very neatly arranged the document that the Count has run off with. It is a list of English agents very close to Marmont . . . only, of course, it is false. By the time Marmont realizes that, it will be too late.

"Last night I had planted the idea in Barnaby's head that John was off to Portsmouth with documents needed by our English agents to get back to our lines safely. At the same time, I actually was to leave for Dover with ample guard to deliver the real documents to our courier. Barnaby must have realized that some sort of trick was afoot and he and the Count decided to take the list from John's home."

"How dangerous for John, though."

"Hardly. He would have offered little resistance had they accosted him along the road. They would have had the list and been off . . . while I got the real papers off at Dover."

"Do you think Lady Boothe gave it away? All she could have said was precisely what you planted in Barnaby's head—that John was off on Friday with the list."

"Ah, Lady Boothe. You see, she chatters, and her husband unfortunately discloses things to her he should not. Boothe was aware that I was off for Dover, though he did not know why. Lamentable ... but there it is. Your papa advised me this morning that in arranging the guard, Boothe happened to hear that I was off. I imagine he allowed mention of it to slip to his wife, who in turn remarked to Barnaby how odd it was that both John Wellesly and Adam Roth were off for the Coast on Friday. Undoubtedly, that is precisely what occurred. Fortunately, John had let it slip to Barnaby that he had the list."

"Oh, I am so glad to have that dreadful business behind us." A sigh escaped her. "But, Adam, why did the Count betray England? After all, we housed his family when the French Revolution threw them out!"

"To be fair, darling, the Count is French, his loyalty naturally would be with the French, and I imagine Napoleon has offered to restore his lands for his efforts."

"Oh, dear, what will happen to him now?" asked Nicky.

"I am sorry, love. It will not end happily for Louis D'Agout."

They relapsed into talk of their wedding plans and it was with some surprise that they found themselves in front of the Beaumont residence.

Grudsly opened the doors wide, his dark old eyes twinkling with pleasure at the sight of his mistress's arm linked within the Duke's.

"Dearest Grudsly, please call Mama to the library—Papa, too, if he has returned."

"Yes, Lady Nicole."

Lady Nicole led her Duke to the sofa and pulled him down beside her.

"Adam? There is one other thing?"

"Yes?"

"When we are married ... er ... what do you intend to do about our ... our ... sleeping arrangements?"

Completely taken aback by this forthright and unmaidenly question, he answered with a look of amusement, "Why, I intend to sleep in a bed."

"Yes, I know, but ... but you don't understand. I ... I

am aware ... well, Mama and Papa, you see, share the same bedroom ... but I am told that many couples of our class do not ... which seems to me a very strange thing. I would like to share the same bedroom ... different dressing rooms ... but not ... not—"

He caught her up in his arms and laughingly kissed her. She pressed herself against the hardness of his body and her arms were about his neck. He spoke softly in her ear, "My heart, my earth, how I want and need you. You delight my soul!"

Nicky was used to straight speaking and wanted an answer to her question. "That is all very well, but does that mean we will share the same room?"

He threw back his head and whooped with laughter. "Yes, my imp, it most certainly does."

"How nice!" said Lady Beaumont from the doorway. "I see you two seem to be on better terms."

Lady Beaumont's daughter then sprang to life, demanding to be congratulated by her parents. A happy discussion ensued and kept them absorbed for some time before the Beaumonts were regaled with the day's adventure. It was some two hours later when the library doors flew open to expose Harry standing in the frame. His fair hair was windswept with far better results than he could have achieved with his comb. His blue eyes were bursting with a strange exultation. "Devilishly glad you are all here! Got those fellows locked up right and tight, Roth. What a damned fine adventure!"

"Harry, don't you want to know what happened to me?" demanded Nicky.

"That's right! Where the devil did you run off to, girl?"

She then regaled him with the night's events, but when she came to the part where the Count had tried to abduct her, Harry jumped to his feet. "What? What? Did I not tell you, Papa? Tell me I didn't warn you ... told you he'd whisper in her ear! Damn—excuse me—loose screw, rum touch, jackanape!"

Nicky sighed. "Harry, sit down and be quiet." She waited for him to resume his seat and finished her story without interruption. This again involved a lengthy debate, which ended in Harry's muttering darkly that wine on the villain's shirt was not enough, he wished it had been mustard!

Nicole relaxed against the sofa, saying with a sigh, "I think we have had our share of adventure!"

This was something her parents readily agreed to, and after a few minutes Harry, and then his parents excused themselves, leaving Nicole in the Duke's capable hands.

The Duke's lips lingered tenderly on Nicky's neck, and he whispered, "You will have to learn that my Duchess must not climb out of windows, and then back through them again . . . she must refrain from going out into the night without proper escort on dangerous missions. My Duchess must not get abducted—"

"Oh, you abominable wretch, you make it sound as if it was all my doing!" she interrupted.

He chuckled. "And she must never, never refrain from being what she is, for I love her with all my heart, my precious imp!"

She smiled tremulously up at him and gazed into his eyes as he said softly,

> A perfect woman, nobly planned,
> To warn, to comfort, and command;
> And yet a Spirit still, and bright
> With something of Angelic light.

"I believe that Wordsworth wrote that piece so that I would be able to whisper it to you, for it suits you as it could no other."

She looked at him and sighed and then a thought struck her. "I love you, Adam Roth . . . and you must never forget that you are not to whisper anything ever again for anyone else's ears but mine!"

He threw back his head and laughed before gathering her up in his strong arms and assuring her of this once and for always.

Sylvia Thorpe

Romantic tales of adventure, intrigue, and gallantry.

☐ BEGGAR ON HORSEBACK	23091-0	$1.50
☐ CAPTAIN GALLANT	23547-5	$1.75
☐ FAIR SHINE THE DAY	23229-8	$1.75
☐ A FLASH OF SCARLET	23533-5	$1.75
☐ THE CHANGING TIDE	23418-5	$1.75
☐ THE GOLDEN PANTHER	23006-6	$1.50
☐ THE RELUCTANT ADVENTURESS	23426-6	$1.50
☐ ROGUES' COVENANT	23041-4	$1.50
☐ ROMANTIC LADY	Q2910	$1.50
☐ THE SCANDALOUS LADY ROBIN	23622-6	$1.75
☐ THE SCAPEGRACE	23478-9	$1.50
☐ THE SCARLET DOMINO	23220-4	$1.50
☐ THE SILVER NIGHTINGALE	23379-9	$1.50
☐ SPRING WILL COME AGAIN	23346-4	$1.50
☐ THE SWORD AND THE SHADOW	22945-9	$1.50
☐ SWORD OF VENGEANCE	23136-4	$1.50
☐ TARRINGTON CHASE	23520-3	$1.75

Buy them at your local bookstores or use this handy coupon for ordering:

FAWCETT BOOKS GROUP
P.O. Box C730, 524 Myrtle Ave., Pratt Station, Brooklyn, N.Y. 11205

Please send me the books I have checked above. Orders for less than 5 books must include 75¢ for the first book and 25¢ for each additional book to cover mailing and handling. I enclose $_____ in check or money order.

Name_____

Address_____

City_____ State/Zip_____

Please allow 4 to 5 weeks for delivery.

Historical Romance

Sparkling novels of love and conquest against the colorful background of historical England. Here are books you will savor word by word, page by spellbinding page.

☐	AFTER THE STORM—Williams	23081-3	$1.50
☐	ALTHEA—Robins	23268-9	$1.50
☐	AMETHYST LOVE—Danton	23400-2	$1.50
☐	AN AFFAIR OF THE HEART Smith	23092-9	$1.50
☐	AUNT SOPHIE'S DIAMONDS Smith	23378-2	$1.50
☐	A BANBURY TALE—MacKeever	23174-7	$1.50
☐	CLARISSA—Arnett	22893-2	$1.50
☐	DEVIL'S BRIDE—Edwards	23176-3	$1.50
☐	ESCAPADE—Smith	23232-8	$1.50
☐	A FAMILY AFFAIR—Mellow	22967-X	$1.50
☐	THE FORTUNE SEEKER Greenlea	23301-4	$1.50
☐	THE FINE AND HANDSOME CAPTAIN—Lynch	23269-7	$1.50
☐	FIRE OPALS—Danton	23112-7	$1.50
☐	THE FORTUNATE MARRIAGE Trevor	23137-2	$1.50
☐	THE GLASS PALACE—Gibbs	23063-5	$1.50
☐	GRANBOROUGH'S FILLY Blanshard	23210-7	$1.50
☐	HARRIET—Mellows	23209-3	$1.50
☐	HORATIA—Gibbs	23175-5	$1.50

Buy them at your local bookstores or use this handy coupon for ordering: